ᴎ

# RED PLANET

Immortality or Humanity

By

Michael Mendoza

Book 1 or 2 of the Heathen 'twin' books

Author: Michael Mendoza
Title:    Red Planet
© 2018 Katie Phythian Publishing Limited
by Amazon

**ISBN:** 9781792181177


www.michaelmendozabooks.com


www.blackstar-redplanet.com

## DEDICATION

"Writing a book is like having an affair. It steals both physical and mental attention from the ones closest to you. My four-year affair has been with these books and my loved ones have not only been complicit but have actively encouraged it. For that I'm eternally grateful.

Like most, this affair has come to an end which should be a good thing. Sadly, as you hug me close to welcome me back into your world, I must confess to looking over your shoulder as something interesting catches my eye."

*To Blossom, Sid and Brahms especially*

**Michael Mendoza** author of Red Planet & Black Star

## My Death

*"My death waits like a bible truth*
*At the funeral of my youth*
*Weep loud for that - and the passing time."*

**Jacques Brel**

# CONTENTS

Acknowledgments    i

# TWINS

We were unaware of a project with similar characteristics to this one, so no apt title existed in the publishing world. 'Twins' was as good a description as any. Both books were released on the same day and both books are individual freestanding novels. By sharing the same characters, timelines and interwoven stories they share the same DNA.

Its left to the reader to decide which to read first, to read them at same time or simply enjoy one. Each choice offering a different experience of the overall project. Like twins, neither book depends on the other whilst each is inseparable from its sibling.

**Katie Phythian**

Glossary of terms

| | |
|---|---|
| **The Dome** | The City of Heathen as referred to by some. A dome in figure of speech only. |
| **Mother** | The Saviour Machine, a central non governing algorithm for the management of humanity and its needs. |
| **The Outside** | The area beyond the safe confines of the dome or outer boundaries of Heathen. |
| **The Chase** | An area of Heathen reserved for legal (mostly) yet unsavoury activities. |
| **V-World** | A simulated virtual world. It has all the benefits and experiences of reality but because it takes place in the brain it is completely safe for users. It is used for gain, social interaction, sexual joy, adventure and gamesmanship of all kinds. |
| **SIM** | Simulated environment in V-World. |
| **Reality** | Any space occupied outside of a normal virtual environment such as V-World. |
| **Reality Junkie** | Those with a taste for adventure in the real world. |
| **Shlep** | One who spends his life in V-World. |
| **Rationalist** | Opposite of Shlep - One who might not be an adventurer but still prefers reality. |
| **Humanist** | One who believes in living as primitive 21st Century man once did before the shutdown. |
| **Shutdown** | The systematic shutdown and deletion of all digital information, cause unknown. |
| **Pre shutdown** | The period prior to the above. |
| **Moonage** | A primitive time where humanity was confined to its own planet. |
| **TVC 15** | Example of post shutdown calendar. T=twentieth Century V = 500 plus 15 years. Yr. AD 2515 |
| **Drone** | Robotic device at varying levels of ability and intelligence. |
| **Luddites** | (Hominid) Organic human body with computerised brains. Undetectable to other humans. |
| **Speks** | Specification drones which have no ability to communicate with organic humans. |
| **Hack or Hack Code** | A spoken or written sequence that can give access to drone programming for interrogation, maintenance and reprogramming. |
| **Dude** | Hacker, re-programmer and fixer. |
| **Juve** | An allocated young adult - juvenile or young person. |

| | |
|---|---|
| **Kinsperson** | Humans who share the same or similar gene pool or a main string. |
| **Comms** | Any device attached to the brain stem to provide communication with others or with a sage. |
| **Verism** | These are environments that are simulated but in the real world as opposed to a virtual world. |
| **The Major** | (Major Zero) Legendary saviour of humanity post shutdown, designer of the Saviour algorithm known as Mother. |
| **Net** | A Public area of V-World for comms and being online. Comms also works in a real environment. |
| **Black-Star** | The name given to an element unique in the universe. |
| **Lazarus** | A cruise ship designed to take reality adventurers to orbit Mars and return. |
| **Diamond Dogs** | A term referencing items that seem valuable and yet are not. Diamonds, gold, art etc |
| **Euthanise** | The time when humans are allowed to end their mortal existence at 130 years to make way for others. |
| **Migration** | A scheme that allows euthenisation (See Euthanise) at any age dependent on personal choice. |
| **Sage** | A computerised intelligence and assistant with an algorithm that is passed from generation to generation. |
| **T.I.N. Machine** | Totality Intervention Nexus short form for a time travel device or belt. |
| **Mag Pod** | Magnetic road transport common in Heathen. |
| **Merge** | Portable device attached to the back of the neck to brain stem. As opposed to implanted version (Fuse) or comm unit. |

ONE

Vic Jones straddled his Midnight Silver Tesla model X across two spaces in the centre of the car park. He could see his breath in the morning chill as he clambered out, inadvertently leaving the door slightly ajar and activating the warning signal. Huffing to himself he turned and slammed it shut, made an about turn and strode to the rear of the vehicle. Popping the boot Vic leant inside, quickly unzipping a small black bag that lay on top of a larger open holdall. The vials inside were still intact, held against the side by elasticated holders. He closed the package and placed it back in the larger bag on top of an array of tubes and other medical paraphernalia. Zipping it shut he jerked it out and threw it across his body. Climbing up the concrete steps towards the main building, he glanced over his shoulder to admire his new car for the last time. He agreed with the salesman, the colour really did add an air of sophistication. The paint job had doubtlessly given unending pleasure to all who'd cast their eyes upon it during the 6823 miles it'd travelled. Ironic that unlike him, this beautiful machine had many more metaphorical miles left in the tank. The sweeping tyre tracks had created a huge glistening and under the circumstances ironic question mark in the morning dew, punctuated by the vehicle itself. Casting an eye to his left he expected no further traffic along the office driveway for the time being. It was hardly visible, covered by aged pine trees that slumped like broken old men on either side. The place Vic had chosen to kill himself was as unsentimental as he was, a building that belonged in the history books, in fact it was in them. The 16th Century Haddon Hall having once been a residence, later invaded by dated outbuildings that probably looked cutting edge in the 1970's. The tech company who bought the place had seen fit to hide them, half buried amongst the pines with curved moss covered roofs. He strode the final set of steps two at a time and headed towards the imposing main door which was straddled by two stone columns. Slamming the door behind him, Vic checked his watch and marched purposefully past the offices and directly to the library at the rear of the building. The heating system had fired up and the warmer air inside was inviting, intensifying the smell of paper, oak and leather. Antique bookshelves lined the walls and in the

3

central area there were three melamine white tables and a scattering of plastic chairs. Vic paused for a moment to admire an unassuming but grainy black and white framed image with the inscription 'James Hiram Bedford' (April 20, 1893 – January 12, 1967). By the window was the only piece of period furniture that might be appropriate in a room such as this, a green leather wingback chair beside a low circular table. Vic positioned the holdall on one of the melamine reading tables and unzipped the bag, removing items and meticulously laying them out across its surface. The smaller bag was placed carefully to one side and he arranged the remaining items into some kind of order. There were clear plastic medical tubes and fittings wrapped in elastic bands, syringes and large needle heads, another bag contained cloths, bandages and cotton wool.

The next ten minutes were spent methodically moving between the melamine table and the Georgian style wingback chair he'd die in. He erected a small collapsible drip stand and arranged tubes from the three vials into the back of a device which he attached to a remote button. Satisfied he stood back and made a final mental check that everything was in order before glancing at his watch. He'd designed the device so that once he hit the button he'd not need to intervene any further in his execution. He'd be incapable of doing so anyway once the sodium thiopental rendered him unconscious. The next automated stage would be the injection of pancuronium bromide which would induce muscle paralysis and respiratory arrest; finally potassium chloride would stop his heart.

Vic sat in the chair and from here could see the steel blue sky darkening ominously. Inserting a cannula can be tricky even for a professional but he found doing your own with one hand close to impossible. He might later joke how this was the most painful part of the process, if only he'd known at that moment this would be far from the truth. He eventually found a vein, resulting in a steady deluge of blood pouring across the back of his hand and dripping from the tips of his fingers onto the carpet. Mrs Barnett wasn't going to be able to get the stain out but he'd no reason to fear her wrath. The hastily bandaged right hand stemmed the flow enough to allow him to get back to the task. There was a burning sting below the reddening bandage but enough movement to press the button on the remote control to release the chemicals.

The crows sounded agitated outside in the grounds as the sun rose higher breaking through the grey overcast sky. He pondered whether the damp autumn morning may brighten later as it had yesterday, he'd be long gone by then.

In years to come when people asked about his death his answers would disappoint and their incessant curiosity completely missed the point. No one ever asked how the plane felt when you flew to Florida for the Winter. Whilst on the plane you knew you'd get to Florida, likewise whilst dying, he knew he'd be resurrected. The only difference being you might have a rough idea when the plane would arrive, not so in the latter case.

He had control at least, which was almost unique in the case of death and eliminating most of the doubts and fears. Growing old was one, he was 68 but still of sound mind and body, if you didn't include the terminal cancer. There was the question of pain. He'd no experience to speak of so 'should be none' is as close as he can say right now.

Vic looked at his watch, it said 9:25. Nathen's petrol guzzler would be growling its way up the pine ridden access road at any moment. Vic took an envelope from his inside pocket and placed it carefully onto the table by his side and weighed it down with an ashtray. He'd made allowances for Nathen not coming down immediately to find him, perhaps making a coffee before getting curious. Vic's parking had been designed to instigate a modicum of arousal, if nothing else just to complain about Vic's driving prowess. At last Nathen would make his way to the grandiose library and find his friend sat peacefully in the tall leather wingback chair. Not the brightest of buttons in the mornings he'll surely notice the tubes and equipment then perhaps the envelope. All this depended on Nathan's punctuality, which was impeccable and him finding the body and reading the letter. Timing was critical, Vic's corpse would have to be fresh, something as simple as a traffic jam or flat tyre for Nathen might mean Vic actually died permanently. Finding his friend dead, their numerous late night conversations would take on a whole new meaning, the note inside the envelope would confirm his suspicions.

The grandfather clock ticked away the last seconds of Vic Jones' present existence. With a clunk the chimes whirred into life, Vic looked up at the grainy black and white image on the wall for one last time and without a second's hesitation, Vic pressed the button. Watching the chemicals pour down the tube and into his veins, a triumphant smile spread across his face. Before the echo of the final chime had faded, Vic's head slumped onto his chest and he was gone.

□

Coming back to life was going to be altogether different experience to being born as a baby, argued Vic. Reasoning that no one can remember being born because they had nothing to reference it with. They'd no power of deduction, intelligence or experience on which to gauge what's going on. So naturally, he expected a different experience when he was reborn, resurrected, thawed out or whatever you chose to call it. He was no baby, he'd said. He was an intelligent and articulate 68 year old man who had plenty to reference. To his surprise and confusion he'd been dead wrong on this. It was exactly like being a baby again and in some respects worse for the same reasons.

The first thing he remembered were voices. He wasn't sure what they were at first. Not 'who' they were, but 'what' they were? He'd no concept of anything which fortunately included voices, fear and pain. There shortly followed a warm dizzy feeling as if someone had opened a sluice and torrents of liquid were crashing around inside his head. It would only be later that he'd put words to what he felt. Was it knowledge, was it water or drugs? It made no difference; he'd no words for those things yet. He told the medical staff later it was like waking up in ultraslow motion. Over time Vic became aware of himself and his own body. He started to become aware that he could have thoughts. Feelings and sensations started to arrive before finally he could hear his own heartbeat, but was unaware of where the sound came from. He'd planned on being dead for a very long time indeed and yet emerging from an indescribable blackness his first emotion was concern because he'd a realisation of the passage of time. It was maybe around ten minutes since his last conscious though, since that smile, seeing the chemicals running into his diseased body. It was like finally getting off to sleep and then being disturbed.

He was completely paralysed and every muscle in his body ignored his commands. Then there were the memories, not real memories, more realisations; realisations that he existed and that the universe existed. Within his universe were all the objects of everyday life from planets, stars to chairs & lampshades. Everything he knew was entering his world like players on an immense stage. Once everything existed on his stage he started to build his own story and existence around it all. His consciousness shifted and he felt rather than saw a needle, which was as tall as him in a dark room with scratches so deep he could put his fingers inside. That was just a feeling, but he actually saw a wheel inside an orange wall, it was hidden beneath the plaster but he knew it was there. He became confused, how can a man be a shadow, and then he heard the smell of sweet cherry tomatoes. Vic had deep enlightening thoughts which would disappear in an instant, it hurt to try and remember them. He remembered entire lives that weren't his and when he probed, his ability to scrutinise his thoughts was as illusive as the thoughts themselves. He was left with nothing but a frustrating memory of a memory without the detail, merely the theme.

Existence and consciousness started returning and he was now becoming aware. Vic started to remember that billions of different things existed and as a consequence so did he. Yes, so did he. Now it was all quickly falling into place.

"Can you hear me?" the voice again, it came from the centre of his head but this time he knew it was a voice.

It was another person's voice and he didn't recognise it. It wasn't Nathen, but who else could it be? It sounded whispered and urgent. Of course he could hear, he understood the question but had no way of responding. Instead he ignored it and hoped it would go away, Nathen would find his old lifeless body. If he ignored the voice they might go away and he would be allowed to die. It distressed him to choose Nathen because he'd played no part in the planning and yet he needed someone strong and someone who cared. If it had all gone according to the program then his body could be dealt with very quickly. Vic left clear instructions that his body was to be preserved in a Cryonic state indefinitely. He couldn't pass the responsibility to any individual and so had made his survival a company matter. After all, he knew that companies could very easily outlive friends, family and employees. By the time he was thawed everyone he knew including Nathen would probably be long dead. As for the company; that would still be there, he hoped.

Another voice interrupted his thoughts but more distant. "Everything is proceeding normally, vitals are excellent."

Then another voice. "Is he alright?"

"Don't worry its quite natural, it's going to take some time, his senses are returning."

Vic was now whole again, complete. He could feel everything, every part of himself. He started to remember very recent thoughts. That's when the fear hit him, just before the incredible pain. As a child he fell off a push bike at high speed, grazing every limb, crawling to the side of the road in agony. That memory was as vivid now as the day it happened. Every part of him ached and his brain felt inflated enough to burst through his skull.

All the planning had failed, they'd resuscitated him. It had failed after he'd gone to great lengths to ensure everything would work. There was no way his body should have been found until his alarm was raised shortly after his death.

What could possibly have gone wrong? The dosage may have been miscalculated or an unexpected visitor had raised the alarm? He was aware of a green blinding glow on the other side of his clenched eyelids. The chatter continued around him. Voices whispered in his ear. Metal was being placed under his eyelids, cold and yet this didn't add to his discomfort. He felt his eyelids prised open but saw nothing but a blinding watery light.

He was in a chair and although he couldn't move he knew his wrists were fastened to the arms. Vic started to see again as water streamed down over his pupils. A blur of bright lights and movement presented itself to him. The water cleared, someone wiped his eyes and he was in some kind of hospital. A strange looking place; like some kind of communist state medical facility. He certainly wasn't at Nathen's anymore. What appeared to be the very latest medical equipment was all around him along with several medical personnel in white coats. This conflicted with the room which resembled an old tube station or warehouse. Ten minutes ago he'd died and somehow he had ended up several miles away. Presumably he was in the Royal London or even London Bridge Hospital, there'd been so little time.

"Welcome," said Bluu softly. "How do you feel?"

Faces started to come into focus but all the voices seemed out of sync with the mouths.

"Mr Nova, are you feeling ok?" said another.

No he wasn't feeling ok, he felt like he had been hit by a truck and every nerve in his body felt like a hot ember under his skin. Who the hell was Mr Nova? Were they talking to him?

He saw a face come into focus and was aware of a pleasant relaxing odour. As the water flushed from his eyes he could see the nurse up close and other men in the background.

Her voice reverberated deep inside his cranium. "Hello Nova. Welcome. My name is Bluu," she smiled.

Vic opened his mouth to speak and then everything went black.

TWO

The deep blackness of this jungle night would be dispatched into the light of day at a breath-taking pace. The Sun's towering tangerine and red searchlights fanning out across the sky like a shell. The rivers swirling eddies fractured the golden light whilst the dense jungle obscured all land beneath a blanket of green. Tall branches swayed in the breeze, reaching out across the river to shake hands with their counterparts on the other side. The gleaming sunlight turned the canopy from deep green to autumn gold in seconds. The explosion of light cast long shadows through the treetops. The jungle came alive in response, providing a relaxing dawn chorus of tropical birds, excited to begin the day.

The air warmed and quickly became muggy as flies buzzed around the lifeless bundle of fur that lay on a sandy riverbank. The blanket stirred and an arm reached out from underneath, followed by a mop of greasy hair. Doctor Touchreik managed to role away from the breaking dawn hitching himself up on one elbow. He hadn't slipped any deeper than into a light doze throughout the entire night. A troubled man whose nightmares tormented his sleep and his waking hours; his one consolation being that today might be an opportunity to resolve those troubles for better or for worse.

He kept his eyes closed and allowed the warm sun-rays to cast across his face, interrupted every few seconds by a cool breeze. He enjoyed the moment without stirring, smelling the moisture in the air and hearing the familiar soft rumble of thunder in the distance. That sound signalled the 120 seconds he had, before the storm and the tropical rain arrived, stretching he rubbed his eyes with the back of his hands.

"Close please," he said in a loud clear voice. The forest, riverbank and storm ridden dawn sky faded to nothing, replaced by his own bedroom. Duke, his sage shut down the holographic imaging program and lit the room to 40%. The silver bare walls were visible for a moment until the internal decor began to rearrange itself to morning mode.

As Duke reset the room, the walls decorated themselves in elaborate coverings depicting nature and plant life images. Pictures and

9

ornaments appeared in holographic form to enhance the decoration and the lighting shifted colour to accommodate tired eyes. The division between some physical items, hologram and decor was impossibly vague and judging the physical space was an arduous task for the naked eye. One of the tall shrubs sat in a pot to the left of the window but its outstretched branches moulded into the wall covering with no visible join in any dimension.

Algeria rolled into a sitting position on the edge of a huge circular bed layered in luxurious fur coverings. Gigantic artworks filled the walls on either side of him as the dimensions expanded in front of his eyes. A biblical burst of sunlight entered through a two story window at the bottom end of the room. Augmented or not he still felt the warm glow on the side of his face.

Drake always said it confused him to use a random wake up program but Touchreik liked the variety. Some days it might be a tropical beach, a jungle scene or even an interstellar sunrise observed from Jupiter, the jungle river was a particular favourite. His wake up program might be random but there was one morning ritual that wasn't. That was the sound of one of his most prized and well used physical possessions. His ancient caffeine generator was an expensive museum piece that Ramona had given him as a gift to celebrate the millennia in 2499. He'd paid for it but still, it was a nice gesture, however he'd noted to close financial access after that. It was a copy but it ran well and professed to give caffeine in a way utilised by organic coffee beans, at least that's what the designers claimed. In honesty, it didn't taste much better than a 4D version but he loved the ritual, the noise and the smells it produced. Unlike caffeine fabricated by Duke or any other 4D machine its taste was random, impossible to get an identical flavour on every occasion but that was its magic.

He dropped his elbows onto his knees and combed his straggly hair back with his fingertips. Reaching out blindly he snatched a robe with his right hand without lifting his gaze from the floor. He gestured with a wave and the large artwork in front of him changed into a mirror. He looked drained, developments over the preceding seven days or so were beginning to tell. Scrubbing his cheeks vigorously with his palms he rose to his feet and pulled on the robe. Slipping his bare toes into a pair of white silken house shoes, he padded into the food prep area.

The steaming caffeine was waiting for him and he whipped it off the table in a single motion before turning left into the life room. He ignored the small spill he left on the black marble worktop. A tiny dome shaped drone shot from a gap in the end wall and ingested the stain at lightning speed before returning to its resting place, all before Touchreik had left the room.

"Duke, tell me it's not 7am," he groaned.

"Good morning Doctor Touchreik," said a cheerful disembodied voice. "Yes, I'm afraid this is the case."

Algeria tapped the back of his neck to initiate the intelli 3D display and his daily itinerary appeared floating in the middle of the room. He was conscious the day was going to be fairly mundane, some of the time in the reserve and some to check on some lab samples. There was one activity in his personal stream flashing in red. It just said 'meeting'. There was no detail such as time or place, additional files or attachments just one word 'meeting'.

It was this meeting in particular that may determine whether there would be any further 'day' to concern himself with.

Twenty minutes later and fully clothed Dr Touchreik was beginning to look human. He'd chosen a low key outfit consisting of a yellow slim fitting suit, white shirt with high collar. A garish tie and white brogues completed the look. Though he'd attempted to tie his hair back the shorter strands still hung irritatingly over one eye. Fatigued or not he'd built a promising career by 36, a young man for his position and even younger when you considered his career path as research director for pre shutdown analysis. History was seldom a subject to attract the young, something he could attest to from his lectures. Human history reaching as far back as the Moonage might be something more akin to those beyond a hundred years old. This ancient time had fascinated him his entire short life, before the Dome had ever existed. How or why Heathen had acquired the nickname of the Dome was long forgotten but it was far from being one. Heathen was a towering supercity built from steel and glass. Nearly 500 years previous the world's data had shut down along with its civilisation and Heathen became a sanctuary for those left behind; a single bastion for humanity on a desperate planet. Growing and improving over the early decades as it hoovered up the last known survivors from societies 'outside'. Today, 70 million members of the human race remain huddled in this expansive city we call Heathen, it's provided a stable and peaceful environment for hundreds of years and will continue to do so for hundreds more. Touchreik was fascinated by the period prior to this, before 'Mother' began to manage humanity; 'Mother' being another affectionate nom de plume for the 'Saviour Machine' a data cloud system based on Mars, it was in all manner of ways 'Mother' to all, managing and caring for humankind with a love that knew no limits. That love was reciprocated in almost every level of society, on a morning like this he would be reminded that didn't always mean everyone in Heathen.

Touchreik collapsed into a large white leather armchair, taking a moment to compose himself. The living area was as cavernous and bright as the sleep area with large shrubs and trees in gigantic pots almost blending with the panoramic holographic green views through the three story windows. The sunlight coming through had subliminally shifted in colour and angle to simulate the shifting of time.

Algeria reached out and touched a few menus in the centre of his vision and brought up some ball sport news. He punched one of the headlines in free space and two holographic people appeared, although they appeared as solid as anyone such was the quality of Duke's projection. They were both sat on his settee opposite and continued to chat about a V-World ball sport result from the previous night. Touchreik stared them down intently as was his habit, interrupting and talking over them, today he was particularly venomous.

The blonde female presenter sat upright in her seat.

"May I congratulate you on a record breaking season," she said to the young man next to her.

"Yeah me too," said Touchreik waving sarcastically.

"Thank you," the man replied.

"It's been a long journey to perform as you did last night," she continued.

"Guess how they did that!" Touchreik slapped his knee and then had to hold his coffee cup upwards as some of the boiling liquid landed on his thigh.

"It's a long season, a long competition but we stuck together and worked."

"Oh worked on what?" The pair on the settee continued chatting, oblivious to the Doctor's remarks. He sat in his chair leering at the player, looking for any signs he was lying.

He'd mutter, "yeah right," and, "Huh you're kidding me?" at appropriate times.

After five minutes he became bored of abusing the proud athlete.

The interviewer finished speaking and then addressed Algeria as he stood to walk away. He drained the last of his caffeine whilst avoiding the black grains in the bottom of his cup, ignoring her eye contact as he passed.

"Coming up soon Pierrot with the latest entertainment news but first a break."

As Algeria walked towards the bathroom a tall handsome man came out wearing a chef outfit and carrying a tray of sweet smelling 4D food gels. As the man picked one up to offer it to Algeria he reached around and tapped the back of his neck and the man disappeared.

"You seem convinced they are influencing in that team," said Duke softly.

"Absolutely my friend, can't be done. Seen the stats?" he mumbled.

Duke gave a soft cough. "I see the latest fantasy movie has signed up a million actors on its first night," sparkled the cheerful electronic voice of the Duke.

"No," said the Doctor without looking up. He was no fan of immersive filmonic experiences anyway unless they were history based. The Duke carried on regardless, offering interesting titbits of media like a hospital visitor at a bedside.

"Caveman to be regenerated," he piped expectantly.

"Go on," said Algeria pausing at the mirror to pull down an eyelid with a finger as if counting the veins in his bloodshot eyes.

"Mother is pleased to announce that a 23 year project is finally reaching a conclusion. A complete cryonic man from pre shutdown will soon be ready for release from quarantine. Nicknamed 'the caveman' he was discovered amongst samples kept by the Tom Zero expedition to Mars, scientists believe he dates back from as early as the Moonage. Initial worries that the 21st Century man could harbour harmful and ancient bacteria similar to those outside the dome have proved unfounded," cried the Duke excitedly before pausing for reaction, getting none he continued. "Tests have been completed and he has been passed safe to have contact with organic life forms. As the man is from pre shutdown it's felt his knowledge of organic human history will be a useful addition to the historic data banks. From his records it seems he entered cryonic preservation in the late 21st Century, possibly as early as 2015. His poor physical condition delayed the project for over two decades."

"Keep me up to date with that," he said snipping a nasal hair.

"I certainly will it sounds very interesting?"

Algeria ignored the comment, but mentally agreed, it did sound very interesting under the circumstances. He walked back into the life area and plucked a piece of paper from a bowl on the side and stared at it intently. It was obviously from the stranger who'd accosted and threatened him last week. Most historians would remember the Cryonic human, over 20 years ago. Touchreik had been no more than a juve at the time but even then he'd an interest in such things. It'd been an exciting idea to think this ancient man might be thawed out, perhaps live or even communicate with us. Then the whole thing faded from the spotlight and was forgotten, the last he'd heard was there was too much damage to the body for it to be of any use. So it appeared that wasn't the case after all, someone had been busy repairing the damage for 23 years? If they'd solved that problem then it could be very exciting. Since all data was lost in 23rd century then a person who lived in 2015 could teach us so much about our past. He refused to allow himself to become over excited about the thing.

He had other more immediate and concerning problems. Serendipitous as it might feel, his first concern was not whether he might be in a position to work this project but whether after today he still had a career at all.

Today he was likely going to be blackmailed, as of yet he had no idea what for, by whom and why? He stuffed the crumpled piece of paper deep into his pocket and prepared to leave.

THREE

Vic's second return was dynamic and instantaneous, from dead to alive in a split second. A burning light stung his eyes and his instinctive reaction was to try and cover them with his hands. Instead he was forced to dip his head under his armpits finding his wrists restrained by leather straps on the arms of a chair. Squirming, he attempted to bury his face beneath flailing elbows. Mercifully, it turned out he was wearing sunglasses which reacted rapidly to the light and the scene before him slowly came into focus. The stinging pain behind his eyes subsided after one last piercing stab. For the first time since his death he felt mentally alert and yet this was far from the case with his physical state. The act of simply raising his head took an almighty effort and it was now that he perceived a third belt loosely placed around his waist. As intended, it was preventing his flaccid body from falling forward onto the tiled floor. He stole a moment to take stock of his surroundings but there was no solace in what he observed. He was strapped into a wheelchair that sat square in the middle of what could only be a stage or raised platform. It was in what resembled a lecture theatre, instead of seats it had glass booths that cascaded up and back to around ten levels. The smell of almonds and lemon filled his nostrils and the chequered floor was so polished it reflected the surroundings. The booths that filled the wall in front of him curved around and together resembled the eye of an insect. Each lens was a tinted dark booth, curving and bulging towards him. He could see movement behind every pane but the silken mirror finish inhibited any detail. Inside each one he could make out shadowy figures jostling for position. They reminded him of royal boxes in a theatre yet they were devoid of golden garlands made of plaster, no ornate fronds or royal crowns. Occasionally he spotted a door open at the back, slightly illuminating the figures inside. People appeared to be stood in open doorways and on tip toes to see through into the room.

He'd expected some kind of interview or triage nurse to explain where he was, perhaps even a doctor or consultant. It could be some kind of reality based illusion caused by the drugs? At one point he thought he might have died after all. Logically he had to be in one of the local hospitals, there'd been little time to take him elsewhere. But what was with the freak-show? His neck muscles burned with the effort to lift his head once more.

There was a hush from the gallery and then an electronic ping, similar to what one might hear in a foreign airport before an announcement. There followed enthusiastic applause and cheering from another room nearby. Before Vic could see anything more his chin dropped under the strain and he saw his bare knees protruding from a crisp white hospital gown. The muffled applause wasn't coming from another room after all; it was from the glass booths. The sound of cheers and clapping slowly died and there was another long silence. He could hear his own heartbeat before he physically jumped at a loud electronic thump followed by a second ear piercing feedback. A clear male voice began to speak, the volume in the room was at a deafening level.

"Good Morning Mr Nova," the voice echoed around the cavernous space, the man speaking paused to clear his throat nervously with the mic still open. Vic could only stare down at his knees waiting for the burning sensation in his neck muscles to subside so he might look up again.

"My signature is Burroughs."

Nova? That name again, who the hell was Nova?

"Entree to Heathen." A slightly less enthusiastic ripple of applause followed. "We are very pleased to have you here with us," he continued. "I understand that you may be a little unsettled and we hope to make things as tranquil as possible for you. Please be assured you are quite cherished and free from danger."

Vic was unable to lift his head but he pushed his eyeballs upwards and everything blurred as stinging tears ran onto his cheeks. There was no doubt the man was addressing him.

"Your present condition is robust and healthful. You are going to need some time before you are fully roving again. We will transport you from here to a familiar household where you can spend the next 7 days becoming able bodied."

The speech stopped and he could hear some whispering as if a hand was over the microphone. Anger burned inside and he had no way of expressing it. The way his suicide had gone wrong was one thing but to be revived and find himself here was another thing altogether. That's if he was revived? The situation was so incongruent that he could no longer ascertain what was real. Was he dead or maybe in a coma? If not then this was one almighty cock up. He'd need to speak to someone as soon as possible to sort this mess out. It just didn't make any sense.

Even if they'd mixed him up with another patient, the Mr Nova, it still didn't explain why he was here. No matter who bloody Nova was.

Then a wave of dread, what if he hadn't died? They might start cutting him open, right here. The panic gave him the strength to lift his head long enough to make out a door sliding open to his left. A tall figure entered just outside his peripheral vision. He had to move, had to let them know he was alive. The figure approached him from the side, moving with a smooth cat like gait. The echoing clatter of footsteps stopped abruptly behind the chair. He felt a jolt like maybe a brake coming off the chair and his head rocked.

The voice spoke again. "May I acquaint you with Bluu who will be looking after you and I am very much looking forward to meeting you individually very soon. Thank you."

He heard the mic click off followed by more muffled enthusiastic applause. They must know I'm alive, they're speaking to me? The chair jerked and spun, whipping his head to one side and the feeling was like someone tugging sharply on his hair. His wheelchair careered towards the side door which slid open again milliseconds before they collided with it. Vic was still too weak to lift his head for very long, least of all look around. He was pushed along wide corridors with the same chequered pattern of reflective tiles. A million scrubbings had seen off the reflective surface on the stainless steel walls giving them a brushed effect. As they meandered along he saw feet coming from doorways and stopping to watch them roll by, hearing occasional whoops and clapping as they passed. The air was cool but stale, reminding him of a butcher's shop or an empty fridge. He watched the floor whiz past under his bare feet before the chair stopped abruptly at a pair of dented, scratched elevator doors. Once inside the chair was spun briskly to face the exit. Feeling motion but unable to judge whether he was going up or down Vic caught sight of the person pushing him via the mirrored elevator walls. She didn't strike him as a national health orderly. Probably female was as close as he could get to the sex of the individual, tall and wearing what looked like white leather pants? She smelled good too. The instant he became conscious of the smell he was catapulted vividly back, until now having forgotten his first return. Now he could remember the voices, and the passing out, but the smell was the same. Maybe this was a private institution, an ambulance crash maybe? They weren't going to let him die in the street just because he wasn't in BUPA? It was definitely not like any hospital he'd ever seen either in looks or procedure. The lift doors opened and a warm gust of air greeted him. The perfumed musky odour replaced the clinical lemon, almond smell they'd left in the theatre. There was a definite change of atmosphere in this area, more like the Hilton or Savoy hotel. He stared down at his bare feet as they hovered silently over deep red carpet along oak panelled corridors. The chair halted sharply, the waist belt doing its job admirably. A burst of light from his right indicated a set of double doors had been opened by his companion. His chair was whisked round and he was pushed inside feeling the sharp tug on his scalp once more. Vic struggled to look up; it was definitely in keeping with an up market hotel. To his right he could see another set of open double doors which housed a luxury king size bed. In this room which was some kind of lounge area there was a glass door, half slid open with a white organza curtain gently blowing in the breeze. Then, thank Christ, yes it was. To his immense relief he saw the London skyline through the gap as the breeze blew the curtain gently inwards; the London eye, the Post Office tower, not too far away.

Bluu clicked on the chair brake and came around to the front. Crouching down in front of him she began undoing the straps whilst occasionally stopping to stroke his cheek with the back of her fingers. He'd been completely unaware of the bodily fluids she wiped from his nose and mouth with a cloth. She smiled up at him as she threw the remains into a tray by his side.

Her voice was crisp, masculine but kind. "Now do not concern, everything is going to be fine. I hope you find items to your satisfaction."

He summoned his strength once more to look up into her eyes or at least he thought she was a she. It wasn't easy to be sure if she was a boy or girl.

"Where am I?" he whispered in a dry hoarse voice.

She looked at him with large kind eyes, the make-up, even to a man looked crude. The bright whites of her eyes made her look youthful. Mid-twenties or possibly older judging by the tiny crow's feet. She had a natural shimmer to her skin, white eyes lined with deep blue eye shadow. Her mousy brown hair was cropped short, natural yet pasted close to the scalp. She had on a white leather fashion outfit based on a military style with a double breast jacket that stretched across her muscular physique. As she crouched down the material across her thighs and shoulders strained and creaked. Stretching to bring her head lower than his she stared up to meet his gaze.

"You are in Heathen, at the science institute," she said smiling kindly. She spoke in a tone one might take with a dog or cat frightened by a thunder storm. "Please don't concern, I'm sure you'll find everything to your contentment. I am here to care, be assured of that." A reassuring air hostess grin followed.

"Look, listen to me," Vic groaned. "Who knows I'm here? I need to get out of here."

18

Bluu stared up at him, as if embarrassed or unsure how to deal with the situation. Without lifting his head he stared down at her, his bloodshot eyeballs straining, as he summoned all the strength he could. He spoke purposefully. "Get me someone in authority so I can find out what the hell is going on," he spat the words through his slavering mouth. Bluu stood quickly, lips quivering. Physically she was tall and well built, masculine and yet her reaction was feminine. Bluu regained her composure but the moment she did so Vic caught a glance of his own reflection in the full length mirror behind her. Bluu began to speak again but the words meant nothing, they were just a background noise to him in light of what he saw. The vision before him set his heart racing and his palms and armpits became wet.

"What the fff?" he croaked hoarsely to himself as tears ran down his cheeks. He was aware that Bluu was still speaking but he heard not a word. He tilted his head to try and see around her legs but she was still chatting about the facilities and the importance of him as a guest; how he needn't worry and all that kind of crap. Vic summoned all the strength he had to scream.

"I said, move!"

Bluu stepped quickly to one side, silenced by his outburst.

"Oh my God," he said each word individually and slowly as his mind absorbed what he was seeing. He looked down at his hands, then his bare feet. He looked weak as expected but, he was not a weak 68 year old man as he was maybe an hour or two ago. What he saw in the mirror was not that at all. What he saw was a weak young man, clearly in his mid-twenties just as he remembered himself when he was that age in fact. Of course he was thin, pale but absolutely not 68 years of age, more like early to mid-twenties, albeit completely bald. Not just his head but eyebrows, everything. Some kind of swimming cap with tubes attached was fitted to his scalp. The tubes passing over his shoulders like plastic dreadlocks.

"Jesus Christ they did it," he said to himself.

"Did it?" queried Bluu.

"What year is this?" he whispered, mesmerised by his own reflection. There was no reply.

"Miss, err Bluu I asked you a question," he said a little louder as calmly as he could.

"The year is TVC15," she said nervously before realising he wouldn't understand that format. She bit her bottom lip to make the conversion for him. Her clothes creaked once more as she crouched to eye level again.

"The year is TVC15 Mr Nova. T for Twentieth Century, V for 500 plus fifteen years. That would be, yes, to you that would be the year 2515."

FOUR


Despite the uneasy quietness around Barnbrook in the daylight hours Touchreik had never felt threatened, even at night. On rare occasions he'd seen citizens sitting around in the tree lined square, dozing in the cool breeze as it whispered through the leaves. The surrounding buildings channelled sunlight into the square in peculiar ways. The residence was a compliment to the designers whose usual predisposition might be towards interiors. In the case of Barnbrook they'd undoubtedly found time to entertain themselves by planting 'easter eggs' within the structure. These weren't visible to everyone and it was tenants who lived in the upper floors, those who might have switched off their augmented windows who admired and reported them. The rooftops and square were adorned with intricate mobile sculptures, designed to play with the sunlight as it poured in at differing angles. Whichever apparition these honoured residents saw when they looked down was entirely dependent on their location and time of day; a bird in flight in the morning, a man surrounded by twinkling stars at dusk. One had reported how the small pond in the centre had turned a luminescent sapphire colour one autumn evening. These visions were renowned for shifting before witnesses to the spectacle could be brought to the window. He'd heard there was a fellow on the 19th floor who meticulously recorded these sightings but the reason for doing so was as much a mystery as the sightings themselves.

Heathen was a world very different from the one Touchreik studied as part of his work. In 2515 few found the need to venture beyond their own homes and few did. The Saviour machine catered for all physical needs and the virtual world allowed citizens to work, play and socialise anywhere their minds could dream of without ever setting foot outside. The supply of food, clothing and other resources was integral to the structure and completely automated. Heathen provided an excellent minimum standard of living and so few were motivated to improve it. These things made Touchreik a bit of an oddity in two respects. The first being that he had an occupation and the second, that he physically attended it. Even those who chose employment would rarely need to attend in person. V-World's ability to tap directly into the human nervous system meant all virtual experiences whether social, work or fun were as close to reality as reality itself. The benefit being that V-World was a completely safe environment with no accidents or mag pod failures to worry about. The rules of a V-world sim could be defined by the user or the sim itself. A day at work doing a laborious labour intensive task could transition to space adventures and war games from the very same seat. Since Mother had made so many DNA changes to the pool over the years, V-world had eliminated the need for physical intimacy, something very well provided for in the virtual world. In lots of the latest generations of humans the useless organs of reproduction had been removed altogether. Even socialising and sports were mainly experienced within V-world, it was simply the centre of the universe for most. It was for these reasons that the Doc was unusual in seeing so much of the square below on his regular commutes, albeit from ground level.

The Barnbrook apartment block and his work environments were secure, as was the transport system. However, the apartment foyer between the transporter and entrance was effectively a public space. A paved area that ran alongside the square with benches giving the ambiance of a place one might meet and chat with friends. It was reasonably well lit but he'd seldom find himself out after dark and even if he did his Augmented Reality Device could be switched to infrared. In all the years he'd lived here he could hardly remember meeting a single individual from his block; that is until last week.

He'd been returning home after a late shift at the institute having returned later than expected from a field trip in the reserve. The door of the mag slid down as if waving as the transporter pulled away. Touchriek was tired and pinched the top of his nose as he walked briskly towards the block door. As he pulled his hand away and opened his eyes he noticed a figure walking towards him, at the time presuming he was from his block. The man, although he couldn't be sure at the time strutted forwards with his chest out and arms waving in an exaggerated manner.

They passed each other under the streetlight and the downward beam gave the man a sinister appearance as it deepened the shadows across his face. In the moment he had to give closer inspection it appeared instead that the shadows had been painted on instead, exaggerating his features. On his head he sported a shoddy improvised turban which revealed greying sideburns in front of each ear. The man was tatty and dishevelled, definitely not from this sector, that's if he was from the dome at all. He was dressed in rags pulled around his body and what looked like similar improvised shoes on his feet. He'd strutted, purposefully and arrogantly past him. The Doctor quickened his pace and caught the man's grin out of the corner of his eye as he unsuccessfully tried to avoid eye contact. Touchreik walked on through a trail of pungent odour, a dirty earthy smell he recognised. The Doctor's job took him to the 'outside' occasionally and he recognised that odour immediately. The man could have been a humanist, he certainly looked the type. Putting his head down Touchreik quickened his pace towards the sanctuary of the main door.

Humanists were a particularly unsavoury group of extremists but he'd be unlikely to encounter one here. They shared an insane belief that society should relinquish the help of machines, including the Saviour Machine. Not content to stay on the outside and live like animals they chose to harass civilised human beings, live on the fringes of society; intent on spreading their filthy germs and philosophies amongst the decent people of Heathen. Their activities causing power shutdowns, grid disruption, software problems. If this was one of them he'd be up to no good, there was no doubt of that.

His heart rate elevated and just thinking about them made him angry inside, making him wish for a confrontation.

He got one almost immediately.

As the man had passed him he felt the hairs on the back of his neck bristle, daring him to look round.

"Doctor Touchreik," a voice from behind him said sarcastically, as if greeting an old friend. The man knew his name? He was certainly not acquainted with this character in any respect. The Doctor took a few more steps taking him closer to the secure entrance before turning around. His eyes darted nervously, to see if there was anyone else to offer any moral support, more importantly whether this scumbag was alone.

"Do I know you sir?" Touchreik said.

"Do I know you, I know you. Doctor Touchreik," the man repeated mockingly, stressing the word Doctor. "Oh you will know me Doctor, in a few years, you're looking well for your age." He approached Touchreik and put an arm up high on the streetlamp, watching him intently. The odour was solid and warm in Touchreik's presence.

"Incredible," the scum whispered to himself studying the Doctor like a specimen in a jar. The Doctor opened his mouth to speak but the man placed a finger on his own lips. "Ssshhhhhh!"

The man took his arm off the post and stood with his hands on his hips revealing his twisted yellowing teeth in a grin, looking the Doctor up and down.

23

"Old school shoulder surfer, you don't look the type. I know about you and," he paused to lower his voice, "Ramona."

The Doctor's heart skipped and he felt the blood draining from his face. He felt physically sick. Ramona?

Maybe he heard wrong, surely not, only he knew.

"Ah, Ramona A. Stone, the female good time drone," sang the scum.

"I've no idea what you're talking about," said Algeria.

"Neither have I," giggled the stranger. "But I was told it might get your attention and it appears to have done so."

Touchreik frowned, furrowing his brow. He had to think fast because it was impossible that someone else knew about Ramona. "Who, who told you to mention that name, how do you know my name for that matter?"

"That's not a conversation for now, but let me tell you what is." By now the stranger was circling him, hands on hips and walking on his toes. Without realising the Doctor had backed off towards the door a little further but the man was closer, intimidating.

"This is important. I'll be dropping you a little note, when we're ready for you," laughed the scum.

"Who's ready for me?" he said.

"Like I say, a conversation for another day. I wanted to see you for myself, make sure you were not lying. Well I have seen yer!" he had stopped circling now and looked as if he was turning to leave.

"Don't fret over Ramona, it's our secret. I'll be in touch Doctor Touch-reik." He enjoyed that rhyme. Spinning he snapped, "OK?"

"There must be some mistake," the Doctor shouted after him, his voice trailing off as the man turned to approach him once more.

"Are you Touchreik?" pointing angrily into his face the smell stronger now and beads of sweat on his forehead. Deep shadows cast across his face, some by the dim light and others painted on giving him a devilish appearance.

"Yes, but."

"Well there's no mistake, note, action, get it?" Turning quickly he walked away, before he disappeared the Doctor heard him shouting from the darkness.

"We are going to save the world at last," his words echoing across the empty courtyard as he skipped away. That was all last week. He'd gone over the meeting many times in his mind since. 'I wanted to be sure you weren't lying,' or something like that. He'd never met the man before, how could he have lied? Regardless, it was too risky to have contact with Ramona until he knew what this scumbag was after. Then the note had appeared telling him when and where to meet. Interesting because it was hand written which indicated a level of intelligence he wouldn't attribute to the scum he met downstairs. There could be more than one blackmailer? He'd demanded a physical meeting, close to the Doctor's place of work. The meeting place was well inside the Natural Selection Reserve which was off grid. So he knew where the Doc worked, he knew about Ramona and then this morning the news about the caveman.

Dressed and ready to leave he felt a bit more alive, passing the hallway table the door slid open. "See you later Duke."

He felt for the note that had been left for him the night before and pushed it deep into his pocket. It gave instructions to head for a section of the dome in a corner of the Natural Selection Living Specimen Museum. It suggests that there has to be a reason for discretion. Not only that, but it was going to be very convenient for him to visit unnoticed. He didn't know whether that mattered but it was a hell of a coincidence, his meeting was right next to his physical workplace.

Blackmail, he was almost sure it would be blackmail. Perhaps he was a soft target, certainly not a man of means. Sending that little message about Ramona, letting him know how much they knew, and if they knew he was having a physical relationship with a drone, then they did know a lot.

He picked up his bag and doubled back to grab a meal gel from the fridge on his way out.

"You are aware of your meeting this morning Doctor?" Duke sounded concerned. "I have no details on file, do you need any assistance?"

"Oh, I'm fine thank you," said the Doctor with a twinge of guilt at keeping a secret from a machine. Although Duke was not technically Mother it felt the same as lying to her too. Even though the cloud or 'Mother' as she was known controlled everything; was everything, Duke was independent and could be trusted with just about any personal data. Well most personal data, even Duke didn't know about Ramona, the only person who knew about Ramona was the Doctor himself; that is until last week. He stepped outside and climbed into a transporter as it slowed to meet him and settled into a large suede armchair for the short trip to the Institute. The pod was an egg shape craft, lay on its side with the bottom part flattened. As it approached it looked like the entire front half was transparent. Pulling away the grim grey view through the windows was replaced by a colourful augmented display of the outside world. The whole system moved about 6 inches off the ground on an invisible magnetic field.

He voiced his destination and settled down with his tablet to flick through some data relating to the day's events. The transporter pulled up to a crawl outside the Institute and he picked up his case and stepped onto the pavement. There were wide green spaces around the expansive building complex. The three-story C-shaped structure was clad in gold reflective glass and approaching it felt like the building was reaching out and embracing him. Scanning his DNA at the unmanned security point he was at his station in minutes, albeit a couple of hours earlier than usual.

He took a look around before removing his security chip. Then he reached around to the back of his neck and removed his augmented reality plug in, and placed them both in a draw, quietly sliding it shut. Five minutes later he was outside on the sidewalk again walking briskly towards the Natural Selection Park, a 15 minute walk at a sharp pace. The Natural Selection Park was an expansive display area open to the public throughout the year. There's a voluntary ban on any kind of modern communication equipment, location chips and apps. It's frequented by students and old school organics who love the idea of being off grid for long periods of time. Lots of museum piece transport systems, natural plant and animal species are cultivated. It's meant to represent the 'outside' as it used to be when species including humans relied on random DNA selection and physical reproduction.

The hired 21st century transporter was waiting for him on the parking area. It was an accurate replica of an old wheeled self-driven transport. Inside was the optional map he had ordered to locate his expected meeting point. He fingered through the cumbersome piece of paper and got his bearings using the signposts outside the reception and hire. Without his augmented reality device he felt exposed almost straight away. He'd no access to cloud data or location, he felt naked. The transport had no navigation or automatic drive system either. He pressed the accelerator and nothing happened until he remembered gears. He pulled the gear stick into drive and jerked off into the wilderness in a cloud of dust.

Like most people the Doctor very rarely had an opportunity to drive himself and was enjoying the thrill as he wound down the window and enjoyed the morning air. This area had been acclimatized by Mother to have false seasons. To serve everyone's tastes an entire year took around 4 months so there were ample opportunities for visitors to catch autumn, winter, spring or summer. He drove for around half an hour before he pulled off the main highway and spotted the old service station he'd been watching out for. There was no carbon fuel needed, the vehicle he was driving didn't have an internal combustion engine.

The whole thing clunked and puffed out fumes just for effect. Underneath the bonnet was a regular solar generator. However the service station served as a landmark, there should be an old track almost cutting back on itself about a kilometre ahead. Pulling into the imitation fuel stop he found it deserted. He spread the map on the seat and fingered his route down the narrow lane to a small mark he had made earlier. The paper almost slid off the seat as he pulled out and headed off again and almost missed the turn, breaking hard. He reversed slightly and then used some of the opposing lane to swing the vehicle round and guide it down the dusty, bumpy track through some trees. Weeds were growing up the centre of the track and got higher as he passed a few large gateways to either side. He felt invigorated by the smell of warm damp air as it wafted through the window. Perhaps those simulated odours were accurate after all and were appealing to his primeval past. In a fraction of a second he almost cried out for the vehicle to stop before he remembered to press the brakes. One more quick look at his map and he was pretty sure this was the place.

Just gateposts but no gates, he pulled into the driveway and made his way up towards an old dilapidated but grand 21st century house, three stories high and still in reasonable condition though clearly uninhabited. His palms felt moist on the steering wheel as he spun the vehicle around the redundant fountain and stopped facing the exit. He switched off the engine and looked around, considering his escape should he need it. What if the driveway is blocked by an oncoming vehicle? There was an expanse of land around him and he imagined this vehicle would at least get him to the woods to his right if he needed to escape.

It felt like dusk even though it was morning but the climate inside the reserve bore little relation to the outside on any account. There was nothing but the sound of nature. That warm summer glow, the low sunlight was bright and yellow. He sat up sharply when he thought he heard a vehicle, but there was nothing. Touchreik rubbed his temples and checked the map once more. His own vehicle crackled and cooled in the morning air.

Half an hour had passed and he began thinking about heading back. He was expecting a vehicle and was focused on the driveway entrance. Then he was distracted by a movement in the corner of his eye. Something moving across to his right, near the woods. No, maybe mistaken. Wait. There it was again; a flash or reflection from the low sunlight. He watched, squinting. It was a man.

There was a man coming out of the woods and heading across the field towards him. He was slow and appeared quite old, could be a renter or something, maybe even a Marshall. It certainly wasn't the scumbag from the other night. The Doctor stayed put, reaching for his AR before realising it was back at the office. The man was definitely heading straight for him. Keeping his hands out of view he pushed the button down on the door to lock it as instructed at the reception and hire.

The man took an age to make his way through the long grass, maybe it wasn't his meet after all? As the man approached he could make him out a bit clearer and he felt a little more at ease seeing as he appeared older. He was dressed a little strange, walking unaided but with a stick and a rucksack over his shoulder. Red woollen loose fitting trousers with a green patterned shirt. The collar of his thick woollen overcoat pulled up around his bearded face. His expression was further hidden by his large but thin rimmed dark glasses and a tan fedora hat. He trampled across the gravel and reached the passenger side of the vehicle and peering through the dusty glass, he smiled broadly beneath his scruffy beard. He looked pleased and relieved as his breath steamed the dusty windows. The man sighed as the Doc wound down the window a couple of inches. Placing his wrinkled fingers either side of his eyes as if wanting to pull the glass down further the man peered through the gap.

He stared for a moment and the Doctor struggled to see what was going on behind his dark sunglasses.

"You made it then?" said the stranger. He sounded familiar, did he know him? For a second he felt all this mystery would be for nothing, just a prank.

"What's this about? Who are you?" said the Doctor confidently.

"Look, there's no easy way to say this so I'll come right out with it. I'm..."

The man paused glancing down in thought as if he might want to go back and reword the sentence but he didn't. Taking a step back he simultaneously removed his hat and sunglasses. With an item in each hand he spread his arms as if to take a bow.

The Doctor could not believe what he was seeing behind the grubby glass window. The pair stared into each other's eyes unblinking for a moment. The stranger stepped to the slightly open window and spoke into the gap.

"As you can see," he said, "I'm you."

FIVE

It was one of those rare moments in life when one might question reality itself. When one might test the other senses to ensure it wasn't a dream, Touchreik did just that; mentally noticing the invigorating aroma of the pines wafting across from his left and the breeze licking the tiny hairs on his face. If this was a dream then his perceptions were deceived at every level. What Doctor Touchreik saw was beyond any normal mental comprehension.

"I'm you." Those words had been spoken to him in his own voice from another being.

The apparition, standing like a scarecrow in the morning light was a tatty, older and unkempt version of himself. He stood motionless, arms outstretched with fedora and stick in one hand & glasses in the other, a waft of air blew his long grey beard onto his left shoulder. The expression of pride, relief and joy in the man's eyes was as much his own. He struggled to grasp the magnitude of the illusion. Locking eyes with the figure, he fumbled behind his back for the door handle and pushed it open with a creak. He reached his right leg backwards and felt for the ground, stepping backwards out of the transporter. Not for a second did he break his gaze as he walked around the front of the vehicle and approached. Their noses almost touched when stood eye to eye, studying every detail in the face. As a likeness he was faultless, greyer skin and slightly thinner in the face. Up close he smelled of stale embers and earth, reminding him of the humanists he despised. Allowing for the older man's slight stoop their height was identical. In terms of build they were a carbon copy of each other. Touchreik slowly raised his shaking hands up to the man's face and grabbed his cheeks firmly. He remained expressionless as the Doctor pulled at the beard, rubbing the cheeks with his thumbs as if the skin might peel away. Then he stepped back and turned away to study the wooded area the man had emerged from.

"How've you done this?" he whispered, hands on hips scanning the horizon.

"It's real, I'm actually you. Isn't it obvious?" the Professor dropped his hands, slapping his thighs as if that were evidence enough.

"It's some form of illusion, maybe a virus in the augmented reality chip."

The Professor plopped the hat onto his head and pulled the peak forward. "You're offline," he said.

The Doctor snatched at the back of his neck and realised he was right, he'd left his chip back at the office.

The Professor walked past and for a moment they stood side by side, staring at the horizon. The Professor rubbed the back of his neck and spun to look him up and down.

Taking a deep breath he sighed, "My name is Professor Algeria Touchreik, I was born in the year 2479 and I will be 78 years old this year, on the same day you recognise 37 years."

"Impossible," said the Doctor looking past him.

"Look." The Professor stood square to the Doctor with legs splayed; he whipped the sides of his coat back like a cowboy ready to draw and yanked his shirt upwards to show his belt. It was a crude garment that served no purpose hanging loosely about his waist. It had an oversized chrome buckle and in the centre were eight mechanical dials.

"I am seventy nine years old; I came back in time from the year 2557," he said nodding towards the belt.

The Doctor didn't answer, he stared at the belt and then back up at the Professor. The dials had numbers on them, all upside down. If he understood what the Professor claimed then it only served to add to the insanity.

"Who else would know about Ramona? Even Duke doesn't know, does he? Only we know," the Professor said.

The Doctor turned to look up at the house, three crows perched on the apex barked down at them in the still morning air. He turned once more, as if the man might be gone but he wasn't. He walked away from him across the dusty gravel drive and fell hard onto the bottom step of the old building. The Professor followed him, kicking a stone hard and watching as it bounced under the wooden steps.

"What's going on?" he said to his older self, silhouetted in front of the rising sun.

"I'm you and I've lived your life until the year 2557."

The Doctor picked up a branch and began doodling in the dust between his legs before drumming the end between his ankles.

"Professor?"

"2520," the Professor continued. "I've experienced a number of," he searched for the right word, "phases in my life."

The Doctor studied him as he paced up and down in front of the reddening sky. He had every movement, every mannerism so perfect he could be the Doctor conducting a lecture. "I've experienced the next 43 years of your life."

The Professor walked in a circle looking up and down as if inspecting the place. "It feels like a lifetime, because it was," he said as he stared up towards the stars. "I've been to places and done things that you wouldn't believe possible." He stopped and gripped his stick under his arm.

"A week ago I arrived from my own time and waited for the opportunity for us to meet."

"Where've you been since then?"

"I stayed with friends. I couldn't just walk up to you in the street."

"Anyone I know?"

"No," he paused, "not those friends, friends you," he paused again. "Friends you haven't met yet."

"So the freak with the note was a friend?"

"Jak may have unnerved you but it was vital I got you here, alone." The Professor paused in thought with his arms across his body, one hand on his chin straightening his beard.

"The future I lived could've just been the one that happened to me. I had to prove it wasn't; that it was all going to repeat itself as it did last time. It's important we don't disrupt that for now. That's why I've to be guarded in our conversations," he said looking up at the roof as the crows barked in response.

"What about Mother or the group, we have to tell somebody?" said the Doctor.

The Professor stopped, turning on one heel and rushed towards him. "We tell no one. It's too dangerous."

Seeing the shocked expression on the Doc's face he backed off.

"I'm sorry," he said showing his palms.

The Doc sighed. "You know about my future then, how things are going to be."

"Yes, and that future has to stay intact, events remain untouched."

"Like today's meeting?"

"Yes exactly that. It was designed to have minimum impact and avoid any ripples. So far nothing has changed."

"So why meet today?"

"It was convenient, I take it you were impressed with the South Sector Virtual Ball game results?" said the Professor with a smug grin.

"I've been impressed all season," said the Doctor, eyes widening as he slowly realised what the Professor was saying. "Wait a minute," he said pointing.

"Yes, I remembered, I remembered being right about that and I also remembered oversleeping that morning. That's why I picked today to meet with you," smiled the Professor.

"I'm right aren't I?" said the Doctor excitedly.

"Mmm, yes we were right."

"You know, if this is real we could do very well out of this?" grinned the Doc. "You kinda know things before they happen."

"Ripples?" he said then coughed nervously. "You may not realise now, but we're not actually the same person. Not anymore, people change with age more than you think. It's slow and subtle. Just remember we are decades apart." His eyes narrowed, he looked sad. "Your future changed me," he said. "The future you haven't lived yet. I think it'll change you too." Their eyes remained locked for a moment and in a way the Doctor could see some truth in his statement, being no stranger to changes himself. "Which means, time is getting on we have to get back."

"Back where?" questioned the Doctor standing up.

"Home," said the Professor reaching down to pick up his rucksack. "Don't you see? We have to stay close. It's vital we keep my impact on Heathen to a minimum."

"You're staying with me?"

"Of course."

"I thought you were visiting."

"Visiting? I haven't dropped by to give you fatherly advice. My trip was one way, there's no way back."

"One way?"

"I'm afraid so. We are going to be close for the foreseeable future."

"So we're a pair of Siamese twins, sharing the same food and bed?"

"You've got it. For the time being we have to share our home," he said.

"Our home?" said the Doctor angrily. "It's not 'our' home. It's my home." The Doctor stood up and stormed towards the vehicle before turning on the Professor, "Your home is forty odd years in the future. What about Duke, my work? How can we exist together?" he shouted and threw the stick he'd been drawing with across the courtyard and continued towards the transporter.

"It's temporary, I have a plan, trust me?" the Professor called after him. The Doctor swung open the door of the vehicle, noting the creak and imitation rust dropping into the door lining. Jumping in he dropped into the torn leather seat, sponge exploding through the tear and slammed the door shut with a hollow rattle.

"Trust me," he said to himself with a slight nervous laugh. The passenger door swung open and the Professor peered inside as if waiting for an invitation. The Doc opened his hands in a gesture on his knee, raised his eyebrows and the Professor climbed in beside him. The Doc sat for a moment with both hands gripping the top of the steering wheel, staring across at the woods as if it was guilty of spurning his older self.

The Doctor turned the key and the vehicle fired to life. "So what now? Can we go back a few years and then there will be three of us?"

"Honestly?" said the Professor shaking his head. "I've no idea. I have a spare belt. I had to bring it with me. These are the only two in existence and I couldn't leave one behind, besides I am not sure how many jumps can be made with these things."

"Well surely there are others?" he paused. "Who'll come after you," said the Doc twisting in his seat.

The Professor looked away scanning the landscape. He sighed. "It's very unlikely for a number of reasons," he said. "Start driving and I'll explain."

The Doctor shoved the lever forward and pressed the accelerator. "So, about the other time travellers?"

The Professor bobbed around in the passenger seat with both hands overlapping on his stick taking a deep breath.

"Forget what you may think you know about time travel, traditional logic doesn't apply. There are limitations to time travel that aren't worth the explanation. The time travel devices I have require a unique element to work and to my knowledge there are only two in existence, one in each of these belts."

The Doctor powered up the slope and the vehicle bounced onto the main road once more as he spun the wheel hard to the left.

"The second reason is that it's a dangerous and risky business. I was given almost no chance of succeeding."

They picked up speed on the main road back to the reception centre and passed no one as they cruised along the rolling smooth tarmac. The Professor looked across waiting for eye contact. He stared for a second then looked down dropping the large floppy hat onto his stick. Finally as he looked up the Doctor saw the look of dread in his eyes.

"At the moment there's a single and very important reason why no one will be coming back from the future," he said twisting himself round and resting his elbow on the back of the seat. "Unless we change something, there is one very important thing here." He pointed downwards at the tatty brown seat with the paper map on it. "In my past and your present then there will be no future for anyone to travel back from."

The Doctor hit the brakes and pulled over to the side of the road. The Professor looked away out of the transporter window and dropped his head to observe the last of the planets still visible in the brightening morning sky. He looked paler still and his expression became undeniably serious.

"That's the reason I'm here," said the Professor. He took a moment to let the words sink in and then broke into a smile, slapping his younger self on the shoulder.

"Let's go," he said. "I need a caffeine, that machine of yours is gonna breakdown forever next year so let's enjoy it while we can."

SIX

The pair exchanged no words on the remainder of the journey back to civilisation. Professor Touchreik as deep in thought as his young counterpart. He'd jumped decades back in time but the voice in his head refused to accept it. "Look around buddy, nothing's changed. Dead people are still dead and old people are still old, more importantly buildings that were bulldozed years ago are still bulldozed." That voice worked perfectly until the occasion he was faced with physical evidence. When coming across the un-dead, the un-old and the un-bulldozed. Then the voice went quiet, it turned away and left him to deal with it. Just over a week ago he'd taken a suicidal leap of faith and survived; now he knew the assignment had begun.

"That's your problem bubby," his comforting voice said. "I'm just trying to help ok." The voice was that of ignorance, the voice that is blind to realities our conscious mind struggled to cope with. That your friend died, or your lover and you will just be dust someday. The people from whom he's acquired the belts had been willing to make the same leap until circumstances changed that. Even the people who had designed the belts accepted that using them was in all likelihood a suicide mission. Their expectations ranged from the wearer's physical contents being scattered across space and time, to them frying themselves where they stood. Touchreik's motivation to attempt the leap went way deeper than the fear of death.

☐

The sun was coming up as the Professor walked up the lane away from the village. Sneaking away from a grieving boys bedroom like a thief in the night, and he was a thief. The night's spoils wrapped tightly around his waist. If it were possible to be elated and terrified in a single moment then that might describe the emotion he felt. After years of adversity there had been no time to pause or rest, and there still wasn't. Satisfied he was far enough from the village he stepped off the track and into the undergrowth. He had no idea how these things work. Would there be an explosion, flames or noise as was the case in fantasy sims or literature? He'd no wish to alert anyone and certainly no wish to endanger life other than his own.

He found a small clearing and looked around in the dim light for the spot he'd pre planned to make the leap. A grey mound protruded from the dead leaves and undergrowth. He made a final check in his rucksack and discarded a small metal fire-maker. Once he was satisfied there were no non-organic materials on him he tightened one of the belts around his waist. He made a quick adjustment to the dials and prepared to leap. He'd been told that the belts would transport only organic materials but which organic materials wasn't an exact science. Standing on rock would prevent him taking a few feet of soil or the odd tree with him. Above the numbered dials was a simple button which would activate the belts.

"Here we go," he thought. "Sayonara, arrivederci and adios cruel world."

He closed his eyes and pressed the button which popped under the pressure and then, nothing. He opened his eyes and looked down at the belt and a cold wash of disappointment ran over him like a wet blanket. Then he noticed the dim morning light fading until suddenly it became very bright again. Shadows drifted across his vision as if someone were shining a searchlight in the forest. His surroundings became blurry and the light became dark and light again, much quicker. He saw his surroundings in a kind of time lapse that increased speed until the day and night became a single blur. Trees and shrubs around him went from huge adult forms to seedlings and back again. In the space of a few seconds he couldn't distinguish the changes taking place in front of his eyes as the universe rewound across the decades. It was as if he wasn't travelling backwards but the universe was, whilst he stood still, frozen in time. At one point he was shoved to one side as a large tree grew next to him. As if he was in a protective bubble, impenetrable to the outside world. Then things slowed, the searchlight again and then stillness. The atmosphere changed instantly as if he'd stepped outdoors on a chilly day. He was thrown to the ground and lay on his back, a couple of metres from the grey rock he'd used as a launch pad. Had he not known better he might believe he was simply in another part of the forest. Physically he was in almost the same location excepting the nudge from a growing tree. He sat up and looked around.

"You crazy, spectacular being, take a look at how lucky you are," he thought, realising it had not only worked but he was alive. He stood up and dusted himself down, after a moment to gather his thoughts he decided to head back to the village. It would satisfy his curiosity and if he really was in 2515 then the village he just left wouldn't exist. The lane had been there a long time before that but was overgrown and unusable to vehicles. Touchriek followed it back into the village and found not only no village as expected but no signs of life. The ancient crumbling buildings that the village had been based around were barely visible but the occupants he'd seen hours before were nowhere to be seen. Some as younger men, others not born yet. It was as desolate a place as it would have been in the year 2515. No doubt time had shifted but how far he couldn't yet say but he had no reason to believe he wasn't bang on target. With his curiosity satisfied he swung round and set off up the lane and started the long lonely walk back to Heathen itself. At the end of the overgrown lane he found the service road that allowed drone vehicles to move around on the fringes, gathering and growing food and storing and transporting items. The roads were well used and maintained for the drone vehicles working on the outside. On more than one occasion as he traipsed along he came across drone transporters going about their business. They would simply stop when faced with human or organic life. Touchreik simply stepped to the side and they would continue on their way, uninterested by the interruption. The drones were part of an incredible feat of automation designed to service Heathen and its population. Those needs included food harvested from the fields, stored and processed inside enormous storage and process areas. Finished product would then be fed into the city by rail tunnel, road or physical drones. This area would likely have changed little over the decades and he knew enough to navigate himself to the storage area he needed. He wouldn't be bothered once inside and could wander around freely. He foraged some raw vegetables from one of the warehouses and pulled together a satisfying meal. After half an hour drifting around he made himself comfortable on a crate of packaging in an area that wasn't chilled and settled himself for the night. If he continued into Heathen it would be dark anyway and he'd have no access to supplies. The lack of an I.D. chip would leave him unable to access services within Heathen such as transport and food, normally freely available to citizens. He'd have to fend for himself until such time as he could gain physical support from his future friends and allies. Better to leave before dawn and give himself a full day to resolve his immediate problems. In the early hours he gathered some supplies in the dim light and set off. The Sun came up as he walked and by midday he could see the outer edge of Heathen City. Its immense profile spread across the horizon and at one point he was high enough to see its towering structures fading into the distance. His goal wasn't too far away and it was no coincidence he found himself on the correct edge of

Heathen. The climate became noticeably greyer on the outer edge until he pushed through. The fog was still heavy and the air thick but it improved slightly once inside the invisible boundary of Heathen. His goal was the Chase; here he would find his allies and friends. Those allies and friends didn't know him yet and worse still they didn't know each other. His first task was to push on into area SO63 and then retrace his steps. Walking the streets brought back memories of days long gone. So much so he wondered if he might bump into his younger self now, perhaps looking for more salubrious pleasures but it would be a little early in the day. He retraced his own steps from memory up to the heart of the humanist stronghold.

Beyond the place where drones and transport systems ended their services, a grey area between the bright green heartland of the city and the true outside.

The Professor's unfortunate experiences in recent years meant he didn't stand out in appearance, odour or demeanour and so had no trouble talking to those he found on the streets. At last being directed to a home where he might find the fellow he was looking for, an old comrade who would have no knowledge of him yet, a fellow called Jak Samian; a man who by now would have made headway as a thought leader amongst the humanists.

Timing was crucial and he was here to intervene in events, but only the right events. The plan was time critical, there could be no more reruns or leaps backwards in time. He'd used his ticket and there was no way back, or forwards. Time was passing and the train of opportunity was only stopping at the station once and he couldn't miss it.

At last he found the man he was looking for and had the advantage of recognition. He couldn't approach him at his own domain and followed him to a bar in SO63. He was forced to loiter outside without funds to purchase anything until the man exited alone.

His appearance made the older man that Touchreik knew well appear groomed by comparison. The Jak Samian of 2515 looked rougher and in some ways more tired, despite being younger in years. As was the way with many humanists his dress was plain and colourless. Touchreik hid in the shadows until he emerged from the bar alone. He hadn't spotted him despite his care to look up and down the street before pulling his fur lined jacket around him. He hunched his shoulders and leant forward as he headed off into the night. Touchreik followed him until he was far enough away from the bar that they wouldn't likely be disturbed.

"Jak!"

He appeared not to hear him and glanced around as if he might be addressing someone else.

"Jak!"

Touchreik quickened his pace to catch him as he hesitated, glancing over his shoulder.

"You addressin me?" he said as Toucreik approached.

"You're Jak Samian. We need to talk."

The next five minutes involved a conversation that was both difficult and intriguing. The Professor was open and honest about his approach, the time travel and what he was doing here. When he'd finished Jak took a moment to think over what he'd said before responding.

"Leave me alone," he pulled his overcoat around his body and began to walk away.

"What if I could prove it to you," said Touchreik.

Jak stopped a few yards away and turned. "How?"

"My younger self lives in Heathen, if we meet him then you'll know my story is true."

Jak took a step towards him. "You're saying the younger you, before you came back is still here?"

"Would you believe me then?"

"He might be cloned out of sync?" said Jak.

"A possibility, but what if I could also predict the future?"

"Ok, so we meet your younger self and you then predict events that you say have already happened to you?"

"That's the idea."

"You should leave." He turned and headed off, disappearing around a corner.

Touchreik shouted after him. "I'm here because you're right about Mother!" His words echoed up the dark streets attracting the attention of a man on the opposite side of the road.

Nothing, Touchreik turned away despondent.

He'd gone a block or two in the opposite direction when the man appeared from an alleyway in front of him. He leant on the corner of the wall on one leg and took a bite from an apple.

"What about Mother?" he said.

Touchreik sighed with relief. "You're right about Mother; I'm here to stop it happening."

"You came back in time to stop Mother?"

"So why me?"

He took Jak's forearm and lead him into the alleyway. "We knew each other, in the future."

Jak looked into his eyes for some kind of clue but there was nothing but sincerity.

"The three of us can do this; I'm trying to get us back together."

"Three?"

"The third is a man called Antoine Feng."

"Who's he?"

"One of you, one of us," said Touchreik.

"Can he be trusted?"

"Feng is a man you'll meet around 2520 and forge an alliance with, you'll build the humanist movement together."

He roared with laughter. "I haven't met my future partner, is that what you're saying?"

"We haven't got time for that to happen, we need to find him and act now."

"It's vital we do this and enlist the help of my younger self."

"Wait, are you saying the younger you is still here?"

"Yes."

"And how do you plan to deal with Mother?"

"That's just it, it's not my plan, it's yours."

He stopped chewing and stared up at him.

"That's right, I'm here to execute a plan you and a man you haven't met yet thought of decades from now?"

"This Feng, he would eventually be my colleague anyway?"

"In my past that's true enough but time travel doesn't work intuitively. Things are happening as they did in my past but this is a clean slate. It starts from now."

"What do you know of my future then, my family."

"You know I can't discuss that."

Jak took a final bite and threw the core under his arm and it bounced up the alleyway. "Here's what I'll do. I'm going to meet this younger version of you. I'm going alone and then we'll talk." Jak turned to leave and Touchreik grabbed his arm once more.

"I need some help."

"How."

"I have no chip, I need accommodation."

Jak looked around disbelievingly. "Ok, first I meet this younger you, then we'll go and find this Feng fellow. Then I'll decide. Come on."

Jak took Touchreik to his accommodation up in the chase. Just like the village there were very few amenities or technology. The home was sparse and bore little resemblance to the loving home he might have in the future. Touchreik had no way of knowing if he was preventing that path in this man's life.

The Professor was made comfortable in a spare room and they chatted further. The conversations they had that night were enough to further convince Jak of his authenticity and he warmed a little. At no time had the Professor hesitated in his discussions other than when he might compromise the future as it stood. The most difficult thing had been convincing him of the rudimentary elements of time travel. Time appeared linear to our concept but it wasn't, which eliminated the common time travel paradox. If the Doctor or even his own mother were killed it would have no effect on the Professor, it just didn't work that way. They may as well be in a separate universe because they could only experience life from their own perspective, there was only now. The Professor had known Jak to be a serious man but his younger self was even more so. Having woken the next morning the feeling amongst friends wasn't mutual. There was no sign of Jak and no one knew where he was. Touchreik stayed around and attempted to remain inconspicuous and expected Jak the following evening, but there was nothing. He was no prisoner but the others eyed him suspiciously, with no motivation to leave he stayed put. After a second night Touchreik was becoming concerned, there was still no news until late in the evening.

Touchreik lay on the bed pondering his next move. Jak and the others may be on his side in the future but he was an alien to them now. The silence was broken by noise downstairs. The front door opened and he heard voices below, quiet and suspicious whispering. He silently climbed from the bed and made his way down stairs into the lounge area. Jak was standing talking to a man who was sat in the lounge chair with his back to him. Seeing him enter Jak gave the man his drink and then looked up.

"Professor," he said.

The man in the chair stood up and turned around and the pair stood together looking at him with expressions devoid of recognition. The Professor stopped himself from running into the room to hug them both. He realised that no matter what they'd been through together, none of the three men knew each other.

"Antoine," said the Professor, his eyes wide.

"Hey," he said with a familiar smirk and turned to Jak winking.

Looking at them both he almost laughed out loud, two naive young men with futures they knew nothing about. He'd last set eyes on them in their late 50's.

"Tomorrow," Jak said with a nod.

He could see that this grim faced man knew this felt right, the three of them being together regardless of how they met.

"Tomorrow I'm going to meet the Doctor," he said.

## SEVEN

The Doctor and the Professor made their way across the square and took the elevator up to the 11th floor. In the unlikely event they met another resident their likeness would certainly draw attention. Pullis was one of the few who might be willing to greet and put them in an embarrassing situation but he'd be able to pass his older self as DNA kin of some kind. Although both wary of anyone approaching the coast remained clear. The Doctor's apartment was three doors along from the lift and as they approached the door opened automatically and they slipped inside. The Professor's subliminal voice of ignorance switched off the minute they entered an apartment that in his memory had been destroyed a long time ago. The decor and smell evoked a sense of time when he lived peacefully in this environment. When the inner voice of ignorance left there was nothing but a dizzy feeling of nostalgia left in its place. An ache to be back before everything he'd been through and reliving these carefree days, a time when he was happy and unaware of what his future held. The ludicrous feeling of stepping back in time forced an involuntary smile.

The surroundings were so familiar, to the left the study, then the small bedroom; perhaps the Professor's accommodation for the foreseeable future. The living space and food prep areas were in a single space, divided by a work-surface. Then there was the main bedroom, the door opened as the Professor approached and stood in the doorway.

"No," said the Doctor firmly.

The Professor looked in and the feeling was overwhelming, he stared at the wardrobe. He was aware of its contents and his heart pounded. He looked back at the Doctor who was slowly shaking his head.

"No," he said once more. The Professor would have loved to see her once more but now wasn't the time to push it. She was part of the reason he'd risked his life to be here, maybe later.

"Duke," said the Doc sharply to his sage.

"Good afternoon."

43

"My friend the Professor will be staying with us for a few days."

"Hello Professor," said Duke. "Will you be giving full access?"

"No." He beckoned him to come away from the door. "Guest access."

The Professor walked over and placed his hand across the scanner by the front door.

"Sir, I need the guest to scan," said Duke.

The Professor kept his hand on the pad and whispered to the Doc. "Same DNA?"

The Doctor shrugged his shoulders. "Duke, never mind with access just change the security setting please to allow for a pet."

"Certainly." It was the most logical solution for now, Duke could allow for two organic lifeforms in the building for now.

The pair went into the lounge area and sat down. "We share DNA, no need to change the settings, you have all privileges."

"Thank you."

"This means I trust you, you understand that? My space is my space. I don't want you in there. Agreed?"

"Agreed. On our life." He smiled before adding, "Joke."

The Professor had seen enough to know that events were reflecting the history he knew but was surprised at how familiar the place looked. He wasn't sure if he expected the decor to be different as some way of proving he was in a different dimension. It fitted his memory perfectly and he was overcome with a feeling of security being here. He was already looking forward to a restful sleep.

"So what about the life I was meant to have, to be a Professor and to do what you did? Will that change?"

The Professor looked around before responding. "Have you ever heard of a mental condition called Capgras delusion?" he said.

"No."

"It's an interesting psychiatric disorder in which a person holds a delusion that a friend, spouse, or other close family member has been replaced by an identical impostor that is completely undetectable from the original."

The Doctor shuffled uncomfortably before allowing him to continue.

"In a way, my entire universe has been replaced. Events in which I don't intervene are following the same path. I don't know the complete answer to your question other than to say by definition that's no longer possible because I'm here. If you're asking me where the life I left behind either went or will go I can't say."

The Professor's time travelling expertise was strictly 'learn on the job' he knew of no one who'd ever done it before. He'd lost count of the conversations over the years. "If no one had ever announced themselves as being from the future then that in itself was proof it was never going to be possible." What they'd failed to take into account was that it just doesn't seem feasible to travel outside your own lifetime. Certainly for no measurable amount of time, the early experiments and calculations had proven that beyond doubt. Secondly, there was the very fact that anyone who travelled back in time made such an announcement would be most foolhardy. A mistake he had no intention of making, at least for now. Small changes could have catastrophic effects, the fact that he had returned to make a huge change was as far from his mind as he could push it. Nonetheless it had required that the Professor stay close to his younger self at all times, when he couldn't he should make as little impact as possible. Now that the first part of his plan had been completed and he was actually here it was starting to feel that travelling back in time to meet himself, might just be the easy part. The task that lay ahead was vast.

"What's that man?" the Doctor enquired suspiciously. "The man who brought the message to meet you?"

"A friend," the Professor lied. He knew what the Doctor was hinting at from his tone. "What's that man?" was like questioning his humanity, but he was no fool. Knowing his younger self, he could probably smell a humanist at a hundred metres.

The Professor had outlined his plan to Jak Samian about the meeting before he unexpectedly disappeared and took matters into his own hands. He knew the politics of his younger self were not shared.

"No red hair, no lightning stripes, ok?" the Professor had insisted. "Turn up with any humanist symbols and we've blown it."

Jak had reluctantly agreed. "He's gonna find out what company you're expecting him to keep sooner or later," he snarled.

"I know him remember, I was him. It'll take time. Believe me, he hates humanist rebels."

"And you?" said Jak.

"What about me?"

"You're the same person right, you're just older."

"Humanity is at stake, you're right after all. Is that what you want to hear?" The Prof walked towards the door glancing over his shoulder before adding. "Incidentally, no I don't like humanists."

A broad smile spread across Jak's face as he stared back out the window.

The Professor knew that Samian was exactly the kind of person he would have found obnoxious as a younger man and somehow he had to gain the trust of the Doctor. With what was at stake and the reason he'd come back Jak wasn't the man he'd mature into. As his young self he'd never believe that Jak and these savages might one day be right, might be the ones who have preserved the skills of survival long enough to save mankind? Never in a million years, yet here he was.

The Doctor let it go for now but it would stay on the boiler in his mind, simmering away but it enabled him to avoid the difficult conversation for another day.

The Professor kept his promise to stay away from the Doctor's room although he stayed around more as if to reduce the opportunities. They spent the week in close proximity, sharing meals but not a bed. As a pet, the Professor was never ejected by the Duke and so it worked well and bought some time. The Professor preferred to be out of the way and avoid the difficult questions. He convinced the Doctor that all was well, the time will come and he may have been initially over dramatic. As the days passed it was becoming apparent how bloody annoying he'd been as a younger man. The bad taste in entertainment systems, untidiness and ignorance to name but a few. Perhaps nature had given us all the ability to forget how obnoxious we were as youngsters because he had no memory of being so. The Doctor's place was exactly as he remembered it and even though it had been knocked down many years previous in his memory it felt like walking into an exact reproduction. It hadn't been condemned yet to make way for the transport upgrades; that would be some way off. Some days just the sound of Duke would make his eyes water. It was a voice he had relied on for many years and he hadn't heard it for decades. Having upgraded him around 2536 and although he uploaded all the memories to his new assistive software he had upgraded the voice and personality too. The Duke treated them both as the same person for all commands because of the DNA ident so the Professor was less dependent. It seemed that Duke's software ident package had no problems at all as long as it treated them as the same person with identical security rights.

The Prof knew he was going to need to stay out of sight for a while. There was also a need to confirm that significant events he remembered were happening again, exactly as they did the first time. Once he had confirmed that, and so far this seemed to be the case, the timing was crucial. The Doc hadn't brought up the subject of 'that man' and the Professor preferred it like that for now. Perhaps to pursue it further would have brought up the subject of his physical relationship with a drone called Ramona Stone? A subject neither of them wanted or needed to discuss now, if ever. Professor Touchreik had some advantage over his younger self but they both knew that the dark thoughts that everyone holds would remain in the dark. Tucked away and never to surface, never discussed even with yourself.

The one topic of repetitive conversation was the reason the Professor had come back. He'd regretted the drama he'd created about the survival of the human race but the truth is the truth. That wasn't a subject that could be dumbed down and it was that simple; humanity or no humanity.

"You can't tell me? Are you serious?" the Doc said. "The end of humanity, you came back to stop it and you can't tell me?"

"Trust me it's vital things happen as they did the first time around for me, for us," the Prof corrected himself. He knew if he was going to execute his plan then he was going to have to tread very carefully. He had long realised how people change over a lifetime as youthful abandon succumbs to stoicism and maturity but this was going to be different. This wasn't going to be like trying to convince his younger self to give up rock/tech for sonic/opera. It went much deeper than that. He still remembered vividly his passion for Mother and the world order, even more now he had spent a couple of days with him. He knew in the coming weeks he was going to have to turn the Doctor's beliefs on their heads. To convince him to kill the one thing he loved above all else. It was going to break his heart; that much he was sure of and yet he could only hope reason would win through.

"We should go to Mother, put a message out," the Doctor said.

"Absolutely not, we must not discuss this in the cloud. Besides, 'Mother' would utilise all its inputs to try and solve the problem and that's the last thing we want."

The last couple of days had been a strain; the Professor didn't help himself by dropping in comments about this and that. How the Doctor might cough without covering his mouth or how he was so critical of others at times. The Professor would comment on his diet and how it could lead to medical complications in the future. Yesterday he was enjoying a soda drink and caught the Professor staring.

"Problem?" the Doctor commented.

"You know you could get joint problems with that stuff?" he replied. The Doctor was growing more and more impatient.

"What do you mean could?" he said staring the Professor in the eyes. "Either I will or I won't."

"2548," he said looking down humbly. "Nothing serious but still, I am only trying to help."

The Doctor finished the drink in a single swig and launched the empty container in the general direction of the disposal. The battered can bounced off the lid and across the floor before a small droid the size of a cat began its slow journey to collect it. Finally pushing it against the skirted wall where it disappeared into a slot.

"I don't suppose there's anything nice I can look forward too?" he said storming into the food prep area to grab another. This was a perfect opportunity, he hated to hold back crucial information but here was a chance to move the plan forward. Time was running out, he thought it was going to be easy to manipulate his own young mind. Not so.

"There's the new project," he said loudly as he went into the life area and sat down. The Professor placed his calves on the settee and flamboyantly cupped both hands behind his head. He closed his eyes as if he might take a nap. The Doc wandered in casually, soda in hand.

"New project?" he said, collapsing into the huge L shaped sofa, "What new project, when?"

The Professor opened one eye.

EIGHT

Vic picked up the dining chair and hoisting it above his head, stumbling towards the balcony. As he swung it over the barrier the momentum was almost enough to pivot him upwards and send him spinning earthwards with it. His bare feet squeaked on the marble floor as his outstretched toes kicked out to find purchase. Rocking backwards he stabilised himself, a mischievous smile spreading across his face as he surveyed the shifting mass of exposed heads and shoulders below. A typical London morning as throngs of commuters hurried to desks, jumped in cabs or sat in a trance on buses as they crawled along the teeming streets. He wasn't sure how much longer he could hold on, if he didn't let go soon he'd surely go down with it.

"Nova!" said Bluu in her scolding tone, marching purposefully across the room towards him. The tone she reserved for all his little signs of rebellion, like putting his head in the oven and switching it on or pushing metal into the electrical sockets. The name 'Nova' was growing on him and he hadn't had an opportunity to determine why they thought it was his. There was little point in rocking the boat just yet; after all if they found out he wasn't Nova, who knows how they'd react? They might be so pissed they'd just throw him back in the freezer, like his first wife Angela might when she discovered she'd taken steak out of the freezer instead of chicken. No he thought best to play along for now and get the measure of them first. Vic Jones had died just over three weeks ago, in his mind at least and had found himself 500 years in the future. He felt relatively fit and healthy with no sign of the cancer that had been eating him alive. In the process he'd acquired a sparkly new 22 year old version of his own body. It was unnerving at first, climbing out of the shower and catching a reflection in the full length mirror of someone who wasn't you. He was visibly gaining weight and strength by the day. Standing completely naked in front of the mirror he'd run his palms across his chest and down to his hips. The skin felt soft and firm, even the goods between his legs looked more attentive and plump. He was being well cared for, if a hamster in a cage can be counted as well cared for that is. The environment was comfortable enough but this

49

didn't represent the world as it really was out there in 2515. In here everything had been put in place to avoid unnerving him, in a way people from the future might interpret 2015 if they'd never really seen it.

Growing up his mum loved to tell of when she'd taken him to the 'Roman London' exhibition. Inside was a mock-up of a Roman Emperor's throne room. As a very young child he'd been duped by the reality of it, and why wouldn't he? Through the opening he could see the roman square, albeit a frieze, but with additional background sounds of a roman market the illusion was complete to a boy his age. He gaped at the spoils of war scattered across the floor, chests that overflowed with gold chains and coins, goblets and ornaments. The memory was all the more vivid because his young mind had spotted an opportunity to solve all the problems his Father talked about.

"Angela, we just can't afford it."

"That boy is growing out of shoes again?"

"Angela switch the big lights off. We ain't made of money."

He'd slipped under the rope barrier with a single, and at the time common sense objective; to pertain a single gold coin from the enormous stash he saw before him. He knew from his mother's bedtime stories how much a single gold coin was worth. Enough to keep them in new shoes and electricity forever, and the Emperor would hardly miss just one. By the time he'd made his move and realised it was made of plaster and welded to the floor, his mother was dragging him backwards by the hood of his coat. As his feet left the ground he realised his crime had been rumbled and the booty he almost had in his grasp was just a decoy. The three weeks he'd been here had taught him a similar lesson; things are not always what they seem. The furniture was inconsistent with any particular period in time, not particularly unusual in itself but most of it was completely non-functional. It was like living in a dolls house where everything was purely cosmetic.

Never missing the irony that he himself was not what he seemed either; the reason they thought he was someone else may have plenty of explanations. 500 years is a long time and there were just as many reasons why he could have ended up in a cryogenic pod with the wrong label on. The pod must have been moved around a lot over time, maybe the label fell off or got swapped with another in some way? The real worry was why they'd thawed out or thought they'd thawed out 'Mr Nova' instead of Vic Jones. If it turns out they only want to experiment on him in a human zoo then he might tell them the truth if it's not too late. Heck, he thought, I might want to go back in the freezer anyway. So until the scalpels come out he was going to answer to the name 'Nova' and that was that. Through his chats with Bluu, Vic was aware that even in the year 2515 or TVC15 as she called it putting people in new bodies wasn't a common procedure. It was the reason they'd done it that bothered him more than anything. Even in his own time he knew bringing back the woolly mammoth didn't mean they were to be set free to roam the plains or whatever it was they roamed. It meant sticking them in a cage so people could come along with their whining kids and gawk at them and take selfies to post on Twitter. Maybe his destiny was to become the star attraction at a freak show if he wasn't already? There's no need to piss them off just yet, there'd been no signs of aggression, quite the opposite. However he couldn't live out his days in a life sized dolls house. It'd even crossed his mind that they might not be human, he could be on another planet for all he knew. Play along, be a good boy and see what happens. At the end of the day who gave a shit about Nova, presumably he was still in a freezer somewhere. He didn't know him and even if he did he wouldn't like him. What sane person calls themselves Nova or Novel or whatever? Let him stay in the freezer for now, Vic was going to get a handle on what's going on first.

In the meantime he'd stand on his balcony every morning and smell the pollution as if it were real. He'd watch the rush hour traffic below, cyclists weaving amongst taxis and cars that were blaring their horns for no reason. The buses from above looked like giant red maggots that would occasionally stop to hoover up unfeasibly large numbers of bodies stood on the pavement. The street below could've been any street around central London.

It was testament to his growing strength that he was able to hold the chair for a few moments before letting it go. Watching as it tumbled towards the passing throngs, a protruding ledge sending it spinning madly downwards. Then, slowly as it got closer to the bobbing crowd of exposed heads, it disappeared. Vic shrugged in disappointment, unsurprised and ambled back into the apartment. It had been only weeks since he was thawed and as his strength grew so did his boredom. He was only here for 'observation' but felt fine and burned up energy by driving his carers insane, convinced that would get him out sooner. An expression of his will to be set free, to explore the mysterious new world he found himself in.

It wasn't that there was any kind of threat or sense of being in-prisoned, that wasn't it. If this wasn't a prison then it was certainly some kind of quarantine from the 'futures' population. To him they were 'futures' because although he knew they were human beings they seemed different to him. Like foreigners or aliens, from a very different culture, placid in nature yet odd in their outlook. The weeks had drifted by and he'd still no real idea what the outside world actually looked like.

Bluu was with him daily, a companion, a nurse or maybe a guard, maybe all three? Either way she'd always been kind and considerate as well as pleasant enough company. In the early days she'd tended to him physically but as he'd grown stronger he became more independent. Bluu switched from physical to mental support, explaining what she could about how things had changed and what he could expect when he left. She was like an ambassador to the futures, passing messages and facilitating his development. At night she'd leave him alone and return the next morning.

It was during these long night hours, particularly as he became stronger that he tested the security. He felt no immediate need to escape; he just wanted to know if he could. It didn't take long to discover that he almost certainly couldn't.

Not a window, door, or ventilation shaft would show a hint of budging. Even the flimsiest window catch or air conditioning shaft was only designed to look flimsy, none of it was. His most realistic chance of escape appeared to be the balcony until he learned it was purely a hologram. A fact he struggled to believe because it was far from the twitchy blue renditions he'd seen on Star Wars, it was effectively real in every way. He passed off his testing of its impregnability as just childish pranks by throwing items over the side for fun. If it was a hologram then perhaps there would be a screen or projector which may be a way out, should he need it. Instead items that were dropped or thrown simply disappeared as they fell, putting paid to any ideas of taking a leap of faith in the hope he might land on some kind of projector. It would take nerves of steel to jump off a 14th story balcony and hope for the best. Since he'd been more mobile Vic's attention had been drawn to what seemed to be an adjoining door. Having fooled around with the lock many times in the hope it might simply pop open like in an episode of Magnum P.I. That's until amazingly, one night when on the brink of giving up, it did exactly that. The lock clicked and the handle gave way. He jumped back and stood in astonishment for a second. Slowly he approached and gripping a handle in each hand stepped backwards pulling the double doors wide. He wiped his sweating palms on the thigh of his pyjamas and stared. There was only the dim light coming from his own apartment to illuminate the other room. He could make out the shadowy shapes of furniture but was unable to see into the blackness beyond. Perhaps there would be a light switch in there? The hairs on his arms bristled from the chilly air blowing inwards and he walked towards the opening. As he was about to step across the threshold, his forehead cracked against what he thought was a glass door. Running his hand across the surface he realised there was no possible way it could be.

The cooler air was brushing his cheeks yet this force field for want of a better description was both solid and invisible. Feeling his way around it like a mime artist, he detected what appeared to be a join in the middle. Forcing his fingers into the gap he pulled outwards like he was operating an invisible bull-worker. It would shift a little yet it soon became clear it was not going to budge more than an inch. Every time he got some purchase on it the force would spring the invisible door back together and threaten to trap his fingers. Closing the existing wooden adjoining doors he slipped back to bed, if nothing else he'd peeked into the real world. No sign of armed guards or alarms going off.

Vic was becoming stronger and more confident by the day and was keen to get out, if they were never letting him out why have a hologram of London? They could just as easily place him in a bland cell. Bluu had explained how the surroundings were to help him feel at home and adjust. Why not just open the window and let him see the future? She'd insisted that time would come but the weeks had passed. He couldn't help wondering if they were hiding something from him.

The 'futures' had certainly done their best to help him feel at home and whether he chose to admit it or not, the quarantine cell disguised as a hotel suite had put him at ease. The view of the London skyline from the balcony was incredibly realistic, along with interior fixtures and fittings resembling a 21st Century hotel suite. Discovering in time that all of it was in the main, false, that light switches didn't work and draws didn't open. The TV didn't work either; there was just white noise when he switched it on. On the balcony he could experience the sounds and smells of the bustling city below. He'd naturally assumed it was real at first and it made him feel closer to home, to his own time. Even now he found it comforting. Discovering it was just a hologram he began figuring out where in London he would have been by checking out the buildings he recognised on the skyline. It was only then he realised how bad its geography was. Everything that he would expect to see was there, but in the wrong places. Yet it was so real, he could feel the cool city breeze, smell the mixture of fresh air and car fumes. He wanted to go downstairs and run out into the street. Sadly the street wasn't there, even if he could open a door.

He would shout obscenities at passers-by below, they always ignored him. On the third day he dropped a cushion off the balcony and watched as it fell, before slowly disappearing. In other ways he had been kept comfortable. Every kind of food he could wish for in any quantities was provided by a kind of room service. He never saw anyone else, just the trolley outside the door. Over time though Vic had come to realise that every meal he ordered would arrive looking hot and appetising yet everything tasted similar. His eyes tricked his brain into tasting different things but deep down he knew that chips tasted like peas and peas tasted like steak. Growing more and more restless every day his curiosity about the outside grew, at least in prison you knew what freedom could be like. Slumping back into his chair he picked up the remote interface and repeatedly opened and closed the curtains. Staring across at Bluu out of the corner of his eye she failed to notice him peering deep into her soul. Vic was becoming very fond of her. Bluu possessed an incredible knack for managing his mood or feelings, calming and reassuring him after having spoken to other futures over the recent weeks on screen. That Burroughs guy and a few others had been on, assuring him he was safe and important and all that kind of thing but she was the only one who seemed to be civilian. The only one who was ever physically here with him. The others had that official, medical tone, but not Bluu. It was like she cared, really cared and he probably needed that. A 22 year old body, a mind with 68 years of experience, in a world where he had no experience at all it almost seemed dangerous, like a baby with a shotgun. He was embarrassed at his growing infatuation and interest in her, particularly in light of her sexuality. Technically she was neither male nor female purely androgynous. He hadn't stopped to bother about that, yet. The plump anticipating goodies that hung between his legs though were stirring uneasily.

Bluu and the futures had reassured him that he would not be confined here indefinitely.

"We have to ensure you're safe to meet the population and vice versa."

There were natural concerns about ancient germs, viruses and such like. Not just ones he might transmit but those he may receive too. There was also the vast gap in culture between him and them. These conversations were his first hint that he was big news on the outside. Vic or Nova as they called him, was being groomed and educated before being introduced to the general population. Like training to be an ambassador to 2015 and they didn't want him committing a faux pas in public. A slip of the tongue at the wrong time he thought, a mention of Shelly's Frankenstein in the wrong circles might not go down well.

They'd given him a new young body, with all his memories and mind intact and he was physically around 22 years of age. Feeling lighter, stronger and virile once more. Physical feelings he didn't notice leaving the party were casually wandering back in. Sex drive, strength and power all slip quietly away in the night, bit by tiny bit unnoticed over the years. Inside this new body all those things had returned in an instant and he felt like a pubescent teenager struggling with boiling hormones and emotions. Does being in an enclosed environment mean a person will sexually gravitate to anything human? From what Bluu had told him she was neither male nor female, not uncommon these days. The male part of her features and her strength was what gave her the machismo with enough feminism to make her attractive, a kind of pretty Peter Pan character. Still juggling with his teenage emotions he felt there was something more that attracted him to Bluu in a non-sexual way. He shrugged it off as dependence, like a kidnap victim falling in love with their captor. But hey he thought it has been five hundred years since he last got laid! He tried the old fashioned approach, asking about leisure, parties and partners but she struggled with those concepts. Her concept of sex, boy, girl, male and female, was that they were completely interchangeable and non-exclusive.

He had a lot to learn before many of the future etiquette and ideas would make any sense. Staring back blankly at the wall Vic's eyes glazed over as he became lost in thought. What had felt to him like ten minutes had turned out to be hundreds of years. His plan had been to thaw out when there was a cure for his illness.

"Cured? Oh no we can't do that." Bluu had explained matter of factly on the day he first saw himself in the mirror. By all accounts his illness was not only very old but was age related. The reason humans had died of such things in his time was because the breeding was done very young. These days it was much more controlled and whilst degenerative illnesses still existed they would appear much later in life. What they'd successfully done instead was to reset his body clock by using his existing DNA to create a younger body. What they had failed to do, up until he had seen himself in the mirror was to actually tell him. Clearly they were expecting him to be pleased, like a surprise, as if someone has valeted your car or decorated the front room while you're out.

"Surprise! What do you think of the new body? Yes that's you in the mirror! While you were frozen we took your brain out and put it in a new 22 year old body. Great huh?"

"Aw, a new body," he should have said. "22 with eyes of blue! You shouldn't have. I love it. Thanks guys." Instead he'd freaked out.

To be fair he'd adjusted surprisingly quickly since and it had been made easier because he felt physically better every day, in fact he was close to full fitness now which only added to his frustrations. He didn't recognise the significance until later but Bluu had gone to great lengths to explain that his legal age was actually 22 years old. There was seemingly some kind of legal lifespan allowance of 130 years. Being used to a life expectancy of 90' ish years it seemed like a good deal. In the year 2515 the act of euthanasia at 130 was cause for celebration. It was a way of giving something back to society, making space for others. Being legally 22 was looking more and more like a steal.

"How come everyone doesn't just get a new body, like I did?" enquired Vic.

"That would be very unfair and selfish," said Bluu abruptly. "Why would anyone do such a thing, Euthanasia is a special time," she said in a quizzical way as if the very idea of cheating the system was the moral equivalent of stealing from the church collection box.

"How old are you?" asked Vic casually trying to change the subject. Bluu stopped and thought for a moment, he was used to her being very decisive, it was a long moment. Finally she blinked and ignored the question completely, that's a lady's prerogative he supposed. She continued to explain how in order to manage the gene pool the computer thing that ran the place had decided that 130 years would be the life limit. From the way he was being treated and what he heard it might never matter, he was clearly a special case. Either way it would be over a hundred years before he was expected to stick his head in the oven so until then he'd be happy to flout the rules. Of greater concern was what the hundred years had in store for him. He felt young, fit and agile but was he ever getting out of here?

Bluu sat next to him oblivious to his piercing stares. As he spoke, her eyes widened as if broken from a trance.

"So is this it?" he sneered angrily.

"What's your implication?" Bluu folded the tablet computer she was using and swung her legs around looking concerned. Her brow furrowed above her deep Blue eyes like a nurse who'd suddenly noticed a blip on a patient's monitor. Sitting up and turning her complete attention to him he chose not to reciprocate, staring at the constantly opening and closing curtains.

"I feel fine, why am I a prisoner in this fucking zoo?" he gazed up at the ceiling. "Are they watching me right now? Like a panda! Maybe they'll want to breed me and get some more cavemen to experiment on!"

Vic stood up glaring down at Bluu as if waiting for an answer, there was none. She looked up at him with hurt and confusion in her huge eyes. A pained expression like a mother being told she was a failure by her only child. She didn't respond in words, the lip quivered, the eyes filled. He paused a second too long and spun around fists clenched with his own nails biting into his palms. He stormed into the bedroom and slammed the door, throwing himself on the bed. Bluu watched him go, jumping as the door slammed loudly. With a shocked and worried expression Bluu reached for the tablet she had set down beside her. Vic launched himself onto the bed closing his fists around the silk sheets before picking himself up on all fours kicking and punching the pillows in frustration. On the other side of the door Bluu calmly tapped and stroked the screen once more whilst hearing his muffled screams over the low hum of the city outside. Vic jumped off the bed and put his fingers behind a high walled dresser to topple it. Realising it wouldn't budge he screamed and turned his frustration on a small table which was similarly fixed. Crazed he ran around the room pulling and heaving at items of furniture. Nothing would move, all of it was completely immobile. He wouldn't even get the satisfaction of trashing the place. Vic went back to the bed with tears of frustration running down his face. Screaming into the pillow like a child until he could hardly breathe. A mixture of snot and tears across his reddened face soaked into the cloth. He thought Bluu would come to comfort him and he wanted her to. Desperately he wanted her to come so he could scream some more, tell her to leave him alone and blame her, but she didn't. After about an hour he'd cried himself to sleep. When he woke up the room had darkened as the simulated Sun had set across the city outside. Vic slid off the bed and staggered over to the bedroom door and slowly opened it. Looking around the empty apartment, aside from the low hum of the city outside there was silence. Bluu was gone, calmly closing the door with a click he turned and went back to bed.

NINE

The next morning Vic came out of his room, shielding his red eyes from the glare of a bright summer morning bursting in from the balcony. He'd been pretty upset last night and still was. He couldn't help thinking that the summer morning was just for him; that the futures had programmed it to cheer up the caveman. Maybe they thought the caveman would like that kind of thing, after all they were used to living outside when they were hunting buffalo, they might have said. Bluu knocked and entered as usual bringing in his breakfast. Pulling his nightgown around him he shuffled across the room without making eye contact. She placed the cup and plate in front of him as he sat at the dining table. It was becoming a pointless ritual now that he could clearly bring his own meals, not least cook them. He looked down at the plate of steaming sausages, eggs and beans along with brown toast and mushrooms. He felt his blood boiling with anger, he had to make something happen, he felt like a rat in a cage. He must refuse to perform for his captors. Without thinking he slipped his hand under the warm plate and launched it across the room sending the food splattering down the gold leaf wallpaper. Bluu flinched at this explosion of anger and looked at him, the tiny residue of food droplets running down her face and clothing. He stood up breathless with anger, his chest and shoulders heaving up and down, his eyes demanding a reaction. He regretted his actions immediately. The pain in her eyes made him feel like an angry father who'd just lashed out at a playful toddler.

Shit, he thought. He could read her mind; she was stunned by his act of aggression. He suddenly felt pathetic; he was a caveman after all. That's what she was thinking, and he didn't want her to think it. He wanted to take away what he had just done and wipe it clean but he couldn't.

"I have a surprise for you today," she said holding back tears and smiling, dabbing her face clean with the back of her hand. He looked away to the floor in shame. "It's time for us to explore and for me to show you our history and what we know of your future. The future you missed."

58

Her voice was croaky like an abused wife trying to reason with the animal she still loved. The double doors swung open and a couple of futures came in. Both were dressed in white lab coats and wearing hospital face masks. Vic wondered if they had been outside and heard the commotion yet they didn't look at him once. Both he and Bluu looked away embarrassed like a couple caught rowing at a party. One of the futures pushed in a trolley with a suitcase size device on it and then left, gently closing the door behind them with a click.

Bluu composed herself. "Today we are going into V-world so I can show you our past, the part of our past that we know about." She looked down at him with that smile again. "It will help you understand things," she paused. "Why things are different now." She was struggling for words, wringing her hands together nervously. He couldn't escape the shame he felt and what she might be thinking right now.

"Hey, caveman we don't run around raping and killing each other anymore like you did. Why not come with me and find out why life is so much better without people like you. I can show you why you really do belong in a fucking zoo!" However, she didn't say any of that at all. She was too kind to say any of it and he'd later recognise how his feelings for Bluu changed that that day.

"V-world?" he whispered to the floor. "Is that it, my quarantine is over?"

"Not quite, but soon. We all want it to be soon." Her palms were forward as if she might have to ward off a blow. This made him feel even more pathetic and he resigned right then to be a better person. He was intrigued to experience V-World having heard so much about it. From what he'd been told it was a kind of virtual reality world of a quality he'd struggled to imagine. He shrugged looking to the floor again avoiding eye contact.

Bluu continued. "V-world is a computer generated place. A three dimensional environment. I have created something special for you. To help you understand," she paused, "us," she finished. He got the feeling that V-world was much more than any computer game he'd known, it had become a central part of life here. The word virtual no longer applied because if you were a brain then this is as real as it gets. Bluu began the standard explanation to prepare him for what he was about to experience. "Imagine you put your hand near a fire or you see the colour green," she said. "How do you know that?"

"I suppose," he thought about this a little more. "My nerves tell my brain, my eyes tell my brain?" he wasn't sure if that's what she had meant.

Bluu smiled. "So if those nerves told your brain you were cold or could see orange?"

Vic thought for a moment. "I would be cold and see orange I suppose," he shrugged. "That's exactly how V-world works."

Bluu reached into the case and held up a helmet not unlike the leather flying helmet that Second World War pilots would wear, complete with goggles. "By wearing this device it can intercept all the inputs that are coming in from various nervous systems and disable them at the base of the brain. It then inserts new ones dependent on which sim you are in," she said. "So as far as my brain is concerned V-world will actually be real?" This scared him.

"Almost, you can't die and there's a finite limit on certain inputs such as pain whilst other emotions can be accelerated," she stated handing him the helmet. "All you need after that is a world to visit called a sim, you can decide on the rules within this world, like whether you can fly or not and anything else you want. So when you are in a sim, and enjoying adventures then you can do so in complete safety."

"I see," he said. They obviously had some different ideas about safety these days if intercepting and disabling brain function was considered rudimentary. Bluu continued.

"sims can be public places where others around you are real people or private where the other people are in fact artificial intelligence bots, there's little difference in the experience."

Bluu had gone on to explain how V-world had gone way beyond games and adventures. By setting certain rules people could not only socialise but, for those who chose to, experience a cooperative work environment. Vic was astounded to find that because life was so leisurely many enjoyed the challenge of a group task with high demands or monotonous time conscious duties. In effect their job was now their challenge and pastime. Traffic jams, paperwork and office politics were the new Grand Theft Auto. In the same way as they achieved nothing in a game the same was true in work type environments, it was to experience different worlds. V-world allowed humans to work, play and even have sex from their own armchairs, actually being in reality was a secondary requirement. Bluu continued to bring him up to speed as best she could and intermittently assured him it was safe. He felt like a caveman being coaxed into an aeroplane. It took a few minutes to get things ready with Vic being overly polite at appropriate points as if it might lessen the effect of his earlier savagery. There was no mention of his recent outbursts and soon they were ready to go.

"This is your first time in V-world so it can be very disorientating," Bluu explained. "First of all let me explain that nothing you see is real, it's easy to forget that. Everything you experience is through the helmet. If at any point you want to leave just do this." She raised her right hand with the thumb protruding outwards and placed it on her chest whilst using her left in a similar fashion to flick her forehead outwards in a single movement. He mimicked her. "Good," she said. "That's it." Bluu seemed a little nervous, maybe more nervous than he was. As if she'd baked a cake she proudly explained that the entire simulation was designed by her, with a little help. Explaining that most of the time they would not be with the general population but in a private simulation. There were various methods of experiencing V-world but the helmet was as good as it gets without an implanted chip.

"Sounds good, kinda like having the latest Xbox with a wide screen TV and quadrophonic sound." She looked at him puzzled as he sat down next to her.

"Ok," she said making the escape move once more. "Take these and put your helmet on." He looked at the four green pills in his hand with his palms still open. "Nutrients, sugar and protein," she said and dropped her goggles. He swallowed them in one gulp, put the helmet on and dropped the goggles over his eyes. He sat silently for a moment, completely blinded by the glasses through which he saw nothing. "Are you ready?" she said excitedly.

"Ready," he said nervously adjusting himself.

"Here we go."

TEN

Without warning he felt an immediate rush of panic as the air was sucked from his lungs. His skin felt like shrink wrap as it tightened around his body. Then as quickly as it came there was a release of pressure replaced by a breeze, a calming breeze like he'd been pushed out of an air conditioned building onto a hot street. Then he could see, it felt like he'd opened his eyes but they had already been fully open. They were both stood on what looked like a busy London street. Vic looked down at himself to see he was wearing a green silk two piece suit with bright red shoes. A high collar shirt and garish tie hung neatly around his neck. Nothing she had said could have prepared him for the reality he was experiencing. Next to him was Bluu, he could tell it was her but she looked different. She had on a dark business suit with her hair flowing down her back. It was a different colour too, it was much darker. She looked over at him. "How do you feel?" she said smiling.

"Where are we?" he asked looking around. Realising what was incongruent about the scene before him. Mainly it was colours, like when someone fools with the brightness and contrast on the TV. This was exacerbated by the people who wore clothes in an array of primary colours with equally bright hair. The fashion was wrong but other than that he was standing in a London street. Actually standing in a London street, he could feel, hear. Just like that hologram outside his window only now he was actually in it. He reached out to touch a table at a cafe they were stood outside and he knocked on it. He smelled the calming waft of perfume as a woman brushed past him on the walkway, the smell of a city returned as she disappeared into the crowd.

"I created a simulation to help you understand, it's London; what do you think?"

"Amazing," he said. Bluu beamed with pride jumping up and then stopping herself wrinkling her nose in a smile. He didn't mean the street or sim but just the reality of it all. This was reality in every way but she clearly misunderstood his compliment and he allowed her to.

"I had a little help," she said, "but I'll tell you about that later." Bluu pointed across the road. "Let's sit there." Beckoning him over to a park bench on the other side of the street she ran across and he followed darting between slow moving cars, having to dodge a speeding bicycle in the lane between them.

"This is a good simulation of what Lon-don may have looked like around 2045," she said pointing around at the throngs of people and pronouncing Lon-don in two broad syllables. "We're not sure where you were at this time but it was the next stage in the technological revolution," she shouted above the city bustle. "It was as a result of the light-age."

"The light-age?" He questioned, his heartbeat rising.

"Hundreds of years ago, even before your time a man called Albert Einstein claimed.."

"Yes, I know Albert Einstein!" interrupted Vic excitedly. Bluu looked at him raising her eyebrows. "You know, I didn't know him. I knew of him." Vic corrected himself.

Realising 500 years had introduced some misinterpretation, even in the same language. "Well of course he was a famous scientist, centuries ago," she continued. "He had put forward a theory on how light could possibly be treated as a particle, something unheard of in your time. By applying Planck's theory it could.."

"It could be used to develop light processors," said Vic finishing her sentence for her. She trailed off giggling and squinted at him curiously. This was all so elementary to her, probably learned it all in school. Here she was trying to explain it to him, like explaining an iPhone to Faraday. She reverted to a more basic translation. "If light could be used in computer processors then we would have optical computers. This idea was perfected around 2045 and was the beginning of a revolution in processing speeds and artificial intelligence."

"2045, that would be about 30 years after they put me in the freezer," he said gazing into nowhere as he absorbed the scene around him.

Bluu looked back at him nervously. "Err, yes," she said slowly. Vic knew plenty about the principles of light technology but it was almost certain Nova didn't. Still, to hear they had finally perfected it was stunning if not entirely surprising. Vic was busy picking out the differences in this Lon-don to the London he knew. There were still numerous old buildings, Georgian, Victorian or whatever they were. Were they originals? Who knows but he wouldn't have been surprised to see so many of them outlive the twentieth century's lifeless glass monoliths a few times over. The vehicles and cars didn't roll on wheels, they looked like they did but they hovered quite low to the ground. It took a second to tune in to the fact there were no drivers or steering wheels on the vehicles, some had no windscreens at all. The thing that was really timeless was that hustle of a big city, the chill of a busy Monday morning in the air and people who had places to go as quickly as possible. The traffic was calmer, not calmer drivers but the traffic was actually calmer as if every vehicle was going to get where it needed to go. Could cars look more relaxed?

She pointed across the street at a bright red driverless London bus, it was of a more futuristic design as if inspired by its original. To the left some drone cleaning robots were busy sweeping the pavement.

"Can you imagine how that affected technology? Particularly Artificial Intelligence and the field of automation and robotics exploded. Manufacturing, food production and everything else became artificially intelligent. Everything was efficient and connected to everything else. Your fridge could predict its requirements and talk to every other machine in the food manufacturing process right back to the field or factory. In time output and efficiency were so high the tax system became pointless and was turned upside down. Gainful employment went the same way and it was the system that provided for everyone. The days when you were slaves who worked for your government were over and so went government too."

"No government?" This was all sounding better and better thought Vic. "No taxes?"

"By 2068 what used to be called the World Wide Web became intelligent and autonomous. It had access to millions of other experiences and data. This meant it would not only search but think and provide answers much quicker than organic life forms. It would have been super intelligent because it had experienced every problem and could come up with an answer much quicker. Around this time the Web started to manage more and more of the data, food production and management of resources. Along the way it made more and more decisions."

Vic watched as people walked faster and faster in front of his eyes until they became a blur of reds, greens and blues, clearly symbolising the passing of time.

"Communication and technology peaked as artificial intelligence and robotics advanced at an incredible rate. There was nothing humans could not dominate and control. Soon it was technology creating technology and artificial intelligence could actually theorise and deduce. Humanity eventually had the technology to reach out to its nearest planet, Mars."

Like a theatre stage curtain the streets of London collapsed to the ground and disappeared. The bright city colours turning into the empty blackness of space. Vic watched in amazement as the surface of Mars materialised before him. He crouched down picking up a handful of dust which ran between his fingers noticing how some of it was on his shoes. They were both still dressed the same, in street clothes. As Vic looked up, an enormous spaceship the size of a medium office block silently landed a hundred yards in front of them. Blowing dust in its wake as it came to a halt. Vic's eyes widened as Bluu continued her commentary "By the year 2110 the new World Wide Web has intervened in global debate and is starting to make decisions. Alongside this it made sense to take all written data and digitise it, making it available to everyone. Paper data became redundant. This data and art archive was stored across the web; it is around this time that we think it happened."

Bluu's voice seemed to crack a little and she may have had a tear in her eye as she turned around. Vic followed her gaze and had not realised there was a space station about another three hundred yards behind them. Huge hangar doors rolled upwards in the side of a hill giving a sense of scale. Shimmering red and green neon lights burst from the opening and flickered and went out for a moment before coming back on again. Like an office block might burst back to life after a momentary power failure.

"A self-sustaining colony was being established on Mars led by Major Zero. It was during this time that the data crash happened, we are still not sure how or why but it could have been some kind of electronic weapon or virus. Perhaps in your time you had wars which were fought with bombs or armies. By 2068 that would have been pointless, the people or nations who owned the data were much more powerful. Whatever happened in those weeks would have been the technological equivalent of a nuclear bomb. In stages across the world from South America, Australia, France, Germany, UK and all around the world. Every single electronic device burned out and failed, destroying the data of the entire world and disabling technology. In a matter of weeks it would devastate the planet and leave the colony on Mars stranded."

Vic heard a voice in his ear like he was listening to a radio transmission. The voice sounded distressed, urgent. "Ground control to Major Zero, can you hear me Major?" There was white noise then further voices, garbled but undistinguishable. He could not make out anything being said, just the tone similar and urgent. Then the first voice once more. "Major, there's something wrong, your circuit's dead. Can you hear me, Major?"

Bluu interrupted. "The entire network across Earth was shut down every single piece of electronic equipment ruined and unusable. Human beings so dependent on technology left in the darkness with no way of fending for themselves. All historic data destroyed and very few humans survived the aftermath."

The scene fast forwarded once more and a temporary structure was built. Large pieces of a space ship were being cut and welded together. He could see the thing being built in time lapse. Lots of activity around the space station as figures came and went through large loading bay doors. Loading and unloading items onto a waiting craft. Much smaller than the other one and not quite so sleek, it was different and he soon found out why.

"What about those guys?" he questioned.

"Yes," she said respectfully. "The Major and his team were stranded on Mars with as little hope of survival as anyone else. As it turned out they were to be the ones who saved the human race from extinction. They would be the ones who created the world we have now. A world with the City of Heathen."

"Are you telling me they survived up here," he said tailing off, noticing his use of the word here. Remembering he was not actually on Mars.

"From what we know they did much more than survive. An ancient space race was turned on its head. The Major and his colony spent years developing a way of returning to Earth to create the Heathen project," she paused again. "I'm telling you this so that you know the truth," said Bluu gravely.

"Why would I not believe you?"

"Not everyone believes this version of events, when you go out and meet the people of Heathen you may hear other stories about the Major."

Bluu looked deep into his eyes. "They are not true," she said as if it was a command instead of an opinion.

"What was to be a colony using some of the Earth's brightest minds to populate Mars actually ended up returning to repopulate Earth."

They watched as the makeshift craft fired up and took off into space. As it did so he could see the loading bay doors closing, there were people inside?

"I saw people in there, is that right?"

"We think it's unlikely the makeshift craft would have been able to bring everyone home. In all likelihood there were some left behind, we can only guess. In the time it took them to return to Earth the most advanced society in the universe as far as we know was reduced to a medieval existence."

Vic felt like a ghost watching the general goings on from another time and another planet. Bluu continued. "Meanwhile on Earth there must have been devastation and mass starvation with a return to a tribal existence. Far worse than in your time. That's why we need you now, why you were regenerated."

Vic's heart skipped a beat. "Need me?"

"Yes," she said. "You come from a time before the digital age, a time when there were written records of human history. By the time the shutdown hit everything was digitised, pictures, photos, historic records, the names of presidents; virtually every piece of human knowledge was in the web and when that was destroyed, so was our history." Vic drew a breath and brushed some Martian dust from his sleeve.

"So the only knowledge that was left, every invention, event, life was lost? The knowledge of the entire human race now consisted of what was in the heads of Major Zero and his crew?"

"That's exactly it. Thousands of life samples had been taken to Mars for storage, a kind of life blueprint backup. Amongst those samples you likely remained undiscovered for hundreds of years. It was miraculous that eventually your existence came to light. When you were found we were so excited that we could regenerate you, hoping that you could teach us so much." Vic scratched his head. "Yes," he said as confidently as possible.

"That's just amazing."

"By the time Major Zero and his team had returned to Earth the human race had been almost completely wiped out," said Bluu raising a hand in a pointing gesture. She lifted off the ground and pointed towards Earth. "This way," she said.

Vic mimicked her hand movements and found that he too was floating next to her high above the planet. He followed as they both soared towards Earth at a speed so fast the planet tore towards them increasing in size. He felt like a character from the Snowman or some kind of superhero film and yet there was no gushing wind or resistance. It was more like they were pulling the Earth towards them. At last they approached the Earth soaring over mountains and oceans like superman until finally they approached a large city skyline. The pair swooped effortlessly between tall dark buildings that could have been the financial centre of any modern city. They settled slowly to ground level amongst the scenes of desolation. A horrific apocalyptic sight presented itself amongst the tumbled rubble of a once towering city. They stood in the middle of what would once have been a busy thoroughfare. Long abandoned cars burned and rusting, smouldering piles of rubbish littered the street. The breeze sucked battered blinds out of the broken windows of tower blocks which once stood as corporate monuments, now just depressing skeletons of depravity. From the tops of these black monoliths came the faint glow of flame, camp fires maybe perhaps the last remaining humans seeking safety high above street level. Starving dogs scurried amongst rotting corpses competing for the dead flesh with huge rats who could almost match them for size if not ferocity. Battered shutters, half open rattled and hung from shops looted and stripped bare long ago. Vic shivered inside feeling the piercing red eyes peering upon him from the darkness. Small tribes of humans scavenged and fought amongst the debris. Filthy and dishevelled they looked pathetic; wearing what would once have been expensive mink and fur coats, matted in blood and dirt. Items that were once symbols of opulence and wealth now just a worthless piece of improvised survival equipment. Two starving emaciated dogs, once so pampered fought angrily over some scrap of food, so thin they looked like they could have easily slipped out of their diamond encrusted collars.

"This is what was left of our planet by the time Major Zero and his crew arrived."

Bluu held out a hand and began strolling amongst the debris, kicking empty cans and stepping over chunks of concrete and broken glass. She seemed calm and unmoved as if strolling in a park. Remember nothing is real he thought. He convinced himself of that, difficult as it was. The stench of death and piss, the rotting flesh, none of it was real. He felt the heat from the fire as they passed a group of survivors warming their frail thin bodies, eyes empty, staring and unresponsive. One of them muttered something to him as they passed. "They set up Heathen for those that remained and decided that from then on they would never make the same mistakes again. Over population, wars and the battle for resources they answered all of these problems over time. That was when the Saviour Machine was designed."

Vic heard a loud bang coming from an ally to his left followed by a scream. Skipping to keep up. "What's that?" he said.

"A kind of advanced algorithm, it was designed to love humans, to manage resources. We call it Mother."

That wasn't what he meant, he strolled closer behind. "Isn't that dangerous to give so much power to a machine, again?"

"Of course not," she looked puzzled; he was embarrassed by her reaction.

"The resources were plentiful as long as the population could remain stable, the Saviour machine would eventually see to that. Sadly the population was tiny and there was no need to mine steel, cooper or any precious metal. All that had been done long ago."

Vic surveyed a city street full of burned out cars, computers and twisted metal. Bluu stopped and turned towards a shop doorway. "Come," she said stepping through.

She disappeared into the darkness and Vic paused to make a choice. Stay out here or step into the blackness after her. He looked around at the tribes of humans around him, they seemed curious, eyeing his plump flesh. "Nothing is real," he muttered under his breath as he skipped through the doorway. Once inside they stood back in his suite where they had started. "I think that's enough for today," she said as if addressing a toddler who might become over excited.

"Another thing, that sim, the one we were just in. You said you had some help?"

"That's right, I had some help from you, that's how it works. I was able to adapt some of your inputs, we are learning already," she said triumphantly. "That's why nothing we saw is literal. The sims can be contaminated easily with fantasy, dreams and wishes. Usually we would have spent more time cleaning up the environment before going in."

She slipped her helmet off and helped Vic with his, throwing them both to one side. There was a knock on the door.

"The timing is perfect today," said Bluu. She skipped over to the door and swung it open. In walked a tall skinny man wearing a bright yellow suit. The man peered at him throwing his straggly hair out of his face only for it to instantly fall back. He stared in awe at Vic who noted he didn't look medical at all like the others. The fact that he was here in person was a novelty in itself.

"Nova," said Bluu proudly and shot a gaze between the two of them. This gentleman is one of our foremost experts on ancient history and he is going to be working with you.

The man stepped forward. "Mr Nova," said the man confidently. This time his left hand stayed on his head holding the hair in place whilst he held out his right. "I am very pleased to meet you. My name is Doctor Touchreik, Doctor Algeria Touchreik."

ELEVEN

Doctor Touchreik had morphed from a man obsessed with history to a man possessed by it. Each night being driven home in a trance until the transporter pulled up at his sector. Every conversation with the caveman changing the romantic image of pre shutdown life he'd created over the years. A combination of denial and confirmation pertaining to established thinking. It was like taking a painting, the one he'd created of 21st Century life and having to rub out elements and redraw others. Being consumed and incredibly grateful to be included in the project; grateful to whom and for what he thought? The undeserved credit for it fell on his older self, despite the fact it would have happened anyway. According to the Professor it had already happened, a fact he was reminded of after the initial meeting. It never occurred they wouldn't combine their findings and knowledge to accelerate their overall understanding. Any ideas he'd harboured of collaboration and shared experience were soon shattered. At times he wondered how he could ever turnout like the unpleasant and ignorant character he was forced to share his life with now. Touchreik floated up the stairs two by two that evening and burst through into the accommodation, running from room to room. Throwing his tablet on the chair and running around until he found the Professor. "I met him," he cried. "I kept myself calm, was it the same for yo.." he'd thought they would spend the first night comparing notes, dissecting the tapes and the conversation.

The Professor appeared from his room and pushed out his palm.

"No," he'd said stopping the Doctor in his tracks. "We can't discuss it, I was there?" pointing a finger at his lips the Professor continued. "I've experienced it, if we discuss it and I influence your work it could change his attitude or yours, there will be time for that later."

He turned and slammed the door to his room. At the time he'd assumed he meant 'time later' for discussing not a 'time later' for changing attitudes. How very wrong about that he was at the time, and he'd be very wrong about a great many things before this was over. Shocked and hurt by the wasted opportunity he withdrew into himself and pushed deeper into the project, with no way of knowing if his conclusions reflected those of the Professors. If that was how he wanted it then fine, he'd push on regardless. After what felt like seconds in the transporter the door opened and the chilled air broke his reverie. In such a short space of time barriers were being broken and bonds strengthening between himself and the subject. What had started out as a delicate manipulation exercise had become natural, dare he say a feeling of kinship with the sample.

The communication channels with Nova had exceeded expectations, which was both illuminating and encouraging. There were bumps in the road, cultural misunderstandings of course but that had been the point, to probe pre shutdown culture.

The 21st Century life Nova described was very different from the one the Doctor had known and grown up in. He'd described in vivid detail billions of people all mixing, touching and walking the streets. Not just of one City but thousands, all over the globe. Given some adaptation almost the entire planet was habitable back then. In the 21st Century humans interacted, shared space and most interestingly enjoyed physical acts of sex and love. This was no surprise; physical relationships were a necessity in his time. Male and female formed bonds and produced offspring with random DNA in the same way animals do now. Back then there was no Mother to produce young or manage the DNA pool. Studying ancient history was one thing, but to actually have it confirmed by an actual ancient man was another. Touchreik wasn't alone in his tastes but he and anyone who harboured physical desires were wise to be discreet. He missed Ramona, but since that night he dared not see her, the Professor being around was a further distraction and of course with this new position it was even less likely. She'd understand, but imagining the scandal it might cause made him shudder to the bone, he could definitely kiss the project goodbye. In his weaker moments Touchreik felt like the caveman might understand real physical feelings for Ramona, as if it came more naturally to him. Sensibly he'd held his silence it'd be foolish to let his professional guard down. The one person in the world who would understand was the Professor but neither had acknowledged her openly other than his guarded warning on that first day. It had even entered the Doctor's head to ask about her, was she still in his life? Had he left her behind in his future? Those kinds of questions made no sense on so many levels, as if there were two Ramona's, one here and one in the future. However, that was the logic applied by the Professor. He spoke of the past and future as two separate physical places. So in his future could he have lost the feelings for her? If so would he want to know about it? One way or another all relationships end but those thoughts are kept buried deep in the conscience. If any of that was true he'd no wish to find out just yet. A couple of days ago, almost telling Nova his secret he pulled back and came to his senses. It was tough in the days that Nova came from, the past had some benefits and one of them was the acceptance of physical relationships.

For the time being the job meant real world travel and returning late through the square. A mental cue to think about things he'd rather ignore. Stepping out onto the pavement he walked briskly between the towering residential blocks of Barnbrook and for the first time saw Heathen slightly differently. The hiss of the transporter pulling away flicked a switch in his brain and sent him back to a night that felt like a million years ago. The night he'd walked under that streetlamp, where it all started. He paused underneath the beam and looked up as tiny droplets of fine rain fell like shooting stars out of the blackness. The myriad of towering buildings with layers of internal lights for the first time looked cold and empty. Those rooms, staggered and stacked high into the night sky teamed with residents, thousands of people with no motivation to have physical contact with their peers because V-World enabled every level of life from work to leisure.

Touchreik peered into the darkness, half blinded by the light and a shiver ran up the back of his neck. As if the humanist who'd accosted him here might still be hiding in the shadows watching him. There was no point denying it anymore, that man was a rebel. The Professor wasn't willing to discuss his intentions; always some talk of ripple effects, the time will be right or such like. Since the beginning of the caveman project he was in no hurry to 'save the world'. The Professor was relaxed about it all so whilst his little ducks lined up the Doctor would enjoy what he was doing. Occasionally he might feel deflated at the missed opportunity for them to compare notes but pushed on regardless.

The Doctor lay in bed that first night staring at the wardrobe. Inside he knew Ramona waited patiently but how could they meet when the Professor was in the house so he resisted.

Since the Professor's promise of the new project his predictions had been accurate in every detail. They felt like predictions to the Doctor but in the eyes of the Professor it was more experience or memory of old events.

Predictions or experience they were uncanny all the same. The knowledge of exactly how the caveman project would develop, the day Prout would ask him to the meeting with the other departments. How they would confirm that Cryonic man had indeed been revived and might be at the institute. Even offering detail of who would attend and how they'd react. Once the caveman was at the institute it was a near certainty the Doctor would be involved provided he kept his nose clean and stayed out of trouble. Provided there was no talk about him and his infatuation with drones or being seen around SO63. There was talk alright, always had been but as long as it was just that he'd get the project, and he did.

Exactly as predicted the sample was coming to the institute and in a matter of days he was indeed offered the project. Given the chance to work with him and ascertain how much he could add to our sketchy understanding of the 21st Century. The body transplant could potentially have been a huge hindrance to the samples communication abilities; nothing could be further from the truth. Once underway the Professor clammed up so as to allow events to happen naturally. Doctor Touchreik's initial fear that there may be limited access proved to be unfounded. Even at that first meeting they had agreed to talk more and work together for the foreseeable future.

Recently the Doctor felt lighter on his feet, the caveman project renewing in him energy for his subject. It had also turned his department from a remote backwater of science to its cutting edge. For anyone who was interested, and their numbers were growing, his department was now headline news. The last few weeks had flown by as he immersed himself in the work. If he was to get the best from the Caveman then he would need management and gentle coaxing. Tuning into his moods and trying to be aware when he needed to back off a little. The Doctor had been astounded at the amount of detail he was able to recollect whilst other global questions were difficult for him to remember. He almost had to pinch himself some mornings. This was tough work mentally and not as glamorous as some thought. Questioning, analysing and comparing against many of his established assumptions, the weeks had slowly helped him realise how many of his previous theories had been right. The Doctor was fast becoming an established authority on life in the Moonage.

Nova confirmed the idea of the upside down economy where humans worked for governments. The staggering utilisation of ancient electronics to put people on the moon was an incredible feat of his time. In Nova's world artificial intelligence and robotics were so primitive as to be useless. Moonage computing power was still electronic, slow and cumbersome without any form of intelligence. Through toil and hard physical labour they'd managed to feed a population of billions. All using slow organic farming methods with no way of growing accelerated nutrition. Although there are rumoured to be small groups doing that even now it didn't reduce the impact of its reality. Leisure and learning time would have been almost non- existent with their entire waking hours taken up in physical toil. Meanwhile light-age technology, the key to mankind's future was sitting right under their noses all those years hidden amongst the theories and writings of a man called Albert Einstein, long before it was perfected. They still bred physically like animals with a totally random gene pool, resulting in a population that was out of control and many times the sustainable level the only consolation being the numerous deaths from preventable disease keeping the numbers down.

There were many more ancient festivals and celebrations than he'd suspected. They would celebrate their day of birth and many other anniversaries including bonding and accommodation acquirement. There were religious beliefs too even as late as 2015 an intriguing idea in itself that would have been attractive to primitive man. That of a conscious being who acted for and with humans, who was able to judge and punish even after natural death. The Doctor had enough to keep him fully occupied, whatever plan his older self had in mind it had drifted to the back of his consciousness.

At the end of every period with the caveman there was more research and recording to do then sleep, then repeat. He also had the media and the department to keep up to date, the only time for most of that was in the evening. Touchreik kept his work with the media very generic with very little given away.

"Yes things are progressing nicely; we have lots more to do he is fine and well and enjoying Heathen that kind of thing."

Keeping his reports impersonal by confirming or not, various theories on pre-shutdown life. The publicity for Nova had renewed people's interest in history which had to be a good thing. Immersive filmonics based on Moonage themes such as primitive space travel and moon landings were more popular than ever, as were study and experience sims. Occasionally the reason the Professor was here at all drifted, as if by avoiding that thought it might just go away. Being engrossed in the project and finding he couldn't share it with the very person who would appreciate its allure saddened him. He was deprived of the advice, deep discussion and experience his older self could have given. Had they combined their knowledge they might be weeks or months ahead.

The Doctor and his older self, had settled into the routine of life together and the Professor had relaxed some of his rules. They argued less and less too, unlike the early days when the Professor would nag him about his habits or lifestyle.

Most annoying was the subliminal advice and warnings, when it was clear he was using inside knowledge. "You should think about this, or avoid that, as if they were just random thoughts." After a few days things came to a head and although unpleasant at the time the row seemed to have cleared the air. Even the Professor had realised he was breaking his own rules. They no longer shared meals or so much time together which took further pressure off the relationship. Then no sooner had things settled than there was a shift in behaviour. The Doctor returned home to discover the Professor was nowhere to be found. Admittedly at first he panicked somewhat, haunted by visions of his older self, disappearing in a puff of smoke due to some time travel anomaly or other. The Professor re-appeared a short time later, shrugged the whole thing off and stormed into his room with no explanation of his whereabouts. It was clearly not the first time he'd ventured outside whilst the Doctor was not around, so much for ripples. An air of tension was returning as the Professor became more aloof and quiet. As for his movements the Doc didn't ask, if he heard the word 'ripples' once more he'd jump through the window.

Duke had coped by identifying the pair as a single entity, enabling instructions from either or both without issue. The extra waste, food and air they had consumed was gradually absorbed into Duke's schedule without fuss or question. It was noticeable how his older self avidly followed media broadcasts and events with a keener eye than previously. He was getting used to the Professor suddenly crying out excitedly on some news item or other. Each step confirming that history was panning out exactly as he remembered it. The Doctor knew he was waiting for something, some kind of event that would signal the next phase of his plan. In the meantime, there was no sense in kicking a sleeping dog he was far too busy to worry about that.

Working with Nova had been so exhilarating and challenging that he had little time to think about anything else, not least whatever scheme the Prof was cooking up to save humanity.

In time he'd become further lulled into a feeling of security by the business of life and the regular routine that developed. That didn't stop him developing his own theories about his older self's jaunt through time and his thought process following to a logical conclusion. The Professor had clearly become associated with the rebels in his own future. He'd not admitted as much, yet at the very least had befriended one of them and sent him to set up the meeting. Assuming the humanist was still involved with that organisation then somehow the Professor had gained their trust.

But why? "Mankind was under threat," he had said. That was a hell of a statement to make without any qualification but it was obvious where any such threat would come from. After hundreds of years in the care of 'Mother' then it would be the humanists who might be that threat. That being the case, it started to become clear this was about a plan to destroy them once and for all. The Professor wouldn't reveal it until the time is right, so what. He may have good reason to make sure all the vermin were in the trap first. The more he thought about it the more convinced he became. The Professor was cunning and cautious, he was him and that's what he'd do. The obvious conclusion then was that the plan must be to infiltrate their organisation, he'd found a weakness. We were going to put them out of business before they got lucky and harmed Mother. If that's the way it had to be then so be it. For too long they'd been left out there on the city's fringes, living off Heathen whilst wishing her dead. All he needed to do is wait for the call and he'd be there. One thing was for sure, a threat to mankind had to be a threat to Mother and if that's the case the Doctor's mind was already made up. Deep down there was always a chance that the humanists would go too far and someone, someone like him might have to step forward. Psychologically he was ready to do whatever needed to be done for 'Mother' and for humanity. That decision was made, now he waited. If he couldn't trust himself, his actual older self then who could he trust?

☐

The Professor placed his palm on the DNA scanner and involuntarily stepped back, jaw dropping as the panel slid away. To him it had been years since he'd last seen her and looking at her now felt like a reincarnation. Ramona Stone was standing proud and upright, square chin pushed forward with long dark lashes shading her delicate eyelids. Underneath he could detect a slight but rapid eye movement. Pink silicone flesh covered her high cheekbones. The full red lips, the long flowing auburn hair cascading across her curves like a waterfall. He absorbed every detail from the top of her clinging shimmery gown to her exposed painted toenails. Ramona's flush pink flesh made her look warm and alive, though she'd never truly lived she was simply in hibernation mode, a standard procedure for any drone that is expected to be in storage for some time. Even as she slept her personality shone through, the part of her he loved the most the intoxicating laugh, the tireless attention and engaging conversation. He felt his heart pounding like an old man meeting a school boy crush, a beauty locked in time. She looked as dazzling as ever. Professor Touchreik looked down at his wrinkled hands and wondered what she might make of him now. Having never felt deserving of her admiration, her attraction to him had always been a mystery.

He knew the procedure to activate her, it was very straightforward. Maybe just for a few minutes he could say hello and explain. Perhaps time to apologise for something that hadn't happened yet. Something he's done or might do that would end everything for them. She'd laugh so hard when he told her what he'd done by travelling back in time. Before long they would be in deep conversation, laughing and then? Then she would want to know more and so time would slip away, as always an hour, then two. The Professor could imagine it being like it was, chatting and laughing in an endless evening of banter. He wiped away the gathering tears with the back of his hand. He regretted even coming in here now. Leaning forward he kissed her lightly on the cheek. Her flesh was warm to his lips like she might open her eyes at any moment.

She didn't.

"Oh Ramona," he whispered hoarsely through his sniffles. "If there was only some kind of future."

The Professor slapped his palm angrily against the scanner once more and the panel silently closed leaving him staring at his own dull reflection in the brushed steel door. He left the Doctor's room with a sense of shame. Like a father spying on a child, looking for drugs or filthy material while they were out. Making his way outside he slumped into a chair on the balcony admiring the burnished red sunset behind the trees. It had been one of her favourite scenes. So many years since he and Ramona had sat here in this very spot together. Just he and the shameful secret, so shameful he dare not discuss it even with his younger self. They both knew what she meant to them and that was enough for the time being. When he and Ramona had been together for the last time, no one was willing to understand. When she'd been taken from him he thought he understood too but not anymore. Now he knew she might be taken away for another reason and he couldn't stop that either. When all this was over there would probably be a place for physical relationships but never with the likes of her. The Doctor would be home soon and he'd delayed for far too long. If his plan was to succeed there will only be one shot and no second chances. The time for procrastination was running out. He was going to have to share everything with the Doctor. The time to do that had been getting closer by the day.

The thought of it filled him with dread.

TWELVE

It looked like the documentaries he'd seen on the discovery channel about Cape Canaveral. Everything pointed towards a huge screen on the left hand wall. There was too much data to make any sense of. Numbers cascading down and across a map, blips, lights. Fifty or so unmanned desks laid out in rows each with its own myriad of data, buttons and switches. The place hummed with energy and the temperature was stable, air conditioned with the smell of a cool, clean office environment that reminded him of the smell of new carpet. In the centre was a huge high backed chair turned away from him. Minutes earlier Vic had been stood in his suite but still couldn't get used to that outrush of air when he entered V-world. He stood for a moment to catch his breath as lights blinked and various instruments beeped. The chair spun slowly round to reveal its occupant. Bluu had her hands clasped and her elbows on either arm like a bad guy from a bond movie. "Remember, I said nothing is real?" she said. Vic was looking round and nodding at the same time. "Well this is not real within not real," she smirked.

"It's to illustrate the Saviour Machine, the Saviour Machine does not exist in any single place but if it did every input, every experience and every answer would find its way there. Like an algorithm and search engine combined that no longer answer searches but answers questions." Standing she stared up at the screen. "The fact is there is no control room, no authority. The Saviour Machine or Mother as it's commonly known is everywhere. It's us really. It's a little bit like an internet of thought?" raising the notation as if to ask if he understood.

"Ok," whispered Vic still taking it all in. "With no government is there some authority, police or something?"

"We are citizens of Heathen, we are the authority. Citizens are able to take care of anything unforeseen but I can't imagine what?" Bluu seemed puzzled by the concept of authority. "Mother does not exist in any given place but...her servers are on Mars." Bluu noticed his eyebrows furrow.

"Then how can it work things here?" said Vic.

"It's not a server in the sense you might remember. Any instructions from Mars are more global whilst instant decisions happen locally."

"Let me give you an example," she stopped, waiting for a response. Vic stopped scanning and turned to her. "Imagine that enough people wanted to build a leisure space near your living area? In your time that might have involved decision, authority, agreement and of course disagreement. Yes?" Bluu beckoned him to sit down opposite her in a noticeably smaller and lower chair. He nodded slowly. "Well imagine if all the opinions, expertise and past experience were already there? Imagine if all that input could be correlated to show how it could be done, who would like it done and at the other end?" There was a ping as a small slip of paper slid out of the console in front of her. She leaned over and tore it away, holding it up with the word 'yes' printed clearly on it.

"Of course it doesn't work this way, there's no control room like this one but in principle that's how Mother works. The Saviour Machine doesn't need input because that happens instantaneously. That's why we love her, that's why we trust her. What you said about it being dangerous, that it would hurt humans? That's why it will never happen because we are part of it. The Saviour Machine was able to solve problems that had hindered primitive humans for centuries. War, famine, over population and pollution are now managed by everyone who exists. Even though they have no need to consciously consider or vote for anything." Pleased with herself Bluu stood up becoming more animated the background lights blinked across her features. The light appeared warming to her and highlighted her skin tone, the V-World hair colour suited her female form.

"There's no need for government or leadership. Robotics are so advanced that food and resources can be harvested, because of the limited population the materials are all around us. Steel, glass and stone that used to supply billions of people before the shutdown are sitting around on the surface of the planet."

The screen above them burst into life showing images of robotic trucks collecting scrap cars, clearing cities, smelting and recycling components, mountains of electronic equipment being turned into light processors and robust utility robots. There was no sound but he could see the film was being presented by an unusual clown type character who seemed to be explaining what was going on. The clown casually walked through devastated streets, followed by huge bulldozers gathering the Earth's waste. Flyby shots of fields that stretched as far as the horizon, filled with what looked like wheat and green healthy vegetables. It showed what looked like environmental clean-up operations as filthy discoloured seas and desert landscapes gave way to blue oceans and lush countryside. It was like an almighty planetary promotional video showing happy residents, youthful and good looking, enjoying the fruits of robotic labour. Like a car assembly line goods were filtered into conveyors and directly into homes. The whole process was seamless with no human intervention.

"In your time most people had to work for their government. Now there's no work because there is no need, if you want something you just order it and it arrives, most times it arrives anyway."

Vic was mesmerised. "But, how many people are there, what do they do?"

"We are in V-world right now but this is a private sim created by me. But in the grid, V-world is everything. It's where most people work, meet and compete." The screen sprang to life once more showing epic battles, operating theatre drama, plane crashes and high powered race car collisions.

"V-world has always been much more than a game, it's life itself. Imagine the pride and excitement we feel when one of us reaches their time to euthanise. To break away after 130 years and leave room for their race to advance, it's an amazing privilege," said Bluu excitedly. "That's all changed now because those whom we have known and engaged with in V-world and the real world can now still know us thanks to the Salvation Project." Bluu raised her hand and brushed the screen to one side. "After Euthanising a person would have been gone forever, or at least they used to be. We now have the Salvation Project, a way of euthanising and still existing without depriving your comrades of resources. Isn't it amazing?"

Vic stared past Bluu at the blank screen. "I am not sure I follow?"

"At 130 years of age our Euthanasia is the time when a person in Heathen celebrates their demise and prepares to make way for others. But Mother seems to have solved a problem we didn't know we had. At age 130 citizens celebrated their euthanasia, but now it's possible to have both to die and then upload every part of your personality, memories and wishes into V-world and be there permanently."

"You mean you could live forever in a computer game, in here?" said Vic stunned. He said it louder than he intended and hoped he hadn't upset her by expressing his shock.

"Yes, isn't it just wonderful?" She jumped up and down again, oblivious to his tone. I want you to meet someone, come."

Bluu marched across the room towards a pair of out of place gothic double doors. Vic was frozen in place for a second before stepping towards her. Clasping a handle in each hand she stepped forward thrusting them both wide and opening her arms as she did. They walked through onto a high wide balcony overlooking what looked like a busy fifties dance hall. It was crowded with people dancing, drinking and chatting. They stopped what they were doing as they entered. The music stopped too and everyone stood in silence staring for a moment before a spontaneous round of applause broke out. Bluu stepped out onto an upper stairway balcony which overlooked the crowd below. "Ladies and gentlemen," cried Bluu. "Please carry on your fun, don't let us disturb you." she beckoned for Vic to step forward. In a low voice she proudly whispered. "We are now in the grid, all of these people are part of the Salvation Project." Vic cautiously stepped forward and peered down taking a moment to absorb the scene hundreds of people of various ages straining to see him high above them. All these people are dead, he thought. He felt a shiver down his spine, they were all digital ghosts and yet it all looked very natural.

She turned to the crowd once more. "Ladies and Gentlemen, may I please present the one and only Nova." Bluu paused and turned to Vic this time joining in the applause. As it died down the music started up and everyone went back to their business. Bluu took Vic's arm and walked him round the balcony. "They are all absolutely bursting to meet you, how they are keeping it together Heathen knows, come this way." The pair walked around the wide balcony passing small groups chatting, sipping champagne each one trying to steal just a glance at the caveman as they passed. There were pairs of settees and coffee tables set out at intervals. At one of them sat a man who stood up to greet them as they approached. He smiled, thrusting his hand into Vic's and clasped it with the other, shaking it confidently.

"Mr Nova, a pleasure to meet you," he said smiling warmly.

"Nova," said Bluu nodding to the man. "Nova this is the," stressing the word 'the' into thee, "Paul Ambrosius."

Vic thinned his lips, smiling. "Pleased to meet you."

Paul nodded in a kind of salute and sat down, being careful not to ruffle his impeccable suit. Everything about Paul was crisp and clean. His perfect unblemished skin tone complimented his deep brown double breasted suit. Gold cuff links, tie and tie pin gave him a Saville Row look. He was made to measure and bespoke, unbuttoning his jacket and sitting down in a single well practiced movement.

"How old do you think he is?" said Bluu absolutely bursting to tell.

"25," muttered Vic shrugging his shoulders.

"I am 150 years old Mr Nova, not quite as old as your good self of course," he darted a quick look at Bluu and then looked at the floor in embarrassment. "I didn't mean..." he started to explain.

Vic hadn't lost that point. Here he was in a body 22 years old and yet he had technically existed for 568 years something that wouldn't have gone down well with the futures. Was this Paul fella aware of the rule change on his behalf, is that why he was embarrassed. You'll be treated as 22, Bluu had said. With what he now knew, that was quite significant. He was starting to feel like an army deserter, or conscientious objector.

Bluu attempted to keep the conversation on good terms. "Don't you see, we euthanise at 130, at least we used to."

"That's right, I was the first, the very first to enter the Salvation Project," said Paul grateful for the intervention and bowing towards Bluu. "Instead of euthanasia all of my memories, personality, wishes and dreams were uploaded into V-world."

"Isn't it incredible?" said Bluu. "He was the first, Paul was the very first to take the Salvation option."

"It's an amazing project I am here permanently in the virtual world. I can't die. Lots of us are here permanently now. I can change my appearance or sim anytime I like. Nothing has changed, my friends and family still log on." Vic stared blankly. He looked towards Bluu once more. There was an uncomfortable silence and Vic felt he should be impressed, should question more.

"What does it feel like, not having a physical presence?" he asked at last.

"How does it feel for you right now?" responded Paul.

Vic realised how it felt for him right now. He was not here in a 1950's hotel talking to this guy. The cigar smoke he smelt, the music he heard and the feel of the leather chair holding him up. None of this was real and yet.... it was. I suppose that was his answer.

"But I mean you. Are you still?" Vic paused, "are you still you?"

"I most certainly am still me. There's no dividing line, no change over, it's continuous. I can tell you about my childhood growing up in TI's."

"2300's," said Bluu by way of translation.

"Yes, exactly I am 150 years old and before you perhaps the oldest human ever. I am proud to say I can do this, we can all do this without affecting the gene pool."

Vic wondered what he was being sold here, at least that's what it sounded like but then thinking on, no that wasn't it. It was guilt, the man felt guilty. Perhaps I might feel that way soon he thought. Paul was justifying being alive and probably thought about the guy before him. The one who went through with it, he felt like he and everyone else in the Salvation Project had cheated. Vic stole a look at Bluu, is that what he saw in her tone, behind those eyes? Political correctness? These people from the Salvation Project probably had that same deserter, conscientious objector feeling he had. Perhaps they knew it and everyone else knew it but no one would ever say it. Vic was learning fast. There was a much stronger feeling of community here in the future but it went deeper than that, more like ants. A real feeling of everyone being part of this whole freak show, as if you hurt one you hurt them all.

He knew that back in his time people discussed things like humanity, society like they were real. The truth was those words were abstract vehicles to cover up their own selfishness. He always wondered who would be the first in the queue to put their baby on a spaceship to the nearest star to save 'humanity', yeah right. How many would line up to give their lives to save mankind when they wouldn't even walk to work? In his time he'd always known that civil society had a very thin veneer. From what he had heard there had been no society in 2040 when the lights had gone out. Humanity just reduced to savages, ashes to ashes, dust to dust he thought. That was it, everything back to its lowest denominator.

Ashes to ashes...

It was with those words that he experienced what was to be the first of his 'incidents'. Everything faded in an instant, both sound and vision moving away to allow him to think. He felt dizzy and remembered where he was. Could this helmet be malfunctioning? He saw things now, what had Bluu said about the amazing Major Zero the saviour of the human race? That's the truth or something like that, you may hear other things. My mother said to get things done; you better not mess with Major Zero?

His thoughts accelerated like a drag racer on rails. He could see it all now, without the crutches of technology the curtain had been pulled back and the beast beneath laid bare. He wondered for a moment where that had come from? Not so much the thought but more the understanding. Vic knew why and how he was here he knew who Nova was and why this felt familiar. How on Earth could he have missed it all, or forgotten the obvious? Not only did he understand everything completely he knew why he understood, as he reached out to grab that knowledge out of the air, it was gone. An enlightening déjà vu feeling that he couldn't get back. Like having the answer to a million dollar question on the tip of your tongue and then, poof it's gone. He tried but he couldn't get it back. He came back to reality quickly as if his life had skipped a beat. The minds door slammed shut and left him outside without even the memory of what was inside.

In the seconds he was experiencing the incident Bluu had already stood as if to leave and Vic followed suit. Everything turned back up, crystal clear once more. Had he missed some of the conversation, he didn't remember the last seconds. "It's been a pleasure meeting you Mr Nova," said Paul shaking his hand with a slight bow. He pulled down the bottom of his jacket and stood to attention watching them leave. Bluu put her hand on her hip and made a D shape, beckoning him to link her arm as they walked down the stairs. Slowly like some historic king and queen they descended the wide staircase as the crowd parted in awe at both of them. At the bottom they took a sharp right and two people bowed slightly as they pulled aside a thick curtain covering an alcove.

As they passed through, the world became sepia and grey. The air was cold and clammy with the odour of dust filling his nostrils. The dramatic change of scenery reminded him to repeat to himself. Nothing is real he had to whisper it as if reassuring himself. "Nothing is real."

He found himself in a gothic lab like something from an old Frankenstein movie jars of organic material either animal or human floating in stained liquid strewn across shelves. The walls were daubed in what could have been blood or paint. Body parts lay around the floor making him shudder even after he realised they were not real, just parts of what looked like shop mannequins. Strange receptacles, tubes and instruments covered in dust were scattered on benches and tables. In the flickering shadows cast from the low hanging lamps he could make something out against the far wall. Two huge tanks of green translucent liquid stood at the far end, bubbles slowly rising. Tentatively he stepped towards them kicking and standing on rags, broken glass and other debris. An old stone stairway led from an upper level with twisted metal railings on either side. The tank on the right was empty apart from a few severed tubes floating like seaweed in a tide. Shuffling closer through the rubbish strewn floor he didn't bother to look down as he felt something soft beneath his heel. In the other tank he could see a figure, a human figure. Bluu stood to one side as Vic crept deeper into the room, his curiosity getting the better of him. As he drew closer he could see it was twisted and malformed with limbs floating in unnatural ways. It was like looking at a drowned corpse beneath a thin layer of green ice. In the corner of his eye Bluu was gazing at him like a child opening a birthday surprise, fingers across her open mouth. He walked closer and was able to make out the clothes on the man a plain white shirt untucked under a dark nondescript suit floating in an invisible current, revealing the figures midriff. Ankles and elbows disjointed and twisted like a road crash victim. Is it possible that the brain can deny what it sees, as if blinking like a cartoon character will make it go away? Blood rushed to his limbs from his insides making him shake and feel sick. He bent over the table retching dry air and nothing came up. Finally looking up through the tears he could see Bluu laughing, real hysterical laughter for the first time since he'd known her. It was like the sound of her laughter was coming from inside a distant cave. The incongruence of the situation calmed his revulsion for a moment. He saw flashes of her and then the body in the tank through his streaming eyes as his head swam. He was sweating and felt a cold dampness inside his clothes. Vic looked at Bluu who was holding her mid-rift, almost unable to breathe and then up at the body in the tank.

His body, his 68 year old dead body still in the suit, the one he had chosen to die in. Stripped of life and hanging limp and lifeless like a carcass in a butcher's cold-room. There was the bandage on the right hand where he'd covered the cannula and in it, maybe in a bizarre attempt to protect the record was the remote control. The button he'd used to set the poison flowing into his veins only weeks ago and yet in that time 500 years had passed to bring him here. With what must have happened since his death seeing the remote made no sense but for some reason it was right there. But it did make sense, this was a sim, it was not real. The lifeless body had no substance to it like an animal before the taxidermist had done his work. It all made sense now as he gazed across at the empty tank next to it, slowly he looked down at his own open palms and then back again. Bluu was calming down a little now and was just about able to speak.

"I apologise for laughing, please forgive me. I understand how your time may have felt very different about," she paused looking at the figure floating in the tank, and tried to find a word. "Flesh?" she said in a question.

Vic fell onto a lab stool and put his elbows on the table, head in his hands.

"Can you see how you will be held precious Nova? The project to bring you back began 23 years ago."

Head in hands Vic opened his fingers looking up at the empty tank. "Are you saying that this is where my new body came from?"

"It's a complex process but you were regenerated. Lots of elements from this sim came from your deepest thoughts I had no time to tidy them up. A lot of what you experience here contains deeply held beliefs and fantasies. But yes, it took 23 years to grow the new flesh and then it was a simple transition."

Swapping his brain he assumed, spoken as if they were talking about putting a new engine in an old banger.

Vic thought for a moment, imagining his new body growing from a baby and yet never waking or leaving that tube until it was 22 years old.

"So if you put my old brain in this new body." Using both hands to indicate his self. Vic was still thinking his question through. "What about the brain in the young body that you grew?"

Bluu flicked a wrist at him still amused at his primitive reaction to flesh. "It was never conscious," she said confused.

"I know that," said Vic. "but it would have been me wouldn't it?"

"Of course not, that's a preposterous idea. It was never born. We just needed new flesh for you," she laughed at his naivety. This was going to go nowhere and he knew that. Bluu was still giggling occasionally about how he had reacted to his own dead body in a jar, just flesh. It reminded him of when his cat had seen himself in the mirror and jumped in the air. Vic had laughed about that for hours. It was the same for Bluu, he knew that but, seeing your own dead body.

She placed a hand on the base of his back and led him towards an outer door and as they went through he took one last look over his shoulder. 23 years or 500 years he thought, none of it made sense because what made it difficult was his own warped sense of time, like he had sat in that chair in the conference room only weeks before. Vic was even more aggravated at knowing he'd had all the answers moments ago during his incident but no more.

He was led outside to where an old mini 1275GT was waiting with the engine running. Bluu climbed into the driver's side and he walked around to the passenger seat. He jumped in and the door shut with a hollow clunk. He still admired the detail of V-world as he breathed the smell inside the car, a mixture of oil and leather. Once inside the acoustics changed as the enclosed space sucked up the sound. Bluu slipped the gear stick forwards and hit the gas as they sped off from the hotel and into the night. They both stared ahead as the landscape flew past them.

"I think that's all for today," Bluu stared forwards.

The passing street lights lit up her face in flashes blinking faster and faster as the car quickened.

"Where are we going," said Vic gripping on to the seat tighter as Bluu accelerated.

Bluu turned and looked at Vic as a sinister grin crept across her face. Her eyes widened as he saw she was staring right at him, paying no attention to the road. The smile spread in unison with the accelerated speed. Vic looked forwards and then back at her as the engine roared, the dial on the speedometer moving steadily upwards. His heart pounded, he screamed at her to slow down but she wouldn't look at the road, she just stared the same crazy stare. Ahead Vic could see the street lights swinging off to the right as they approached a bend. They were getting close to the point of no return and Bluu showed no signs of slowing down. Vic gripped the dashboard as the road slipped from under them realising they were never going to get around. He smelled the burn of rubber and heard the screech of the tyres as he screamed. Bracing for the impact as the tree tore towards him, he closed his eyes and waited for the shattering glass and crunching metal. In a pathetic attempt to save himself he threw both arms across his face, then nothing.

Silence and darkness along with no sense of movement his helmet lifted but his heart was still pounding.

"Nothing is real," whispered Bluu as she took her helmet off smiling. Vic quickly realised what she'd done putting his hand on his heart to see if it was still beating. He wanted to be angry but he couldn't, not after he'd been such an arse the other day. He took some deep breaths and laughed along politely. He seems to have discovered what makes this girl laugh. She is very entertained by his fear and remembering his cat this upset him a little. Was he some kind of pet, cared for but not quite as important as the real people? How he'd laughed at his silly cat being frightened of its own reflection.

Although this stuff seemed odd to him, that's to be expected in a culture that's hundreds of years ahead of his. He would probably need to adjust and perhaps the quarantine, the trip into the V-world thing had been a good idea after all. Things had definitely changed most people spent their lives and now their deaths in a computer game? But if he was going to live in a world where topping yourself was cause for a party and sex was no longer a physical act unless you were some kind of pervert, well he was going to have to face up to those changes. At least they seemed to be being honest with him it was him that was faking. He was almost ready to face up to it and tell her who he really was but thought better of it. He wasn't Nova he was just Vic, lonely and afraid and he didn't belong here. Falling in love with a person neither male nor female in a time when anyone who even knew the concept of being homosexual died hundreds of years ago. For all this his only sense of freedom from his quarantine was running around inside a computer game.

"How was that?" said Bluu dropping her helmet on the chair.

"Weird."

"Yes I imagine it was quite disorientating for you, take a moment to relax. I hope I'm forgiven?"

"Only if I am," he laughed. The atmosphere seemed slightly warmer now.

"So? what now? what about me? You said I was here for a reason?"

"You can see now how fortunate it was that you were on Mars when the data crash happened."

"So I am the only link to that time, the only witness?" he said fiddling with one of the helmets and wandering over to the balcony. She followed and they both stood staring out across the skyline.

"Yes, your experience of history is valuable. Major Zero and his team were the only civilised survivors of the shutdown. History, inventions, everything had to be rebuilt from their physical memories and recollections. But you are ancient, you are from a time over 500 years ago."

"But what can I tell you, everything seems cool now? Why does it matter?"

"Cool?" she was puzzled again.

"Good, alright," he confirmed.

"To most people, the history doesn't matter but we think that you can bring us back together again, ready for something amazing."

"Back together?"

"You have seen V-world today."

"I definitely have," he laughed.

"You have to understand that most experience V-world as individuals, millions of us in our own accommodation, working, playing, meeting and making love. Never needing or wanting to leave V-world."

"Is that wrong?"

"You're ancient, from a time when people interacted physically and you entertain, make music."

Oh yeah he thought, I am a musician? True Vic had recorded an album and was a capable session musician. He'd even released an album in his youth. A head full of dreams and ideas about what he wanted from his career before he fell on his arse and it never happened. A minor novelty hit followed by obscurity. One failed flop of an album before he had crawled back under the corporate rock having said that he'd done a lot better in that world. It had been the success of his business ventures that had given him a good living and wealth. The very same wealth that had paid his freezer bills for the best part of the last 500 years. As for being a musician, maybe Nova could knock out a tune or two but he doubted whether Vic Jones could. He may well be rumbled if that's what they were after.

"You can bring people out of their homes, into the street to see you," said Bluu pointing outside.

"You mean to play, live?" he said following her gaze.

"Why the hell would anyone come and see me play?" he shrugged. Ok thought Vic here's a problem I didn't foresee. These futures think they have thawed out Nova; they clearly have him down as some kind of rock star.

"You don't understand how important you are to the people of Heathen, your fame is instant and guaranteed."

His thoughts were racing into survival mode, ok he was not the greatest singer in the world but he could hold down a tune. He needed time to think this through but there might be a way he could fake this. From what he had learned so far all of history had been effectively wiped out and he assumed that would include art, literature and.... music! The only reason that the futures believed Vic was a musician was his cryogenic pod record and that had become attached to Nova's. The futures clearly had no idea what Nova looked like or he would have been rumbled the minute the frost melted off his nose. It was also clear they have never heard Nova's music and neither had Vic. Something was developing in his mind and he needed time to think it through but he was becoming excited. Likewise the futures had never heard any of the music Vic knew so well, The Stones, T-Rex and Lennon. He grinned so hard he almost laughed out loud.

"You would like to play live then?" exclaimed Bluu who had completely misread his smile.

Vic beamed from ear to ear as he realised he had the entire twentieth centuries music catalogue to plagiarise. Looks like Lennon's on sale again he thought. He could test it out, play a few hits and see what happens but from where he was standing there was no one going to sue. Besides, he laughed to himself, after 500 years it would all be out of copyright by now. His heart was pounding and he imagined that second chance. Knowing deep down no matter how well he'd done in his life it was always fame that he had craved more than anything.

"Your music will be a great opportunity to share your knowledge with us and help us fill the gap on our history," Bluu continued.

"Let me think it over."

"You can do anything you want, everyone wants to know about the dark ages and the ancient music you made," waving her arms in frustration.

"Understand Nova, the world is waiting to see you." Vic was starting to think he may have got this all wrong. Perhaps he wasn't a freak after all. Mr Vic Jones might well have stumbled on a way out here, this might actually be fun.

THIRTEEN

Vic pushed his right thumb and forefinger across his chest and flicked his forehead with his left hand and everything around him went black. Slipping the helmet over his head he decided to call it a night, it was getting late. He was very pleased with his work so far but maybe he could finish it tomorrow. The last few nights had been spent in V-World creating a sim of his own. Over the last week or so Doctor Touchreik had been showing him how to create virtual world environments. Working with the Doctor he'd been creating scenes from his own history. Using these as templates and with his own limited skills he had developed something for himself. He wanted somewhere to relax that was a reflection of his own time.

The Doctor had shown him how the simulator that created the V-world experiences in private sims could also operate in reverse. This was how Bluu had created their Lon-Don sim to provide his history lesson. It could work as a three dimensional recorder, building a world from memories, fantasy or just thoughts. Once created it could be the scene of any future adventures with its own set of rules. With a little late night fooling around Vic had mastered the equipment well enough to create a sim of his own. The sims were based on recordings of memory outputs using the same helmet in reverse mode. The real skill was eliminating the inaccuracies that came about from the intrusion of fantasy, dreams or personal bias. The subconscious mind has always struggled to determine the difference between what is real and what is fantasy. The result would be contamination of the world he was trying to create. This was not so much a fault in the software but more a fault in the human brain. Memories are never accurate and so there would be lots of things out of place or time. Vic's sim was designed to replicate his time in history and he'd done a satisfactory job. His first effort was pretty good but he was aware someone from his own time would spot the glaring inaccuracies in a second. There was nothing too major though; no dinosaurs walking around or anything like that. Just the wrong car models, technology or music out of place. But seeing as the futures were 500 years out of time then they were unlikely to notice thirty or forty years either way. Anyhow who cares, no one else will see it. He enjoyed his time within a butchered version of the twentieth century. This was not for them or the Doctor anyway, it was purely for him. There were no futures going to see any of it were there?

Vic found his time with the Doctor exhausting at times but this sim was the first of the benefits he'd reaped from his cooperation. The Doctor was a reasonable guy and they had developed a good relationship. Vic had never considered he could become a living, breathing museum exhibit.

Occasionally, Vic got bored or frustrated so they might split their time, sometimes just walking and chatting in reality or visiting the reserve. It's more difficult than it seems explaining every detail about life to someone who has no idea how society works. Sometimes he sounded like an idiot, in fact sometimes Vic felt like an idiot.

Where did the money go that you gave your government? Tell me how you made food? After a while it had got deeper and more difficult.

Where there were gaps in his knowledge Vic had kept the Doctor satisfied with scenes he remembered from films and books which worked quite well. It wasn't like they were made up stories it was just easier to reference things from films and comic books. Oddly there were more problems with the real facts as opposed to the fabricated ones. When Vic explained that an actor had been President of the United States there were doubts. Politics had been a problem for him too and the questions were endless.

"Who was the king of your government?"

"Why did people speak different languages?"

"What was this and that war about?"

"Tell me about colour, racism and religion?" On and on it went.

Once Vic had relaxed a bit and started to make up the bits he didn't know then it got easier, even fun. The futures would never know whether Malcolm X and Jesse Jackson were pop stars or politicians; that was all detail. Later it amused him to think that he might be the man to literally rewrite history. It was harmless and unlikely to cause any damage. The Doc had been interested in sex and that kind of thing too. Explaining to a grown man how we made babies was very odd for Vic.

So in time came the lessons on creating private sims. Vic had become competent enough to create sims that could demonstrate various 20th Century concepts like religion and war. Mostly these were derived from memory or various war films he'd seen over the years. This part came easy because he was a fan of war films but his knowledge and interest in sci-fi proved to be useless here. Not as much scope for made up stories. The weird thing was that living in the 21st century had appeared normal at the time. However, the more the Doctor questioned him the harder it was to explain. At times it was so bloody frustrating, like instructing someone to build a model whilst blindfolded.

On the upside, Vic's quarantine was officially over and he'd chosen to continue living in his hotel suite. Being physically moved to a new location of course but everything will go with him, including the view from the balcony. Unknown to him one or two improvements were included in the deal.

A few days later his sim was good enough, lots of faults but they added a little spice. V-world now gave Vic access to his own reality. He craved the imperfect world he once knew. The bills he had to pay, the chores to complete, the car breaking down. He wanted to go to a movie and a dance; be back in his own time. He let himself believe that was the reason he was building his sim. Right up to the moment he invited Bluu to come into it with him, he believed that. If he was honest with himself he would have admitted that maybe if they were on his turf, things might play out differently. If those physical relationships were as much of a waste of time in 2515 or TVC15 as they call it then she might change her view in 2014. None of those things were thought about; all he wanted to do was be with her.

He kept it as casual as possible when he asked her.

"It's going great, I made my own sim," he said. "Heathen is cool, but it's somewhere to relax, take a break." No response. "I have a few hours this afternoon, gonna give it a try."

"It sounds stimulating, have fun," she said.

Then as he was leaving he quickly turned around as if a shot of inspiration had hit him.

"Hey, if you're doing nothing why not come along?" He paused feeling embarrassed, shoulders shrugged. "If you want." Realising how manufactured that must have seemed but it was too late. By the time he looked up he could see that Bluu may have been about to pass out. Her cheeks were flushed red and there were tears in her eyes. It took her a moment to reply.

"Is that a serious comment, you wish me to escort you into your simulation?" It was as if he had offered a blind man his sight back. As if Bruce Springsteen had asked a fan if she wanted to 'hang out' he almost expected her to throw her arms in the air screaming I'm not worthy, he looked her over.

She was definitely worthy.

This only added to Vic's on-going feeling of self-actualisation after a week of meeting other dewy eyed futures. One by one presenting him with a shiny version of themselves, way beyond anything he deserved.

Ten minutes later they were both helmeted, plugged in and ready to go. Now he was nervous. 'Nothing is real' he thought although in this case it was going to be doubly so. He'd heard that somewhere before?

☐

Bluu stood on the porch of a 1950's white wooden town house with a picket fence to match; looking around expectantly, hands clasped in front of her. Vic rolled up at the end of the drive looking like a kid in his father's borrowed car. Unsure whether he imagined it he thought he saw the upstairs curtains twitch. His heart skipped a beat when he saw Bluu looking more feminine than ever. He remembered this was his sim, his fantasy probably played a part. Her hair was lighter and slightly longer yet still cropped close to her head. Dark makeup highlighted her huge puppy dog eyes and a million freckles crowded around her tiny nose. The flesh she revealed between her baby doll red dress and knee length boots glowed with youth. Bluu waved and skipped across the drive, her red dress flashing her knees as she ran and jumped in the passenger seat. Vic crunched the gears of the monstrous swaying Cadillac and Bluu was too polite to notice he almost stalled. He wore an ill-fitting white dinner suit with a matching bow tie. The warm night air played with the curl on her forehead as they cruised into the suburbs. Bluu squeezed his hand over the gearstick as if they were shifting it in unison and smiled. A few miles out of town he pulled off the main road and onto an improvised dirt track, scraping the underside of the beast as he did so. The Cadillac bounced along until they reached a cordoned off area. Spinning the wheel he pulled into a drive-in 2D movie theatre were rows of featureless nondescript vehicles all pointed expectantly at the large silver screen in front. The film was about to start as they occupied the one free spot on the back line.

Laughing and talking they paid little attention to the film itself. A senseless story to do with a space alien visiting Earth in the 60's from what Vic could gather. On another day he may well have related to it but tonight was different. The pair ordered fries and cola even though they had no money for the food or the movie. This was his sim, so what.

After the film they drove giggling into the city some miles away. During the course of the drive they'd managed to cross several decades as well as several countries but Bluu failed to notice, he didn't expect she would. Pulling the car up outside a warehouse building to the gasps of queuing girls there may have been guys he wasn't sure, he didn't notice them. Skipping around, he opened the door for Bluu and took hold of her forearm, leading her past the nodding doormen and down the stairs. A flickering neon sign above the doorway read 'Dschungle.' The doorman had smiled slapping him on the back as he waved them inside. They hit the dance floor in fits of giggles as the crowd parted to give them room. The music played and they danced and danced till they were dizzy. Pushing through the crowds to the bar, Vic ordered two Martini's.

As he turned to hand Bluu a Martini a drunken German man in military uniform nudged his arm, spilling the drink on his suit. Laughing the man leered at Bluu, offering to buy her a replacement in his gruff German accent.

10 minutes later the pair were running up the stairs in the opposite direction to a line of lawmen, truncheons at the ready. A small drop of blood dripped from one nostril and on to his lip. Behind them an immense bar brawl had ensued between groups of airmen and sailors, neither group consistent with the time zone, neither group cared how it had all started. Leaping into the Cadillac they sped off on the wrong side of the road, the back end gaining traction as they disappeared into the night.

By the time they had reached the hilltop parking spot by the bridge history was of no consequence. In the warm night air they sat above the illuminated cityscape below. The conversation they had was a million miles from any he had with the Doctor. Bluu was not troubled by the drama and violence they had witnessed tonight regardless of its apparent reality. These and much bloodier pastimes were commonplace in V-world sims. It was the fact that it actually happened in his time that had bothered her most. He could understand that in his own way. He'd played enough computer games in which running over old ladies gained you points, a far cry from doing it on the road. Perhaps this was the reason there seemed to be little or no commonplace violence or cruelty in Heathen. Bluu reached over and dabbed his nose with a hankie. In all the time she had cared for him physically this was different, affectionate. She pulled away a little embarrassed and he guided the conversation back to their earlier altercation at the club. His shock as the drinks tray had crashed down on the man's head, before the chap had hit the floor she was dragging Vic through the crowd and up the stairs with the cops tearing into the drunken mob below as they sped away.

"Did you have family?" she said from nowhere.

"Of course," he said before realising that wasn't what she meant. She was referring to having a real organic mother and father.

"I have heard of family, it sounds nice. Like having special friends forever," she said naively.

"Yeah I suppose so," he said remembering his closest friend Nathan who must have done everything asked of him or he wouldn't be here now. It was hard to grasp the fact he would have died centuries ago.

The subject switched to relationships and particularly physical ones. Bluu had asked about his, whether he had left anyone behind. Even she was talking like he was from another planet and that's how he felt. It took a humongous effort to realise that he had not moved very far physically, he was still here on Earth. They were on a virtual hillside right now but up in the sky the moon was enormous. The same satellite lump of rock was still hanging in space and acting upon the hearts and minds of the earthlings as it always had. This was his world and he wanted to show it to Bluu with all its faults. He couldn't explain most of it to the Doc, but where else could he go? Soaps and boy bands, wars and TV?

When they finally kissed it felt real, physical and he might have been happy with that, Bluu was. What he didn't understand was whether it meant anything in here. Could the adventures in a simulation be carried into reality? Could feelings for someone be taken outside? He would soon find out, in the meantime he would go along with it, after all this was better than any game. That much was clear from his own physical reaction after he had reached across the gear shift and kissed her. In this so called computer game her warm hand on the back of his neck, the soft moist mouth were the only reality he wanted. If he could freeze time right now he would have done. Afterwards he said the L word and she did the same. He knew he felt it as deeply as she did right then.

"You like older men then?" he joked.

"What's 500 years in a relationship?" she responded.

"I'd stick with you baby for a thousand years," he said and he meant it, right at that moment he meant it. He had no idea how soon those words would come back to haunt him. Despite the short lived illusion Bluu really loved him but, just for a short while. Once the game was over and they were back in reality, maybe not. The futures may as well be aliens as far as he was concerned and she was no different. But right here, right now he was head over heels.

FOURTEEN

"Manhattan Chase! Are you serious?" The Doctor had mentally committed to helping the Professor with his plan to eliminate the humanists. He knew he would do whatever needed to be done, but to go up there? He hadn't thought it would involve going up to the far end of the Chase.

"I'm with you, I support what you need to do but do we really have to go up there? It's too dangerous."

"I haven't told you my plan."

"I'm not stupid, it's obvious you found a way of getting rid of them," said the Doctor staring into the cold store and grabbing a cooled soda. His shoulders were hunched and tense as he ripped at the lid taking a long guzzle. The Professor's jaw dropped as he looked away squeezing his temples. He hadn't considered this for one moment but of course. What else would the Doctor think? Certainly not the truth, he'd never have guessed the real reason for him being here.

"We have to talk. It's time for me to explain what happened to me in my future," he said. The Professor beckoned him to sit down at the table. The Doctor obliged, noticing the concern in the Professor's expression. Indicating to one of the chairs at the feed area, the Doctor swung into the seat.

The Professor slid down at right angles to him.

"There's something you have to understand before I begin. I'm sorry if I appear deliberately vague or withhold information but I have to consider what might happen if something goes wrong, if something happens to me. I can't put you or anyone else in a position where you know too much about future events, ok?"

The Doc nodded. "That kind of knowledge could be dangerous if events continue on their original path as they appear to be doing."

The Professor waited until the Doctor had looked up nodding defiantly.

"Everything that is happening to you now happened in exactly the same way to me. Aside from my involvement of course your life now matches my memory of events perfectly and so do the events of

97

Heathen." The Professor spun in the chair and placed his elbows on the table, hands clenched.

"I was offered the opportunity to work with the caveman just as you were. I don't need to tell you how incredible that was for me because you are experiencing it now."

The Doctor nodded in agreement.

"I can assume that everything else I am about to tell you will happen in the future we are now in." He stared downwards as if seeing what he was describing.

"Nova had started to tour Heathen, meeting people physically. I spent a lot of time with him and Bluu and was around when that happened. You're currently witnessing his popularity grow, bigger than we imagined. As for me I'd never been happier, it was a dream project." The Doctor looked up now and met his eyes.

"Was?"

The Professor continued. "Is he working on his music at the moment?"

The Doctor shook his head. "No?"

"He soon will be, shortly after that he will announce that he is to tour with his show. The V-world tour will finish with a physical performance with people physically attending his shows as they did in the twenty first century. This show will be the biggest physical live event in living memory. During the early shows a few of us were given some information about the Salvation Project. How it was ready to go to the next level. In a few months the backlog will have been taken up and the Migration Project can begin."

"Migration Project?"

"Yes, it's the same as the Salvation Project, human personalities uploading into V-world forever. The difference is that anyone can do this at any time young and old. Any living human can euthanise whenever they want. If you can't see it now then you soon will, but the caveman is becoming very influential. He will not only launch the Migration Project but be the first to take it up."

"To euthanise early?" The Doctor was surprised and puzzled. "An interesting idea," said the Doc in deep thought.

"Known only to a small group of us Nova agreed to do this along with his partner after the final show."

The Doctor interrupted. "You mean a physical partner like they had in the twenty first century?"

"Possibly, some suspected that but it would be a natural thing for him, as we both know. It wouldn't matter anyway once they were both living in V-world permanently."

The Doctor was trying to focus on what he was being told whilst processing everything else. A physical partner would clearly have to be Bluu.

"They will agree?"

"It happened after the very last show in the Market Square attended physically by thousands with many more thousands outside and millions watching or experiencing in accommodations. This event took the project to immense levels of excitement and the rush for places began. Over the following months and years millions took up the offer to follow them."

"It sounds amazing," the Doctor was upright in his chair excited at the prospect. "So Salvation is opened up to everyone and not just those due to euthanise? Why will that be a problem?"

The Professor stared back. "Maybe it wasn't?" he said thinning his lips in a wistful smile.

The Doctor worried now. "Meaning?"

"After that night it was clear many people were moving over but it all fell from my attention over time, it dropped from the media too." The Professor's tone became guilty, as if he had missed something. "Years passed since the caveman had gone inside and he had given me permission to keep a copy of his brain trace."

The Doctor almost leapt off his chair. "Wow, that's going to be amazing, you mean everything?"

The Professor ignored his enthusiasm and continued. "Of course, so as you can imagine this was a lifetime's work sifting through fantasy, reality, genuine and false memories to build a better picture of the ancient world. I was lost in this research for a time until years later something happened." The Prof looked down at his hands nervously flicking his thumbs together.

"Go on," the Doctor was fascinated now, eager to ask about the brain trace discoveries. "I didn't find out till some considerable time later but Mother was reducing her reproduction of organic humans."

"Because of migration?"

"Presumably."

"It was years before any of this came back to my attention."

"What about the trace, from the caveman?" said the Doc eager to hear more.

"There were problems with it, things I couldn't understand which make sense now but those things are for you to discover for yourself."

The Doc was bursting with anticipation. "But."

The Professor held out a palm to silence him again. "Years later, there was an outage and it caused a few software problems."

"Humanists?" asked the Doctor knowingly. Sat upright now, buoyed at hearing how exciting his life was going to be. A full memory trace will be a first. He was already working on how he would approach such a mountain of knowledge from the past.

"Yes, I expect so." The Professor waved a hand at him with disregard, keen to head off any diversion from the topic. "It caused a few software problems. But it wasn't just the software that started to become a little buggy. It was also my..."

The Professor looked his younger self in the eye. "My assistant, Jagger."

"Your assistant?"

"He'd been with me for years and we'd worked well together. He shared my love for the work, we socialised. But after the outage I noticed little things that were not quite right like forgetting, ignoring certain statements and repeating things. The sort of things you might not notice."

He paused before continuing. He was aware he had asked Duke to switch to private mode but he looked around all the same.

"Things you might not notice unless you had spent a lot of time with... a drone!"

Doc's eyes widened. "No, your assistant was..." The Doc was stunned. "that's not possible, how could you not know?"

"Without the outage I would never have known. But something had changed, I looked into his eyes and I could see," he paused, "I could see nothing and everything at the same time. Then I wondered how many of us are left? How many organic humans were still here on the planet?"

"Now hang on here," the Doctor had become concerned at where the conversation was leading.

The Professor placed a hand on the Doctor's arm to quieten him and soldiered on with his story. "I kept quiet and carried on. Eventually through friends I made the acquaintance of a humanist named Jak Samian." The Doc shook his head in disgust.

"Jak Samian and Antoine Feng, I believe you have already met one of them. When I met them they were leading the humanist rebels, remember this all happens many years from now. Over time I heard lots of stories, rumours from them. Most of it was nonsense of course but I also learned things. Things I had either ignored or had refused to hear in the past. None of us were sure if anything was going on at the time. Slowly over time the things I picked up from the caveman's memory trace started to make sense. How I acquired the time belts is another story that I can share, once this is over. For now let's say I had the chance to acquire them and despite the risks involved decided I had to try and come back. I had lots of time to think back about my life, time to find an opportunity to change things if I could make it back here in one piece. My plan depended on everything happening as it did the first time around. Up until now this seems to be the case. When I arrived the first thing I did was seek out Jak, he was dubious about my story naturally, but became convinced after coming here to see you for himself. After that meeting it was clear to him that you and I were actually the same person. Remember I first met him years from now but when I arrived he had not met Feng and was considerably younger than the first time we met. I told him his future, told him they would one day work together and he was to find Feng." The Prof paused before looking up. "He has done that now and we have to go and meet them both."

The Doctor closed his eyes tightly in deep thought. "I am confused here, what are you saying to me?"

"This is not about destroying the humanists. Don't you see yet? They're right."

The Doctor stood quickly sending his chair crashing into the wall. "Have you lost your mind? Are you saying that all the time I have kept you here, protected and fed you, you've been involved with those savages?" the Doctor was screaming at him now. "Just go now, leave," he screamed turning him away with a wave.

"Calm down please just listen to me." The Professor approached him as he backed away, waiting whilst the Doctor absorbed the information. Grabbing his elbows across his chest the Doctor hugged himself. "So you're saying that Mother is trying to wipe out humanity, this is bullshit, this is impossible. We have been into V-world and met those who have been in the Salvation Project, we all have." The Doctor was becoming excited again, raising his voice.

The Professor touched his arm once more speaking softly. "I am saying the opposite, I am saying that the Salvation Machine was designed to love humans, that's how it's been since the Major."

"So why would it harm us?" he pleaded.

The Professor realised he was going to have to spell this out, shaking his head. "It's the love that could kill us. I remembered what the caveman taught us about religion. My research into his trace showed how it went much deeper than that to a desire that humans have held since they could think," the Professor spat the word 'think', it was his turn to become animated now. "We have both worked with the caveman. Religion was real to them."

"Which means?"

"The one thing every human being has craved since time began. Immortality! The promise of eternal life, Mother, the Salvation Machine has found a way to give us all everlasting life in V-world safe in Mother's arms forever. It's what we have craved for thousands of years and she can satisfy it. It was in the caveman's brain trace and its hidden deep within ours."

The Doctor tried to speak but he couldn't get any words out. Picking up his glass he took a large gulp and swallowed hard, gasping for breath. He pointed angrily in the Professor's face. "You have spent too much time with them they have lied to you, corrupted your mind."

The Professor shook his head in frustration. "I worked for decades on those traces. That craving is a human trait it doesn't need religion that was just convenient. But no God had ever delivered on that promise, only vain hopes and lies but now.... now Mother may have realised she could do it."

"Lies, humanist lies," he said turning away. The Professor grabbed his shoulder spinning him back round.

"Is it? The Salvation Machine had stopped reproducing organic life?"

The Doctor froze as the Prof continued. "Why do you think that was? Organic life was redundant and eventually there will be no one left." The Professor tasted the salty droplets of tears that had run down his cheek and onto his lips.

The Doctor stared at the floor shaking his head. "This isn't true, it can't be?"

"I saw it happen, I spoke to the survivors and met some of them." Wiping his cheek with his sleeve. "I was a survivor."

The Doctor began pacing around the room like a caged animal. "They aren't survivors they're humanists, you stupid old man, I'm ashamed that I turned into you. You're pathetic. You came back here for this?" he screamed attempting to laugh through his tears. "You actually believe them?" The Professor didn't look up as the Doctor approached whispering into his ear. "All they want is to destroy Mother that's all they have ever wanted." Slamming his fist on the table he picked up the cup and threw it across the room. The Professor flinched, ducking involuntarily. "You have no idea how many people had gone into the project."

The Professor spoke calmly now, without tone. Wiping the spit from his beard the Doctor uttered something as if to speak. "Let me finish please," said the Professor holding up a palm.

"Just before I made the leap I checked and a lot of the systems allocated to maintenance were shutting down as the living organic humans reduced in number, there may have been very few. I had to make the leap back in time, I risked my life."

The Doctor folded his arms, studying then seemed to have realised something.

"Why?" he screamed. "Why did you come back here, you could have left me alone. Mother will take care of everything. I wish you'd never come back."

The Doc turned away but the Professor grabbed his arm and spun him back round.

"We've got five years! That's all we've got. After that humanity begins her downward spiral towards extinction. Are we going to stand by and be the last? I know you." He pulled in close to the Doctor. "Millions of years of evolution and thousands of years of civilisation, the shutdown, Major Zero, the City of Heathen built from the ashes and humanity survived. Will you really just step aside now?"

There was a long silence before he spoke more softly. "So now what, you want me to go to the Chase with you and hear more of this rubbish?"

The Doctor stared into the eyes of an older version of himself. He could see the pain and felt it too he felt the tears well up. Arms out stretched the Professor grabbed his younger self and they hugged each other tightly. They rocked together and sobbed for what seemed like an age.

At last the Professor pleaded, his voice broken through tears. "Come with me, please hear what they have to say, that's all I ask."

FIFTEEN

On the first morning in his new home it felt like nothing had changed. But things had changed, he was free now and his quarantine was over. There were many things that hadn't changed of course the underlying noise of traffic from outside in the city of Lon-Don, the basic layout of the apartment and its contents. The difference was that he was now in a completely new physical location, the draws opened and so did the doors to the outside. The Lon-Don view was still augmented and so was the atmosphere outside. Vic was half buried in a warm cloud as a cool draft wafted against his face, disrupting his bliss. Opening his eyes he saw that the balcony door was open but the idea of closing it was in no way appealing to him. He had no wish to move a single muscle for fear it would destroy the heavenly position he found himself in. He resisted for a few minutes before realising it was ruined whatever he did, he was awake now. He casually rolled off the bed and padded barefoot across the warm floor to close it.

Half way between the bed and the door he stopped dead when a disembodied voice spoke out. The sound so clear it was almost inside his head.

"Good morning." It sounded male, quite camp and came from no discernible direction.

He stopped in his tracks. "Who said that?" said Vic looking around cautiously. There was raucous laughter. Vic walked in circles as if it might provide a better perspective as to where it was coming from.

"I am your religion God, you will obey me," the voice said, vainly attempting to sound deeper and more masculine followed by more laughter.

"Who's there?" shouted Vic looking up as if that was where the answer lay.

"I'm Leon. I am your sage," said the voice.

"Sage?" he questioned.

"They were right, you really are a caveman," the voice sniggered. He still couldn't place its location. "Where are you?"

Another snigger. Vic was slowly creeping around the room trying to keep him talking so that he would eventually give himself away. "I can't see you?"

"No I expect not, there's not much to see I can assure you." Vic stopped between rooms looking in every direction. "I manage the building and I am here to offer assistance."

"But where are you?"

The voice giggled once more. "Oh you mean my physical presence, 3 kilometres away at the offices of Jareth Accommodation."

Vic relaxed, he felt stupid as he realised he'd been startled by the air conditioning unit. Naturally it wasn't a huge leap to assume that the 'futures' had come up with some kind of voice activated building management system a giant leap from having to turn the thermostat up and down. Even in 2015 they were doing most of that by phone. It wasn't long before he realised this was more than an air conditioning unit.

"It's time you go hygiene and get robed, we have a lot to get through and Bluu will be on her way very soon. I can't imagine what she will think if I don't have you ready."

"A lot to get through?" said Vic to the ceiling.

"I have to complete your induction into the property. I calculate that your lack of intelligence might increase the time required to complete the task," said Leon without the slightest hint of insult or irony. Whatever this device was it looked to be taking the role of a butler. Had this thing been here in the room instead of three kilometres away he might have picked it up and thrown it out of the window. He wasn't going to rise to it, it probably meant no harm. "Ok, go for it," he said.

There was a long silence. "Go for what?"

Vic sighed. "So I lack intelligence?" he mumbled to himself. "Proceed with your induction," he said loudly. The bloody thing even had the nerve to give a little insulted cough.

"Ahem, alright. Welcome to the Jareth V9 Accommodation pod. For your convenience its initial physical layout has been set to your original plan with some special improvements. It's fully customisable and has over 40 panoramic views including 10.." he coughed again. "Ancient modes."

Vic watched as the scene from the balcony changed very quickly like flicking through TV channels. He was even feeling slight changes in atmosphere as they did so. A chill followed by a heated breeze and different smells too. Instead of differing views it was more like being dropped in different places instantaneously.

"The structural interior is fixed but also has over a hundred different customisable interior designs." Thankfully he didn't choose to go through them all but Vic got the idea. When he changed a layout it was like being in a different place. It was as if you could move to a new house in the blink of an eye. He could spend the weekend in the equivalent of a chilly mountain cabin and flick a switch to be at home in your familiar surroundings. The building itself was just a shell.

"Can you turn it all off?" Vic interrupted.

"Turn it all off?" Leon repeated.

"Yes," said Vic.

There was the pause again, he thought he was gone. Then suddenly everything disappeared. Vic found himself stood in what looked like a shell of a building it had plain walls and reminded him of one of those Chinese paper homes. There were solid objects too but they were made of the same material. It was as if he was standing in a 3D canvas. He took a few steps that echoed around the room and looked out through the balcony window.

"Ok," he said. Hoping the machine was still there. "Put it back on." There was silence for just a moment too long and Vic was on the brink of thinking he had reset everything to zero. Like the time he'd reset his phone to the Polish language and couldn't get it back. He was starting to become concerned when everything started to reappear. At last he was stood right back in the familiar bedroom he knew so well.

He took a walk round the apartment and everything was just as he remembered it and then he saw it. The adjoining door, the one he had tried to open but couldn't because of the force field. Slowly he approached and took hold of the two handles in the oak panelled double door. Twisting his wrists they gave way and he pulled as both doors swung open.

The interior was no longer a reflection of his room. He cautiously stepped cross the threshold for fear of banging his head again. He couldn't believe what he saw inside.

He had stepped into a wide square lounge area with a low glass table surrounded by four sofas. In contrast to the room he had just left there was a Caribbean breeze floating through the balcony window. On the outside a wooden terrace and a beach complete with hammock and palm trees. Waves were crashing against the shore and running back down bleached white sand. Here he was at ground level when in the other room he could be 14 floors up above London. That wasn't the most amazing thing. To his left and behind half glass there was what could only be a fully functioning recording studio, sound booths for a full band and an endless array of instruments. On the far side of the lounge area was a glass door and inside what could only be a dream come true. He darted across the room and opened the door. Inside it smelled of leather and the sound was dampened to almost zero as he entered, his footsteps merely a mellow thud. The room was rammed with an array of classic musical instruments and amps. He spotted a Marshall 200 stacked with a few others in the far corner. Stood up on one of many racks was what looked like a Gibson Les Paul Lemon-burst and just behind it the Sunburst model. Holy shit there was a Custom 1957 as well as the 1968 in Gold. He slowly walked around running his fingers over their curves. There were also Fender Telecasters and much more. Picking up the Lemon-burst he gently caressed it and picking it up fingered a few chords. When he strummed it sounded awesome, not even plugged in it sounded incredible. He felt the smile on his face stretching his skin uncomfortably and consciously relaxed.

But how? These were real but the designs, the tiny marks and scratches. Of course, they will have been plucked from his memory like they'd done with the sims. If these were all built from his memory then it's likely that in this room he would have a collection of the most valued guitars in history. He looked up at the double neck lead guitar hanging high on the wall and across to the 96 Paisley Stratocaster and left the room. Dazzled he closed the door with a quiet click.

"You like those then? Musical instruments for your pleasure," said Leon.

"For my pleasure," he repeated under what breath he had left.

"If you would like to come this way," said Leon. A light flashed across the floor in the main room and he walked through and into the kitchen area on the far side. An area previously unused as Bluu had provided all his meals. He had always taken it that was the reason there had never been any appliances in here.

"Food prep with the latest in 4D technology," said Leon. Looking around there still seemed to be none of the usual implements. There was a long kitchen style island but no sign of a fridge, toaster or kettle. Just two parallel work surfaces and a single high level oven type device and a drink dispenser.

"Is this it?" he said disappointedly.

"Sir, this is it!" said Leon stressing the word 'it'. "Allow me to demonstrate." There was that annoying cough and he put on some kind of butler type tone. "Can I offer Sir some refreshment, breakfast perhaps?" Vic wasn't keen on the idea of cooking for himself. But in light of the fact that he was retired and only had to pop next door to be on a writing holiday in Monserrat then he might find the time.

"Cheeseburger and large fries, go large," said Vic sarcastically.

"I can replicate animal although it's generally immoral but.. however my formulas still contain all the nutritional value of the natural creature," breezed Leon.

Vic was relieved this wasn't a cooking lesson. Besides, they are bound to have some kind of home delivery in the future? "Oh well if you're cooking then I'll have the works full English breakfast menu with black coffee, fruit juice." There was silence again for around thirty seconds and Vic was wondering had he offended the sage. Then a light illuminated in the cubicle and the door became transparent. He opened it and inside was his complete order, on a tray with cutlery and plates. He was sure it looked as fresh as it would be tasteless. Still you can't have everything. If he was independent now and having to be self-reliant then if that meant asking Leon for something then he could manage that.

"Your views, waking arrangements and decor are all optional. You need only ask."

"Does that thing make Guinness?" he said.

The machine paused. "Mm do you have a formula for that?"

"Never mind," he said.

"You can get yourself steam cleaned in here as you know." A light flashed behind him. Yeah, he knew how to get washed and dressed in 2515.

Finally you may wish to order items such as clothing, artwork, that kind of thing. Another light flashed and he followed it to another door which he had previously never entered. Inside there were a few chairs around a central stage, on it was a small table. In the corner a large garage sized sliding door.

"We can shop together or you can shop alone. If you want to make a purchase then I can do it for you or you can use the console. It will be delivered through here in good time most often within the hour." A hundred objects, real objects came and went on the stage. From bags to chairs to clothing and then disappeared.

"Cool, the very latest in home shopping and how do I pay?" said Vic realising he had no method of supporting all this.

"Pay, oh dear no," said Leon. "Who would you pay? There 'is' no one to pay," said Leon confused. "Most requirements are unpaid, only luxury items are paid."

"Yeah I suppose so," he said.

"We really must get on, we need to get your AR device fitted before Bluu arrives."

"What the hell is an AR device?"

Leon sighed. "Really?"

"Really," repeated Vic sarcastically. Leon continued as if unsure whether the human was having fun with him again. "Your Augmented Reality Device. It is fitted to the back of your neck and taps into your brain stem. It enables you to access 3D menus, get loce data and media."

"What's a loce?" asked Vic.

"Location data." The machine sounded exasperated. "It tells you where you are, where your friends are and enables you to navigate in physical space."

Vic had already switched off at the bit about brain stems. "I think I'll be just fine without an AR," he said.

If a machine could be flabbergasted then Leon was. "How will you know where you are, where your friends are. How about information and media?"

"I'll just ask someone for directions," he said and walked through his bedroom and into the steamer.

Vic was finishing dressing. There were quite a few items of clothing he didn't recognise in his wardrobe. Probably some kind of futurist starter pack he assumed. He pulled out a camouflage boiler suit and cream overcoat finishing the job with a comfortable pair of cream pumps. It felt a bit extreme but by their standards he had dressed down. Nonetheless, he felt more liberated in TVC15 after all he was unlikely to bump in to the lads from the Red Lion.

"Bluu is here," said Leon from nowhere. He rushed out of the dressing room to get the door before realising that would not be necessary. Leon had taken care of that and she was already in the lounge area. As if to prove the point of how conservative he was dressed, there she was sat in a black and white French style top and chunky striped mini skirt, impeccable make-up with huge dark eyes and pink lips. Her high heels made her look 7 ft tall. Perched on her head with the tiniest tilt was the smallest top hat he ever saw. It was more like a cake decoration perched on her tight mousy hair.

"How do you like it?" she said looking him up and down.

"The place? Amazing," he said opening his arms.

"We put some extra space in," she said waving the tiniest purse he had ever seen.

"I know, the studio is pretty awesome."

"I'm sure you'll like the instruments."

"I prefer the 68 Les Paul to be honest," he said disapprovingly.

She frowned in disappointment.

"Kidding, joke remember. Ha ha humour."

"I thought you might like a look around Heathen today, just us. Before the eh," she paused. "The official introductions."

"Before I'm paraded before the masses you mean?"

"You'd never believe how excited everyone is to meet you."

"Be careful you don't lose him dear he has no AR fitted," interrupted Leon.

Bluu looked at him concerned. "No AR?" Like he was a child refusing to wear a coat.

"Bluu please have a word with him. What am I supposed to do when he leaves this building? He may as well jump down a black hole. I will have no idea where he is, I can't communicate."

"Don't worry about it ok," said Vic winking at Bluu.

"Nova it's a good idea to have an AR fitted. It can be switched off if you want. What if you got lost?"

"He will ask directions he said," interrupted Leon once more.

"Can Leon be switched off?"

"Of course I can, you only need ask."

"Then switch off."

"That's all well and good but." There was silence.

"So what are we doing today then?"

"We have a transporter outside which will run us on the mag system over to some air transport. We can get a great view of the City from high above. Would you like that?"

"Sounds great to me, a tourist flight across Heathen."

Ten minutes later they were sat in a Quad-pod and heading away from the apartments. It was disorientating when he fooled around with the controls. With the false view up it looked like they were travelling around 40 miles an hour as the green pleasant landscape passed them by. When Vic switched it off and they could see the real landscape they were travelling at four times that speed easily.

When they arrived at the air centre it was nothing like an airport more of a rooftop car park with the Mag pods offloading and people travelling up escalators. Still not crowded, the whole planet seemed to have a feeling of Sunday afternoon. It looked designed for crowds but never really experienced any.

The upward escalator was about ten people wide and had handrails distributed across its width. At the top there were various craft and Bluu led them to a slim mean looking beast. It had no wings but he could see what looked like jet outlets half hidden in its body. A smaller craft took off quite close to them and gave off no pressure or dust. They stepped inside and made themselves comfortable.

"Where would you like to see first?" said Bluu.

"Not sure really."

"Let's circle some of the residential areas of Heathen." The craft lifted off and they started to get a sense of scale for the place. Although a mishmash of different sized buildings there were newer more modern areas with row up on row of residential towers. There was a wide open highway hub crisscrossing the city. These eight lane highways still held little traffic. They passed over public spaces and these were like the streets, relatively uncluttered. The city area was interspersed with green fields and trees. The buildings themselves were like an architect's dream. They flew in between structures of endless shape and size. There appeared to be no organisational flight paths as they flew under walkways which served to join buildings together. Passing so close he could have touched them, a stark reminder they had no visible human driver on this craft. Then they headed out across the Nature Park which was a lush landscape which went on for miles. Bluu explained they were not allowed to fly low over this area.

All in all Vic's futuristic fantasies about flying cars, robots and spaceships had been generally a disappointment. If an alien race were to arrive here they might think it relatively uninhabited.

That's until they reached the outer fringes of the City. Here he was able to witness the sheer scale of the robotic machine that provided for humanity. It was so much bigger than what he had seen in Bluu's V-world simulation. With the visualiser off they sped across fields with acre upon acre of crops being grown, harvested and processed.

They passed a railway system which had at least six lanes feeding into the city itself. At a certain point they would snake into tunnels, laden with parts, machinery and containers.

There were also automated voyagers which were driverless trucks. At its far reaches it seemed there were no more resources and the City ended leaving dusty roads that snaked away over the horizon. In the distance they were able to make out these mammoth vehicles the size of a mansion crawling to and fro.

They reached a far point and they were alerted to return because the vehicle could not operate further out. Although over hundreds of miles across Heathen looked quite small from here.

They headed back to the air park and as they walked back to the mag system Vic was recognised. A family group were getting out of a mag transporter and made their way over to them.

"Mr Nova, I hope you don't mind but it's an absolute pleasure to meet you," said the female of the group. Her companion followed suit. "Hello Mr Nova." Vic said hello and they took some images. They were pleasant and spent a few moments chatting. Finally they had made their excuses and left. They made no effort to disguise their chat as they left.

"He's very nice and speaks quite well too, and seemingly quite intelligent. I'm very pleasantly surprised."

During the course of the day he had gotten a feel for how this city functioned. The world of robotics had gone in a different direction than the visions portrayed in his schoolboy comics. There were no humanoid robots like Marvin or whatever he was called in the forgotten planet. Instead most automated tasks like waste removal and food delivery were kind of plumbed into the city and continued unseen. The machines were very discreet and designed to fade into the background or be built into the fabric of the structures.

On the surface the city was calm and yet as he understood it, a hive of columns and tunnels kept things functioning below the surface. It was inevitable that there would be some humanoid drones for tasks that required direct interaction with people. These were a minority of course. A person would just open their fridge and it was as if someone was loading it from the back, in fact that was actually happening. 4D technology allowed them to manufacture most foods at home from basic ingredients. The replicators were like incredibly complex 4 dimensional copiers. If the machine had the right formula then it could generate any food imaginable, something Vic was well aware of.

All meat style and vegetable products were now grown in simulated environments. The basic ingredients were the same for everything from a mouse to a cow, a sheep to a cat; they just had to decide what they wanted to come out at the end. He could see the attraction of V-world without a doubt. It was possible to lead an army of ten thousand men and be the only real person in the sim. This amazing technology was not the only reason that the streets were so deserted. Even for those who chose to do some kind of work could do most of it in a simulation.

At last Vic felt he had a sense of perspective for where he was. He thought about his twentieth century sim once more but maybe he would hit the music room first.

SIXTEEN

At first sight the future looked very bright indeed. No work, no government and a standard of living beyond most 21st century millionaires. War and conflict were inconceivable and an abundance of food and resources. Bring it on he'd thought but Vic's reality was proving quite different no work didn't mean doing nothing, maybe sitting on that beach outside his window and enjoying the sea breeze strumming his guitar. Touring V-World and working with the Doc were all part of his on-going education, and theirs. Then he was being paraded around reality too like a freak show. He knew he always let them down, he was too normal and he could see the disappointment in their eyes. Had he attempted to pick fleas off them they might have accepted him more. So his quarantine was over was it?

There were times over the last couple of days he'd have considered being in his cell a better option. To say the people of Heathen were enthusiastic was an understatement. What Bluu had said was true, he could use this fame to lever himself into anything.

Groups of people had started to physically turn up wherever he went. A few thousand wasn't many by his standards but to Heathen this was an incredible turnout. The last couple of days were spent being jostled and pushed around the City on a physical VIP tour. His appearances were beamed live to media in 3d wherever he went. A drone was always present above him wherever he went and he'd assumed it was security but not so. It was scanning the event for media clients meaning they could position themselves in prime position in the crowd, without leaving their homes simply by plugging into their VR machines.

First stop had been to meet the team of scientists who'd worked on thawing him out and nursing his new body back to health. They had designed a public exhibition that explained and documented the whole process. He was given the honour of officially opening the facility. It had working models of the equipment used to replicate the DNA and gestate the sparkly new Vic Jones.

Although it was slightly different in reality the horror of what he had seen in V-world had softened the blow when he saw the real thing. At last appreciating Bluu's unorthodox method of preparation, catching her eye for a moment when they revealed the tank full of luminescent green fluid. Casting his eye across his own dead body suspended in the gooey substance, still no sign of decomposition. A little unnerving but a far cry from the Frankenstein scenario his subconscious had chosen to include in Bluu's sim. Thankfully he was no longer as shocked at the concept and gave her a knowing grin. Bluu's smile broadened as she strained to contain herself from laughing out loud. Thanks to her preconditioning he failed to collapse and start dry retching as he'd done last time. The white coats proudly demonstrated the technology that had kept him alive for 22 years until the projects conclusion. Vic's cheeks flushed at the display of naked pictures of himself lay on a slab before the brain transmission had taken place. The audience no doubt more intrigued by the very existence of genitalia as opposed to its actual size or lack of.

There was a 2D video presentation of his birth and a time lapse of his growth into adult form. Various dignitaries made speeches and enjoyed private jokes on his behalf, relating some of his pre wake up ramblings. This was news to Vic he could neither confirm nor deny any of it but nodded and smiled at the right moments. There were humble apologies from the team who had worked on the project for the slight damage to one eye. Vic had made light of it and they were grateful when he suggested it added to his mystique.

Some of the futures he'd never seen before became very emotional, one or two of the nurses bursting into tears when he greeted them. Whilst on the facility he was asked to complete a few basic fitness tests, they connected him to various futuristic monitoring equipment this was more for the benefit of media than necessity. He was declared 100% fit by his chief surgeon who ceremoniously gave Vic some kind of certification. There were roars of laughter when he put his hand on his chest, faking a heart attack. Vic was winning the personality contest without breaking a sweat, he could do no wrong, gratefully greeting endless futures in white coats who had spent years monitoring and maintaining his new 'flesh'.

He was genuinely interested to see for the first time the inside of a mock up cryogenic pod where he'd spent the last 500 years. It was noticeably battered a little on the outside but inside the protective foam was like new. It was much bigger than expected, more like some kind of soundproof booth. The walls lined with some kind of tubular rubbers jutting outwards. With its inner shell removed there was easily space inside for two people to stand up. The media were most excited when he posed for them in its doorway as if stepping out for the first time. Vic squeezed and greeted many more dignitaries at all levels as he made his way back to the transporter for the next leg of his whirlwind tour of Heathen. On his first official day in reality Nova had played his part to perfection and was already winning fans.

As they lifted off from the building they waved to the crowds below and cruised low and fast across the city's gleaming skyline. Vic felt the relief in his facial muscles at dropping the smile that had been plastered across his face throughout the day. Through the windows he admired the kind of view he'd always imagined for the future. Illuminated towers, walkways and a living cityscape rushed by beneath them. It shimmered from neon lights glowing large and small. There were hundreds of people walking through brightly lit parks, malls and arcades.

He stared for a moment at the wondrous futuristic scene before him.

The deadpan look now deteriorated into an aggravated frown. "Turn that off," he muttered.

"Turn what off?" said Bluu puzzled.

"The thing, the scenery below," he said pointing out of the window.

"If you like," Bluu sighed. "The life you see below exists," she said by way of explanation.

He scowled at her without comment.

"Visualiser off," she commanded. At once everything he was seeing disappeared and was replaced by reality. A greyer cityscape, much less occupied than the bustling city he'd been witnessing.

"The visualiser is designed to offer a pleasant environment," she explained.

Vic slumped back in his chair with his arms folded and ignored her. Eventually Bluu switched it back on anyway.

He still didn't get it. The way she was in V-world with him and yet here in reality she was so cold? It was all the wrong way around. The time they spent together in his sim was incredible and the truth was he could easily stay as long as Bluu was there too.

Next stop was the Major Zero memorial where yet more crowds were waiting. On thinking back Vic realised it was most likely here that the scrap of paper was thrust into his hand. A crowd had surged forward grabbing at him as he left the craft before he could be ushered behind a waist high glass barrier. The barrier felt like glass but it was more like the stuff that had divided his room from the next one at his hotel. He was behind a kind of waste high force field still he was glad of it as the small but enthusiastic crowd surged forward.

They spent a couple of hours inside admiring the stories and legends attributed to the Major. There were numerous artefacts and displays paying homage to his exploits. Vic was shown the makeshift craft that had carried the Major and his crew on their perilous journey back to Earth. He stopped to admire a statue of the Major in the central hallway standing tall in his space suit, helmet under his arm, his chest out and one leg symbolically stepping forward. The eyes slightly closed with an arrogant grin, almost a smile. Staring outwards towards the horizon as if seeing things mere mortals would not comprehend.

They were led inside to examine records of the city of Heathen in its early years. There were also hand written notes and models which were attributed to the Mars teams outpouring of knowledge. At that time they had to record whatever they could from memory. Some of humanities greatest minds were required to tinker with well-established inventions with the goal of rebuilding civilisation.

After the last two days he was exhausted and craved some time alone. Vic pulled off his gold encrusted overcoat, becoming less self-conscious about the outlandish fashion of 2515. He felt something in his pocket and pulled out the crumpled note before throwing the coat across a chair. He slowly unfolded it, trying to remember where it had come from and who had thrust it into his hand.

Vic and Bluu had made their way back to the transporter and that must have been when it happened.

There had been that moment of chaos and he remembered feeling something thrust into his hand and looking up. He saw a face pulling away and being swallowed by the crowd like a drowning man. Wide unblinking eyes staring up at him expectantly as they sank from view. The hood hiding what could have been a clutch of bright red hair and some kind of circular symbol on the forehead. Around the man's neck hung a symbol on a chain, a lightning symbol. Where had he seen that before? It looked, no not looked... it felt familiar?

So there on the top was the same symbol, a squiggle like lightning. As soon as he saw it he felt the 'incident' come on. Like an old vinyl record, the incidents were like jumps in his life moments when things were out of place. He was having them more frequently and hadn't dared tell anyone yet. His own description of them sounded too weird a mixture of déjà vu and understanding or an enlightened feeling. It was here again, like the moment you work out the answer to an incredibly difficult problem. Usually déjà vu was a minuscule moment in time, yet in these experiences it was continuous and unnaturally long. It was like he knew what the note would say a fraction before he read it. He knew everything just before it happened, but only just before it happened.

Opening the note he read.

My mother said to get things done.

You better not mess with Major Zee.

Ashes to ashes, fun to funky

We know Major Zees a junkie'

"Where did you get that?" whispered Bluu into his ear making him jump. She'd clearly already read at least some of it.

"I don't know," he said screwing it up disinterestedly and throwing it to one side. Bluu picked it up, reading it herself for a moment.

"I suppose it was only a matter of time," she said sadly.

"What?"

"The humanists, this is some kind of rhyme they use to degrade Mother," she said. "It's so saddening."

Vic knew who she was referring to a group of humans surviving on the outskirts of the city without Mother. A bunch of anti-technology terrorists as the Doctor had described them. Without Mother's intervention they operated independently. Fending for themselves by growing organic foods, scavenging.

"A selfish agenda to return to a barbaric lifestyle, living like dogs," she said. Vic understood the implication in her comments because humanists wanted things to be how they were in Vic's time. They would spread gossip and rumours about the Major, claiming he had left the human race to die. Had created his own sick drug induced Kingdom on Mars.

"Is any of it true?" asked Vic provocatively.

"You have an intelligent mind, what do you see? A world created by Mother, the affection of the people of Heathen towards you?"

Vic shrugged in agreement and walked towards his room. He could feel her eyes burning into him from behind. It made him shudder and he supposed it was all to do with the frosty atmosphere between them at the moment.

He had returned to writing his own music and his enthusiasm for it was growing.

"The music you're making is sounding very good." No longer doubting he was heading anywhere else but to Montserrat. This was his own nickname for the beach side recording studio he had in the next room.

Vic thought 'good' was an understatement. The stuff he was writing right now was astounding. That was the interesting thing. This material was actually better than all the shit he planned to steal from Lennon, Springsteen and the Stones. He felt no humility in even thinking that because he knew it was true. He'd have one inspirational idea and then another. Then before long the songs were pouring out of him, completely effortlessly as if they had always been there. So much of it was influenced by TVC15, Heathen and his recent experiences. There was so much material to work with. Vic needed no set genre he was free to experiment as never before. He'd been prolific in the last couple of weeks. The confidence in being a rock star before he'd written a note set him free creatively.

"Have you thought about playing them live, physically?" she said expectantly.

"I'm not sure, I thought those days were over for me," he said turning to see if she was serious.

"There's not a single person in Heathen would not come out to see you," she said. He stared at her holding eye contact for a moment. She was correct it was a matter of choice. If and when he took his music to the masses he would arrive fully formed as a rock god.

"Good night Bluu," he said coldly.

He turned and went inside closing the door, still thinking. Here he was full of hormones, throwing tunes out like confetti and holding on to the underlying feeling that he was old. He had to realise he was not old anymore he was 22 and a superstar just by walking on a stage and smiling. It was an interesting idea.

In this moment however he was thinking about the humanists. Why had they gone to such an effort to contact him? To Bluu and anyone else he understood how vile and frightening these people would be. He was curious all the same. The general population of Heathen had an underlying feeling of conformity. They were super civilised and happy. Surely these humanists were lunatics, fuck they had to be. Bluu was right, why would anyone not go along with the life that Mother and Heathen provided. The curious thing was that they were living off grid, growing food and probably even fucking each other. The upshot was they sounded a lot like him.

It was still a little frosty between him and Bluu since her post game attitude change. The way everything in V-world was one thing and then in reality, bam it was like it never happened. How could she be so mean? In V-world they were lovers and that was a fact but once they came out it was different altogether. He'd do well to remember it was just for one day unless he wanted to be labelled some kind of pervert.

Vic sat down at his writing desk strewn with lyrics, ideas and songs created over the past week or so. He reached into his suit pocket and pulled out a second note.

Glancing over his shoulder towards the door he unfolded it and began reading.

SEVENTEEN

The transporter circumnavigated area SO63 and hissed to a halt at the upper North East limits of the maintained city. The reassuring landscape view from the windows disappeared as soon as the door had slid open and the cool air rushed in. As the Professor and the Doctor stepped outside onto the pavement the transport unit set off back towards the security of Heathen. Once it was out of sight the silence was eerie. They stood looking around nervously for a moment and then at each other before the Professor headed off up the hill.

"Let's go," he said as the Doctor turned after him.

The atmosphere was cooler and quite misty, fog continued to thicken as they walked further North. Because the Heathen atmosphere was manipulated the smog and cloud would accumulate here quite naturally on its habitational borders. Manhattan Chase was a few miles further South and no longer serviced by Mother or any of her automated systems, they'd be forced to walk from here. The air became moist and cold as they made their way along deserted weed ridden pavements on foot. Sunlight filtered into light greys and blues as it struggled to burst through the heavy cloud cover. The buildings left standing were deserted and nature was winning the battle for dominance. Huge trees had taken root and ripped into the fabric of many of the structures. Some had utilised the glass like greenhouses before punching their way through the windows and reaching for the sky above. Vegetation of various kinds competed for light amongst the shade of concrete towers.

Large areas of pavement were now a mixture of green moss and cracked grey concrete. The patchy fog shifted thick in places and clearing in others occasionally tricking the eye forming figures, faces or creatures that would disappear as quickly as they formed. The Professor clearly knew where he was going, darting this way and that with the Doctor close behind. They pulled their coats tighter and marched deeper into the urban wilderness. The Doctor noticed occasional rebel lightning symbols sprayed or scratched on walls as well as occasional derogatory text pertaining to the Major. He felt nervous and uneasy like a soldier trapped behind enemy lines. Turning a corner the silence was broken by the cry of a child. The Doc instinctively felt the hairs on his neck rise in response. The Professor threw a hand out across the Doctor's chest to stop him.

"Did you hear that?" he whispered

"Help me, please someone help me," cried the pained child's voice again.

"This way," cried the Professor and set off into a side road that would once have been relatively wide but was now just a series of moss covered pathways between trees and bushes.

"Someone please help me, I hurt. I hurt so bad," cried the voice again.

Following the sound they delved deeper, pushing damp branches out of their faces as they went. Up ahead a large tree was protruding between the pavement and an abandoned office block. It's trunk powerful enough to have lifted part of the pavement like an old carpet. From the other side they saw movement, a flash of yellow. Slowly the pair circled the tree as widely as they could to reveal the source of the sound. The boy looked around 14 years old and was partly dressed in a yellow open neck suit with no shoes. A large metal spike was protruding from his chest and penetrated into the tree holding him in place. There was no blood but where he had the ability to move his arms and head the tree had worn away exposing the white wood below the bark. At the points of contact his clothes were torn and shredded. On the floor lay a single shoe with the foot still inside protruding from the severed leg were wires and metal twine of various colours. The boy could have been there for some time, maybe a year or more.

"Drone," said the Professor with a sigh of relief. "Come on."

The Doc stayed still, staring at the drone who attempted to hold out a hand to him, pleading.

"Don't leave me here, I hurt."

The Professor turned back slapping the Doctor on the shoulder and grabbing his collar. "Come on it's only a drone, let's go," the Professor said putting on a brave face.

Not out of care for a drone, but he was slightly embarrassed that their potential hosts had shown themselves for what they were so early on. This wasn't going to gain any empathy from his younger self. They both knew the drone felt no real pain it was just standard programming to display discomfort when necessary.

The Doctor followed slightly dazed as the childish cries for help faded into the distance behind them.

"Don't go please help me."

Making their way back to the main road they finally reached the wide open boulevard of Manhattan Chase. A hundred yards up a narrow alleyway ran off to one side up some steep steps.

"This way," said the Professor tapping his shoulder once more. By now the fog was thick and claustrophobic as they stopped by a door, slightly ajar. There was dim light coming from within and the door creaked as the Professor pushed against it, slipping inside. They found themselves in a dim narrow corridor with wall lights along its length. The deep red walls were punctuated by doors leading off at intervals. At the end of the corridor they found a wide stairway leading into a large open space. It might once have been the atrium of some apartment or hotel building. The space was maybe ten stories high with windows on the left and a plain wall ahead. Cloth draped scaffold walkways filled the right wall. The glass roof was still intact and the air was noticeably warmer in here. They looked up and around the space seeing no one, but feeling the presence of many. There was a loud clank up on the scaffold and a bulge in the cloth slithered downwards from a higher floor before swinging down in front of them. The man landed gracefully on his feet and broke seamlessly into a walk.

"Come on in, you'll catch your death in the cold," said the sneering figure walking towards them.

The Doctor had to consciously close his mouth to hide his surprise and disgust. There were subtle rebel symbols in the city but he had never seen anything so blatant and shocking before. The man before him had bright red spiky hair and the humanist symbol, a red lightning stripe was painted boldly across one eye. The sinewy man wore a white decorated one piece suit with a high collar. The Doctor felt sick and his colour drained. The last few hours had been stressful enough but this was sickening, he just wanted to close his eyes and get home. The pair were led around a large glass tower in the centre which had obstructed their view until now. Despite its size it was brighter in one area upon a raised stage where some furniture was arranged. A table and some armchairs under some bright lights reminding the Doctor of a stage set. He had no doubt that the audience were already here, up at those windows. The whole structure was like a building turned inside out with hundreds of windows across the left wall. Looking up and around again he saw no movement. In front of them a man was perched on a table, slow clapping as they arrived. The first man raised a knowing eyebrow to him.

"Look what I found crawling down the alley," he sneered.

The Doctor was fairly sure the guy on the table was the same one who had threatened him weeks ago. He looked very different now, red high waisted dungarees and thick tattered dark hair. A patch over one eye and without the shaded make-up his face looked a little thinner. A tiny wine glass hung from his right hand between thumb and forefinger.

"Nice to see you again Doctor," he said taking a sip of the red liquid and trying to disguise the involuntary wince.

"This is Jak Samian," said the Professor. "And of course Feng." He nodded towards the other man.

"So this must be," he paused. "You," said Feng in response as they both burst into hysterical laughter. Feng skipped past the two visitors and perched on the table next to his colleague. Lifting one knee he put his arm across the other man's shoulder and they both stared. Maybe they could now be sure, right here side by side the same person decades apart, still pretty amazing.

"How much does he know?" said Jak without removing his gaze as if the Doctor were an animal with no capacity for human understanding.

"As much as anyone can know," said the Professor stepping over to the table picking up the bottle of red liquid. "May I?"

Feng nodded his approval and the Professor poured.

"How's your history Doctor?" said Jak eyeing him closely.

"Not too bad considering it's been my career for thirty years," the Doctor replied arrogantly. "It's my job. Building up a picture based on facts." The Doctor stressed the final word purposely.

Jak raised one eyebrow at Feng in a kind of 'is he really talking to me' look.

"Is that right?"

"That's right." The Doctor gulped hard and took a deep breath.

The Professor took a swig of his drink and quickly put it back down on the table. "Let's get on shall we?"

Feng ignored him. "This is the damn point Doc. Welcome to our version of the beautiful city of Heathen. Ever wondered what that word means Mr?" He looked at them both, standing quickly he walked slowly around and in between them whispering in their individual ears as he eyed them both close up. Like troops being lectured by a Sargent they didn't respond. "Heathenism is a state of mind. You can take it that I'm referring to one who does not see his world. He has no mental light." He made elaborate meaningless gestures with his hands. "He destroys almost unwittingly. He cannot feel any God's presence in his life. He is the 21st century man." Feng spread his arms pleased with his analogy. "If you have studied your history then you will be aware of the word Heathen, and its historic meaning."

"Your point is?" said the Doctor.

"My point is that it was you who came here looking for our help. In doing so you gave us the truth and reason to be what we are."

Jak interrupted. "The Salvation Machine has to be shut down and you're going to help us do it."

"Me!" The Doctor stepped back.

"I thought he knew?" said Jak looking at the Professor who dropped his eyebrows turning to the Doctor. "We want you and the caveman with us."

"What has Nova to do with this?" The Doctor peered up at the rows of windows, imagining the watching faces. He wondered how many there were up here. Hundreds, thousands or maybe just two? Unlikely two, but he felt like he was in a courtroom. Helping those who were up there make a decision, perhaps shifting the minds of the less committed ones.

The Professor stayed close to the Doctor trying to mentally hold this coalition together. "We are talking about shutting Mother down. No one takes this lightly but it's unavoidable. There will be huge disruption and we need people with knowledge of the past. People like you, people like Nova."

"You think he wants this?" said the Doctor.

"Five years, that's all. No one wants this but we have to. People will trust him, but somehow we have to let him know what's at stake. We need him on our side and he is going to have to understand that he is finished if he Migrates anyway."

"How do you plan to close Mother down?"

The Professor placed his hands on his hips and addressed them all. "I think there's an opportunity to launch a virus." His throat dried up and he choked on his words like he was discussing bumping off a dear relative. "A virus into the system."

"Can't be done," the Doctor snapped eyeing the three of them.

"On one particular night we think it can," said Jak slowly walking around the table to refill his glass.

The Professor continued. "If everything happens just as it did last time there will be a short power failure on the night of the physical show, just before the interval. That will give us an opportunity to get in."

"It's been tried before, the Salvation Machine is segregated by firewalls," the Doctor repeated.

The Professor looked around at them nervously.

"Usually that's true but not on this night. This is an organic live event that is being beamed to every sector of the city simultaneously. Mars will be 14 light minutes from Earth. This should give us plenty of time to infect and shut down the cloud."

The Doctor took a step back. Jak looked away scratching the back of his neck.

And there it was, suddenly this whole thing seemed plausible. It was as if the Doctor had been able to deny it as long as he believed it couldn't be done. Looking at these three faces and hearing what was being said he began to see it could. The realisation that they might be able to actually do it horrified him and he felt every hair on his body bristle. Feng just stared right back at him that huge reptilian grin across his face like an alligator waiting for his prey.

"You are really crazy, the lot of you," he was talking to the Professor now. "Do any of you understand what you're saying? Another shutdown, is that what you want?" The Professor walked over to the Doctor, arms out as if to hold him. "I understand." He pushed him a way.

"And so this plan of yours relies on me?"

Jak was back on the table, foot up and elbow on knee chewing some kind of toothpick.

"The Migration starts with that caveman, it has to end with him," he said using the tiny stick between his fingers as a pointer. "We've tried contacting him but you are on the inside. You have to convince him to help us, to tell people what's happening."

"How?"

The Professor stepped forward. "You're with him all the time. He has to trust you because when the time comes he will have doubts. You have to make those doubts bigger and get him on side."

"Mother is going to blow a fuse with or without your Neanderthal friend," spat Feng. "Without you too if that's how things pan," he said nodding towards the Professor his eyes narrowed and his sneer slowly turned into an insincere smile that made the Professor shiver. Remembering how he'd met him before, but decades from this future. He'll be older then and even now there were early signs of his dark temper.

The Doctor hung his head, tears forming in the corners of his eyes. "I want nothing to do with this," he said and turned to walk away. The three exchanged glances and the Professor rose to follow him.

Jak stood on the edge of the raised area and placed his hands on his hips.

"Ramona A Stone the good time drone." His words echoed across the open space. The Doctor froze in his tracks and spun round. Over the Professor's shoulder he saw the two grinning figures. The Professor staring into his eyes slowly shook his head as if in apology, the pain etched on his face. He looked older and more tired than ever before.

"Let's go," the Doctor whispered.

Shaking his head slowly the Doctor turned and continued walking, the Professor followed. He glanced over his shoulder at the two, raising his eyebrows giving a thin smile and a reassuring wave to indicate all was well.

He knew it wasn't.

Feng looked across to Jak's concerned face. Still grinning he shrugged his shoulders and opened his palms.

## EIGHTEEN

"Nova, did you hear what I said?" the Doctor raised his voice. What was it with Bluu, a cultural misunderstanding obviously his feelings for her had grown over time whether inside or outside, hers were confined to inside only. He couldn't find the switch to flick once they were back in reality. Having created the sim, played the game in his own time and on his own terms he thought he'd won her over. Within V-World they shared a passion for each other, outside it was non-existent.

"I'm fine, what were you saying?" he said still in a half trance.

"President Nixon?" said the Doc. "Do you remember President Nixon?"

How could being in love be an element in a computer game, just part of the entertainment? Love, fear, excitement all emotions genuinely felt real in V-world because it was designed that way. It tapped into the brain stem and reprogrammed the emotional centres artificially. Once outside those emotions were discarded, like the fear on a ghost train would feel on the bus home. The only way to make any sense was to make comparisons with what he knew. He'd played violent computer games, that didn't make him a violent criminal. So by the same token, why would Bluu be in love with him outside V-world? He understood that but the incident the day after had really scarred his pride.

Having taken her into his world she'd responded as he'd hoped. It seemed natural to him that things would be different after that. On seeing her the next day he was shocked at her reaction when he threw his arms around her shoulders to kiss her the look of revulsion as she pushed his face away, backing off from him. She just stood there for a moment, they both did, equally horrified for opposite reasons. Bluu's expression of disgust as if she was being molested by her best friend then with tears running down her cheeks, Bluu had turned and ran out of the room. Left standing there open mouthed Vic was clueless as to what he'd done wrong. He didn't see her for a while and even after that things were a little cold between them. In that time he'd considered the situation, tried to think of an explanation. Finally they'd talked about it and he had been right all along. There was clearly no concept in the futures world of bringing a physical relationship from V-world into their reality. He and Bluu had agreed to draw a line under the incident and taken it as some kind of cultural misunderstanding. Little did Vic suspect that when they went back inside it was business as usual, and beautiful business it was! It bothered him, but he soon realised how he was getting better at splitting those two worlds. He still couldn't help fantasising that she was lying to herself to save face. Vic was all too aware that her culture didn't go with physical relationships because it had become pointless. Maybe that was why they had an underground culture with the drone thing, having heard about how these domestic humanoid drones could be hacked and reprogrammed. There were people who kept them for their own physical pleasure. It made sense there would be a market for 25th century love dolls in a twisted world where no one wanted to touch. Vic had seen plenty of domestic drones and he had held conversations with some. There was no doubting their realism even though they were not human. He wasn't sure but there was something about them. Maybe they were designed that way, to be subtly different and to stand out. In this culture any physical relationship was considered pointless. He was humiliated at the thought that he personally was the problem. He wasn't just another human, he was 'the caveman', he knew they called him that. Could he be a pet that entertained everyone like a dolphin at a theme park or a dancing bear? Would the trainer be seen to have feelings for him? Once back in reality his love was lost, that is until they went back inside again. When they were inside then it was instantaneous like nothing had changed, like a drug he soon found he couldn't resist it. If being in love in V-world was just a game then he was addicted. If that was all that was on offer he would take it for now.

"Yes, President Nixon was a king of the City of America," said Vic at last, rubbing his temples with his thumb and forefinger. He'd learned by now to adapt his language to something that made more sense to the Doctor. The best policy was to keep things simple and where he didn't know the answer then any plausible explanation would do.

"Maybe we should end our session?" the Doctor didn't wait for an answer standing up and folding his tablet. Vic was pleased he'd a lot on his mind.

Over time Vic sank deeper and deeper behind the mask of Nova. So much so he wondered if he could ever take it off and be Vic again. He could do no wrong as Nova, the futures adored him. He wasn't crazy about brazen publicity but this just made him more aloof and desirable. If he was expected in any public V-world sim, he would be mobbed by admiring fans. As a result he had security and paparazzi following him around whenever he visited public areas. This disturbed him a little because he'd learned how V-world sims could be quite revealing. Adventures were contaminated by hidden wishes, dreams or fantasies. Since the last time he was in his twenties he'd wanted to be famous and he now had the fame he always dreamed of. When that shitty album he made went tits up he was pushed in another direction. He smiled to himself, realising how naive that music was in comparison to what he was writing now.

Ironically, as famous as he was he found most peace in the real world. Here he could wander freely and almost at will. Not because the fans had no interest in him but because they were simply not around for the most part. Reality was a very quiet place on the whole and when he did run into real futures they would either be too polite to acknowledge him or be in small groups which were quite manageable.

In a way that's why he liked it, the real world was almost devoid of human existence in certain places. The Doctor seemed not to mind reality so much either, for a future that is. On many occasions they'd travelled outside together. Heathen was vast by any City standards, maybe hundreds of miles across. With the visualiser off he would spend hours soaring across huge expanses of land. It was here that the sheer scale of automation could be appreciated. It was like travelling around inside a huge clockwork machine or being inside an engine. There were numerous signs of life but it was seldom organic human, merely humanoid drones going about their tasks. These were the ones whose role put them in contact with humanity. It was these that gave him some comfort that he was not touring a long dead metropolis. There were humans of course, and he saw many of them but they were different in some way. He could recognise them against non-human drones easily. He wasn't sure how, they were just less human he supposed. Maybe a look in the eye or some subconscious connection, he couldn't put his finger on it.

Then there was Manhattan Chase, having travelled to its outskirts on many occasions. The transport would not take him that far and so he went as close as it would. Vic would sit and stare out into what looked like a lifeless ruined city. Mist constantly hanging in the air and without going outside it looked damp and cold. In places the manmade structures had been almost completely overcome by nature. In others, it soon would be as powerful trees had lifted curb stones and distorted pathways. The transport would travel slowly across its boundary without daring to cross an invisible line.

'My mother said never to play
with the gypsies in the woods,
and if I did she would say
naughty girl to disobey'

He still had the paper given to him by the strange character, the
one he later found to be a humanist. It was cryptic but he'd done some
discreet research to make any sense of it. Maybe that had been the
intention, to encourage him to find out? If not for Bluu's reaction, and
then other people's he might never had investigated further. When they
subtly questioned his sanity he felt it best to drop the subject altogether.
They were too dismissive he thought, overly dismissive. The other
reason was his own compulsion as he called it.

The 'incidents' it was the best description he had so far. In one of
them he'd seen those same words given to him in the note but written
differently. He knew there was some kind of connection. On bad days
Vic questioned whether he'd ever been thawed out at all whether this
was some kind of coma or delusional episode.

'My mother said
He was our hero
You better not mess with Major Zero'

Any everyday future he'd mentioned it to had reacted quite
strongly, particularly the Doc. The Major was the central demon for
these techno terrorists and they relished insulting him. His research
revealed they held an opposing view of this national hero. Spinning
tales of how the Major was not the hero related to in common folklore.
How he left humans to become virtually extinct before he intervened.
Enjoying drug fuelled orgies whilst humanity ate itself almost to
extinction back on Earth. Finally they say, he returns to feed off the
scraps. There are even crazier conspiracy theories about how if there is
any life on Mars it will be him. That dead planet is more than just a giant
server room for everything that goes on down here. Of course this is
nonsense, unless he is a few hundred years old but it adds to the myth.
Vic wanted to stay realistic and not get drawn in by mischief making
stories and nonsense. Squinting into the gloom he thought he saw
movement, a shadow in the mist perhaps someone watching him,
maybe he is mistaken. There's no sign of life, never had been out here,
certainly not human life up on the outskirts of the Chase. They are out

there somewhere, but after a couple of hours he would usually go home.

Vic was dragged from his trance as the door slid open and Bluu marched in unannounced.

"Hello," she said sheepishly. "Busy?"

"We're done, I'm just leaving anyway," said the Doc snatching his case.

"See you later," said Vic.

The Doctor looked across at Bluu grinning, he never got bored of this ancient dialect. Shaking his head he walked through the door, smiling at Bluu as he passed her.

"See you later too Nova," he said comically shaking his head as he stepped past Bluu, aware it was unlikely he would see Nova later.

Bluu skipped across the room as soon as the door closed. Vic heard the Doctor chatting with someone outside as he was leaving but couldn't make any of the conversation out. Clasping her hands together she opened her mouth to speak but didn't manage to get the words out before the interruption. From outside came the sound of a booming voice, presumably someone who'd come in with Bluu.

"Where is he? The second greatest star in Heathen is not here to greet me. Where is the great Nova," the voice said? Thunderous deep laughter followed, filling the air outside the door. Bluu was beaten to an explanation as the door crashed open.

"Nova this is.." uttered Bluu. A giant of a man stood in the doorway made even bigger by his extraordinary attire. Even by TVC15 standards this was exceptional.

"I am Pierrot my good friend." The huge figure powered towards him. Before he had any chance to acknowledge the man, Vic was gripped in a bear hug just below the shoulders. With arms by his sides he was picked up with the same regard as a baby picks up a puppy arms splaying out from the elbows, defenceless as he caught the eye of Bluu who watched helplessly. At the point where Vic thought he might pass out the man held him at arm's length by his shoulders as if admiring a shirt, albeit with Vic still inside. It was the first opportunity that Vic had to observe what had intruded into his life so abruptly. At first glance he looked like a giant clown from a childhood nightmare. A towering man with a smile painted on his lips across a white mannequin face. An electric blue frilly one piece suit cut off below the knees and elbows. Metallic socks and plimsoles with a pudding hat finished it all off. Vic was suspended in space for a moment before this giant of a man finally put him down, slapping him hard across the shoulder with enough force to rock him on his heels. This resulted in another burst of laughter that filled the room.

"Pierrot will be hosting the final show of the tour," cried Bluu above the laughter.

"Hosting? Tour?" Vic's eyes narrowed inquisitively.

"Nova it's up to you it really is but I know you will.."

Bluu was flushed again, breathless and clasping her hands together in front of her lips.

"Explain," said Vic regaining his breath and his composure.

"It's amazing, but you can think about it," she shrieked.

The monster in the clown costume came back to life cutting her off once more.

"We have plenty of time for that my dear," said the clown pushing between them. Bluu was clearly excited about something but he could see she had given up on getting that out for now. The giant continued. "But let's take care of business. The two greatest superstars on Heathen are to share a stage the biggest physical event in history." He said flamboyantly spreading his arms.

Vic unconsciously backed off towards the wall.

"That's right my dear friend, you are going to be on stage with the great Pierrot."

On stage, with him, what the hell, thought Vic.

"I am going to be hosting the event in the Market Square and if you're going to be on stage with me, we need to do something about your fashion sense."

Pierrot stood back a step or two with his arms outstretched as if giving Vic a chance to clearly admire his own style. Vic did, and it was the least of his worries at this moment.

"Don't worry, I've brought my own people. We will need to do something. You look like a goon in all that 21st Century get up."

The giant clown clicked his fingers and a group of around three or four futures burst through the door and lunged towards Vic.

⌐

So that was how it came about. There were no publicity or A & R meetings, contracts signed or album sales analysis. It was that simple. Bluu had explained about the idea and then held her breath.

"Will you Nova, will you?" She waited whilst the grin spread across his face. Smiling in unison she almost leapt to the ceiling when he said yes. It was worth it just to see Bluu so happy. What he didn't know at the time was, she wanted to see him play but that wasn't the only reason she was excited about the shows.

So now aside from everything else going on in his life he was preparing to go on tour. The plan was to do a handful of shows in V-world and then the climax being the live physical event. A live gig in Vic's world was no big deal, but in Heathen it was all turned on its head. Pierrot, Bluu and everyone else were convinced they could pull the biggest crowd in memory bigger then '83, bigger than the Isle of Wight festival or Woodstock. They were talking about filling the Market Square stadium with over a hundred thousand people with many times that outside. Still, since being here Vic had seen no more than a couple of thousand in any one place. Pierrot believed there would hardly be a human on the planet that didn't experience the show live in some way. Would these people actually come out of their homes to see him? Everyone thought so, Bluu was absolutely ecstatic at the idea and that was partly the reason he agreed to do it.

So it was on, and Nova needed to get a band together very quickly. Strangely that turned out to be the easiest part. Pierrot had some great contacts and they pulled together some amazing musicians almost straight away. At least they seemed to be? There was so much electronic musical enhancement he was unsure whether you just needed to hum and electronics did the rest. Nova had told them time and again to switch it off. It was a great system for getting an idea of what you wanted but it was way too perfect to play live. Nova and the band spent a lot of time together early on but he broke away as the shows got closer. They had the show nailed as far as he was concerned. Pierrot turned out to be a real professional and he was right about the clothes. Nova and his band were fitted out with foil jump suits, platform shoes and the most dazzling stage attire he'd ever seen. They had designed a stage set to match.

If they were right then this was going to be the biggest show ever. As show time approached he decided to relax a little and maybe give some thought to the band name.

## NINETEEN

Vic felt the building rumble beneath his feet at the sheer power created from 100,000 human beings stamping and screaming. They chanted his name Nova, Nova! almost in sync with his pounding heart. The stadiums house lights went down sending the crowd to unbelievable levels of ecstasy. As the stage lights came up he felt a cool breeze across his face as Weird, Gilly and the 'Spiders' ran past him onto the stage waving to the audience as they did, sending them into further raptures. Nova had finally found a name for his band, his own private joke. He'd remembered a conversation with some computer geeks at his office about algorithms they have in search engines spiders or crawlers or something like that. They were robotic computer programs that could help you find what you were looking for. Finding himself living in a world that was run by a computer not least a computer on Mars it was perfect. He had named his band the Spiders. Now he would have everything his way, the way it should have been all those years ago when he had his first crack at fame. The last time he'd put his music out it resulted in utter disappointment. He wasn't surprised of course, not with what he knew now. Looking back he'd no idea how forced and naive his music had been in those days. As the lights came up and the crowd roared Vic thought back to the night he quit music. Feeling like the only musician who'd ever gone home and cried like a baby, seeing their dreams shattered like broken glass. Never in those wildest fantasies could he have foreseen this.

He had fully adopted the name Nova by now. It was the name Bluu used to address him and so he had decided Nova it would be. Having demanded his show promoters change everything associated with the tour, every single reference to his name was to be changed.

"I don't give a shit how difficult it is, just do it!" So it was done, like everything else he asked for was done. As the shows became closer the mask of Nova had welded to him so much it was hardly a mask anymore.

At last the people of Heathen would get the chance to see their hero in the flesh, to almost taste him. Cameras projecting onto huge screens caught a glimpse of him back stage just a momentary glimpse of him in his woollen leotard and feather boa. It was now, it had to be now as the guitars struck up he marched confidently towards the microphone. That was when it happened. As the band finished the intro to the first song he missed his cue. Instead Nova just stared into the crowd as if in a trance.

The band attempted to reconfigure the song and start the intro again, sensing something was wrong. They got as far as the opening lyric for a second time and still nothing. He was frozen, like a rabbit dazzled by the lights. The crowd, realising something was wrong slowly hushed and the music died. Finally a hundred thousand faces just stared up at him, wide eyed. They were almost silent as he just stared, the only sound the occasional uncomfortable shuffle of feet or involuntary cough every tiny sound echoing across this cavernous concert hall. The red, yellow and blue spotlights circling the stage seemed pathetic without any musical accompaniment.

It was another of his 'incidents', this one was strong, powerful. He was aware of why it felt so right to be in front of 100,000 fans. He was Nova and his band were the Spiders. He was no longer Vic Jones and never had been. He could see his past and he could see the future. He knew everything that had happened and everything that would. It had all been staring him in the face, plain as day. He didn't need the humanists to tell him what to do because he already knew. All this, he realised in that instant.

Then, as quickly as it arrived... The realisation he had a few moments ago was gone, everything he'd known only seconds ago had disappeared and he couldn't get it back. Like waking from a dream, where he knew what it was about but could not recall its detail.

Nova raised his hand to block the bright lights from his eyes and gazed at the ghostly faces staring up at him.

Shaking he clasped half a fist across his chest with thumb and forefinger outstretched and flicked his forehead with the fingertips of his other hand. Everything disappeared from his vision and he reached up onto his head and pulled the V-world helmet off the screaming crowd, the stadium and the band all gone.

Finding himself back in the real world rehearsal space. He was no longer in the private rehearsal sim they had designed for the tour.

"Fuck it," he screamed throwing the V-world helmet at one of the futures. "Rehearsals over."

"Hey Man!" The future looked nervous, in despair.

"Don't you fucking 'hey man' me. It's Nova, get it," he screamed into his face stabbing the man's temple with his finger. "You're using that electronic thing again."

The futures had been artificially enhancing his music and voice with some gadgetry that resampled every note to perfection. He'd already demanded that this all be taken out of the recordings.

Angry about that, yes but if he was honest with himself, it was all just cover for the incident. He daren't tell anyone; moreover he was concerned it could happen on the night of the show. He felt it better to keep it to himself for now until he had some idea what was going on.

"But every note..?" said the engineer.

"I don't give a shit about how plastic you want this, I want my music to sound real."

"The notes are great, we are not.." Pleaded the man.

"It's off, forget it. This show is not happening. Leave me alone."

Vic stormed out, slamming the door.

That had been a week ago, the show was off. Fuck 'em he thought. He was happy to stay in Montserrat and write. Admittedly over time he'd calmed down a lot and no one had approached him about the show. This amused if not concerned him somewhat, clearly they had been unaware they were supposed to beg him to come back, pacify him whilst he begrudgingly accepted. This hadn't been the case and he was becoming increasingly concerned especially as the quality of his writing increased exponentially. He was absorbing this new environment into his songs both in reality and V-world. Everything in TVC15 provided limitless new themes on which to write his music, coupled with numerous genres from his own history. He borrowed from jazz, techno and rock to produce a sound that had been long forgotten in time and the futures would love it. Not that he wrote for them, he would have no need to do that. Anything he produced would be lapped up regardless of quality. Even the Doctor hadn't seemed concerned that the shows were cancelled or even questioned him about it. He'd expected that the Doctor if not Bluu would be chosen to make the plea but none came.

It seemed that the futures had decided if he said that's it then that was it. If this kind of behaviour continued he may well have to consider begrudgingly relenting after all. No matter, he was ready.

TWENTY

The Doctor had made it clear he'd no intention of going back up to the Chase, in his anger having requested a more neutral meeting place eventually suggesting Sector S061, a subliminal insult to the rebels which had backfired when they agreed. The Doctor had isolated his location from Duke and expected the Professor would have done the same. Being off grid was one thing, but having to explain why you were in Sector S061 was an entirely different matter. It was one of the grubbiest sectors in Heathen sitting on its outer fringes. By physical human standards it was busy, physical being the reason most people were here. It's narrow, dimly lit streets hid a multitude of sins. If Manhattan Chase was Heathen's human sewer then S061 was its overflow pipe. There were plenty of bodies milling around, few of which had a legitimate reason to be here. On the surface it bustled but it wasn't always clear how many of these people were organic. If the whole place wasn't lit like a cave it might be easier to tell. Truth is there were people here who didn't want to know who was and who wasn't organic. The Mother system allowed certain immoral activities to go on provided most people were willing participants and in sector SO61 this was most definitely the case. A large number of hacked drones for sale or hire boosted the visible population on the streets. The Doctor felt a hint of hypocrisy in his disdain for them considering his relations with Ramona but that was different. They had not lowered their relationship morals to crawling down alleyways. At least SO61 was serviced by Mother which meant it was possible to catch a Magpod into the area. The upshot being you only have to endure its depressing stench once you hit the street. Neon signs reflected in the puddle strewn pavements, washing yellow and purple hews up the dark damp walls. Disembarking at his destination there was no such signs, instead a worn plate on the wall read 'Cafe Exile'. The Doctor stepped from the transport and clunked down a narrow stairwell towards the muffled beat of music. At the bottom he pushed a dark heavy curtain to one side and the odour filled his nostrils. It smelt damp and musky like a derelict building. A bar ran across the far wall and a row of dimly lit booths ran along the right hand side. The bearded man leaning across an under illuminated bar was looking straight at him. The place was empty except for three figures sat in the only occupied booth and he nodded in their direction. The barman stood upright as he approached, drying his hands ready to take his order. The Doctor ignored him and as he passed the man leant back on his elbows and continued reading. The monotonous beat of the music faded in the confines of the booth as he spread his legs and pulled a stool between them. Feng stared straight ahead, his smile too wide as if holding back a laugh, eyeing the Doctor sideways.

"How's it going?" said Jak. At the end of his arm a glass characteristically dangled from thumb and finger. His head shot back as he took a large gulp of the red liquid, slamming the glass down on the table. Dragging his sleeve across his mouth like a pirate caused his lipstick to smudge a little. He looked around nervously much of the confidence from the last time they had met was gone. We're in no-man's land now the Doctor thought, feeling the power had shifted just a little. Jak looked different again, none of the shadowy make up and definitely no blatant humanist symbols. There were hints of grey hair but still the eye patch over his right eye.

"How's what going?" said the Doctor knowing full well what he meant.

"The caveman, everything going as he said it would?" nodding towards the Professor. The three waited for his reply and he paused purposefully, looking up in thought and then down at the table.

"It's been a week since he cancelled the show." There were looks of concern around the table as the three men waited for a response from the Professor.

"Tomorrow or the next day," he paused. "Just as last time, he'll change his mind." The Professor simply nodded in acknowledgement and the two sighed with relief, sitting back in their chairs. Feng threw a look at Jak.

"It looks like we are on," he said scrunching his lips, picking up Jak's glass and taking a slug in acknowledgement. Not for the first time the Doctor wondered about these two. Whether they might be physical? Who knows what goes on up there in the chase, you hear stories.

"It's no concern we keep to the timetable, 7 days. It happens," said the Professor having no wish to rub salt in the wounds for his younger self. Perhaps a neutral location may not have been a good idea. The Doctor caught the eye of Jak looking over his shoulder and spun round to see the barman staring at them.

"It's ok," said Jak. "He's with us."

The Doctor narrowed his eyes at the word 'us' hoping Jak hadn't noticed his contemptuous stare.

He did, and smiled in acknowledgement.

The atmosphere was still very tense between the Doctor and his older self. Even though they had ample opportunity to talk about the implications of their actions, last night had been particularly venomous. The veiled threat to blackmail him by exposing his relationship with Ramona hadn't gone down well. Something the Professor had not seen coming but under the circumstances he supposed it was natural. There had been no resolution or reconciliation and an atmosphere of mistrust still pervaded. The Doctor was feeling the same way and all along both of them had to keep reminding themselves that they were the same person, just years apart. It'd taken the Doctor longer to grasp how wide that gulf was. Not just physically but in mental attitude, to see in real time what he would one day become. Cooperating with the people he loathed and conspiring to kill the thing he loved most. He knew the word kill made no sense and yet that was what they were planning to do. He'd grown to like Nova and working with him had increased the Doctor's knowledge of the Moonage. The more he knew the more this whole thing terrified him. How could the people of Heathen survive in that world if Mother shuts down? The Caveman had asked about the humanists some time ago and he'd told him the outright truth. They were savages, unstable and dangerous and yet he was expected to turn that on its head and convince him to join 'us'! His experience with these scum had not changed his opinion one bit, in fact it had served to confirm his opinions. He had said as much last night to the Professor as they had argued long into the night.

"What if they are using you? Have you thought of that?" he shouted at him.

"In what way?"

"Surely you don't trust them, you went to them with your idea, a theory of what happened or what's going to happen and they grasped it. They don't care what's true as long as you help them shut Mother down."

"I told you what's going to happen, a reduction in organic life support systems; I was working with a drone and didn't know it."

"So on that evidence they'll encourage you to help them achieve what they have failed to achieve in hundreds of years," screamed the Doctor.

"It's organic life that matters, you've learned a lot from the caveman but remember I've studied him for decades, sifting through his memory cast, building sims of the Moonage."

"Organic life matters, yes, I agree, but what about those who live in V-world permanently? Those who have gone into Salvation?" pleaded the Doctor.

"Not again, they are already dead," said the Professor in despair. "They died a long, long time ago."

"What's going to be left for us? Living like the caveman?"

"We won't be completely isolated, we'll still have manual technology, electricity and there are lots of people like you and me who can help rebuild a manual system."

"Physical work? Physical relationships? Living like animals?" The Doctor stared, challenging the Professor to explain how they could go back to that.

He paused. "Yes," he said looking at the floor. "There's no other way."

"Mother could help us if we were to reach out to her."

"Don't say that, it's a Machine."

"It? You already sound like one of them," he spat as he held his gaze, probing for a reaction to his venomous insult.

The Doctor just wanted his life to be the way it was going to be, he wanted to continue with his life and his work. He didn't want to meddle with time, he just wanted to wait and see for himself when he reached the Professor's age, maybe with hindsight it could be different. But to destroy the Saviour Machine he still found it hard to believe he was sitting here now with these two.

"Shall we run through the whole thing while we're together? We won't meet up until after it's done," said the Professor as the two scumbags nodded enthusiastically.

"At the moment we still have confirmation that everything is happening as it did. Let's assume that'll continue to be the case. On the night of the final show there will be a power failure in one of the sectors attached to the Market square. It should be just before the interval, Jak are you able to get in?"

"That's the easy part, once the power goes down we will be able to lock in every sector. No matter what happens, any sector that opens up to that broadcast stream will be locked in, we have the off button." He emphasised the point by performing a slow karate chop on the table.

The Professor turned to the Doc. "You realise what this means? We then control the broadcast and it cannot be switched off. When the time comes we'll need Nova to announce to the world that Mother is closing down. To tell them what they have to do."

The Doctor just looked up like a lost child, he had no words. The Professor continued. "Once we have that then the virus can be uploaded?"

Feng tapped his breast presumably to indicate he had the card on him.

"Will it work?" said the Professor.

Jak thinned his lips "We've used the virus before and it's tested but.." Feng interrupted. "It's never done much damage because of Mother's firewalls."

"This time, it's different right?" The Professor dipped his head staring up at them both in unison. Feng presented as confident, over confident thought the Professor but this was all they had.

"I told you, if what you told us happens. If that show goes out live to every sector then we can get into Mother's main system on Mars."

Jak sipped his drink once more. "We've checked the coordinates, on the night of the show Mars will be 14.38 light minutes away. That will give us a window of 14 minutes to hit her and 14 minutes once she is hit to come for us or drop the firewall, by then it should be too late."

Feng laughed falling back in his seat. "Way too late baby, by the time she realises her system has been infected she'll start blowing fuses, boom." Feng widened his eyes making a slow explosion gesture with his fingers for effect.

Not for the first time the Professor was slightly embarrassed and waved it away dismissively. Feng made it quite clear that the gesture was aimed at the Doctor this snivelling little man who was afraid of surviving without a machine to look after him. He was right too, the Doctor was afraid, maybe because he knew a lot more about the Moonage than these lunatics.

There were times when the Doctor had wondered which was worse. Maybe to allow humanity a graceful end, oblivious to its fate was the best idea? The alternative was a return to the caveman's time, racism, physical war and struggle. To send our society back to that was a travesty, maybe better to just let it die a natural death.

"This is where you come in," said the Professor to the Doctor. "It was during the break that I spoke again to Nova about the migration. He was concerned about what he was about to do and so I reassured him."

The Doctor was aware that they were all staring at him intently, trying to read his thoughts. The Professor continued. "I explained that he would be living in a whole new world within the cloud. I supported his decision. His every desire catered for and he would be with the love of his life forever."

There was an involuntary snigger from Feng that the Professor ignored. "In the past he had become confused within V-world about emotions. In the end he took my advice and well.... The rest you know."

"I suppose that changes now?" said the Doctor without looking up.

Feng replied for him. "Because of what he did, because of his endorsement the Migration Project flew." He poked the table hard with an outstretched finger.

The Professor held up a hand as the three mentally crowded in on the Doctor like they were trying to coax a child? "You will be there, you need to explain to him that he should not do it, I should have done it when I had the chance but with what we know now it's even more important."

The Doctor wrung his hands under the table, rocking back and forth nervously. "What if he ignores my advice and goes ahead?"

"The plan is in place, by the time you speak to him." The Professor nodded to the two men.

"It can't be stopped but more than that, he will have the ear of Heathen. The cloud will not be able to shut him down. Whatever he says will go out. He has to warn people."

"You will have to tell him the cloud he is about to go into so that he can live forever is about to blow a fuse!" Feng laughed again to himself.

"Once the power is restored and that sector is back on line then it'll be inevitable, the cloud will be shutting down for good." The Professor threw a glance towards Jak before continuing. "We really need him on our side you know what happened last time. We can't have that happen again, genocide, the years of the Diamond Dogs. Humans scavenging like animals."

"Some of us still are," interrupted the Doc, looking at Feng.

Before anyone knew what was happening the Doctor was on the floor with Feng's knee on his chest and a loaded ray gun pointing hard into the side of his head. He had never seen anyone move so fast, none of them had. Experience was probably the reason Jak remained calm.

"Not now Feng," he said calmly without moving from his seat. It was hard to know how he could have heard him it was as if they were telepathic.

"If you kill him," said the Professor holding out a shaking hand, "you might kill me too." He knew that wasn't true but it was all he had.

Feng froze, spinning to look the Professor in the eye, his chest heaving with the anger.

The Prof shook his head slowly. "We just don't know." The end of the ray gun pushed hard into the Doctor's temple and beads of sweat ran down his forehead. The barman casually looked up for a moment.

Making no attempt to intervene as Feng slowly returned to his seat and replaced his gun in a single smooth movement. The Professor helped him up and they sat in silence for a moment before Feng finally spoke as if in explanation for his actions.

"We don't need him," he said pointing into his face.

The expression on Jak's face didn't go unnoticed by the Professor. He could see the worry as the veins still bulged on Feng's neck. "Let's remain calm." He spread his arms across the table. "Everyone is needed if we are to make this work." He knew this wasn't strictly true but he did want to come through this voyage with all hands accounted for.

Jak continued as if nothing had happened, cracking nuts and popping them in his mouth. "Feng and I will be amongst the crowds on the night. Don't worry about us, we'll get in," he said with a nod.

The Professor stared him out, he didn't flinch then he slowly turned to the Doctor who was adjusting his clothing back into some kind of order.

"Nova will have doubts when he comes in, that'll be an opportunity to explain what's happening. He'd be a lot more use if he stays out here. We could do with people like him."

"I'll do my best," mumbled the Doctor.

Feng opened his mouth to speak until Jak squeezed his hand.

"We need him on side man," said Jak. "He's a dog, one of us."

The Doctor was deep in thought, working though the plan in his mind. "You know if we convince him not to Migrate." He glanced downwards distracted as Jak gently massaged Feng's manicured hand. Their thumbs and fingers in identical deep red nail varnish wrestled with each other on the table top. "Have you thought about Bluu. They're close, what if she wants to go inside?"

"I'm thinkin' she does," chuckled Feng in some kind of comic voice, looking knowingly at Jak.

The Doctor looked around the faces, glances darting between them. "What do you mean?"

Feng laughed. "Doesn't he know yet?

The Prof squinted his eyes at the two. "I haven't had a chance," he said between gritted teeth.

"What about Bluu?" The Doctor was concerned, noticing the fleeting look of guilt on the Professor's face.

Feng started laughing hysterically, head down on the table. Banging and thumping and every time he looked up at the pained expression on the face of the Doctor he laughed more. The Professor shrugged his shoulders and cocked his head Jak offered a wry smile of embarrassment. They wait until he composed himself as the barman regards the group once more.

"It's decades before anyone finds out," said the Professor.

"Finds out what?"

"Bluu," he whispers. "It sounds silly now, it should have been obvious." He made eye contact with Jak.

"Bluu, as in Blue Gene?"

The Doctor grimaces then as he realises what the Professor is saying his eyes widen. He glares at the three of them, for a moment he feels so foolish. Perhaps it's a joke? He laughs nervously, shaking his head. "No."

This sets Feng laughing furiously once more.

"Yes. I'm sorry I couldn't tell you sooner," said the Professor uncomfortably over the laughter of Feng. "Can you imagine the position it would have put you in if I'd revealed everything right off?"

"So what else is there? How many other surprises have you got in store for me?"

"Believe me, if we fail. If you're forced to live the life I did. There will be more surprises in all your futures than you could ever imagine. That might still be the case so for now except what I am telling you. I can share everything once this is over."

The Doctor stares at the table top. "Blue Gene?" he whispers in a question to himself. "She can't be."

TWENTY ONE

Since that meeting, the Doctor had looked at Bluu in a whole new light. Once or twice she caught him studying her intently whilst her attention was elsewhere trying to see behind her eyes, looking for anything that gave her away; bringing up subjects in conversation that might give any kind of clue, without success. If she really was a drone then she was a perfect specimen and ironically it was her imperfections that made her special neither stunningly beautiful nor highly intelligent. It was noticeably human how she might laugh uncontrollably, make mistakes or forget things occasionally. Ramona was a wonderful example of a drone but it was her perfections that gave her away. The knowledge that she was not human was reassuring, with Bluu this was impossible to determine. He sympathised with Nova, would he have felt the same about Ramona if he actually thought she was organic? If all goes to plan then Bluu will certainly be a victim. No one knew more than he how painful that was going to be for Nova. Whether a partner was organic or not they can become woven into your life. He will be as heartbroken as the Doctor was right now. Sadly, Nova will never know what his destiny could have been had they chosen to leave history alone. He may well have never known that Bluu was non-organic. The pair would probably have gone into V-world and lived in ignorant bliss forever. However it did reveal the extra motivation Bluu had for convincing Nova to Migrate with her.

The Doc appeared unannounced at Vic's but he wasn't around. Doing so was an unusual practice in Heathen but Vic had explained that this is how it used to be. He called it 'old school' just turn up and hang out. There had been no loce devices or quality communication in the 21st Century. He was making a habit of being off grid, finding Bluu at his place she was equally mystified.

"Do you know where he is?" the Doctor said casually.

"No, he likes to explore alone, you know that. He goes off grid and returns when he returns." Bluu was glowing today and increasingly so in recent weeks.

"Don't you think that's strange?" The Doc thrust his hands in his pockets frustrated.

"You would know better than anyone. He is from the Moonage, being offline is natural for him."

"The V-world shows have been incredible," said the Doc trying not to show any urgency.

"Yes, he needs his own time to relax. Even though they are V shows it's been very demanding for him, he is still writing and adding music for the physical show."

"He must have been a huge star in his time, he doesn't talk too much about that," said the Doc.

There was a pause, why were they having this inane conversation? They each wanted something. She stood up nervously, he even saw a bead of sweat on her brow. What amazing attention to detail.

Bluu stood quickly. "Would you like a drink Doctor?" She didn't wait for an answer, walking round the bar and taking a glass from the cupboard. He caught sight of her shapely form under large maroon baggy slacks and an almost transparent yellow patterned top. She had metamorphic features that could display masculinity and beauty at different times, today being the latter.

"Thank you," he said as he stood leaning across the other side of the bar. Bluu poured and slid a glass across towards him. He was conscious of their hands touching for a fraction of a second, perhaps accidentally placing a hand on her glass without picking it up reflecting his body language. He felt the heat below his collar, wondering could she detect his emotions. Their eyes met and he studied the detail of her skin, imperfect and blemished with an organic beauty. She just had to be organic, and yet the Professor claimed to have worked with a very advanced drone without knowing for years. She returned the look, dark eyes and large pupils piercing into him, holding a moment too long.

"I'm glad we are alone at last," she said softly looking down, fingering the condensation up and down on her glass. The Doctor felt flushed as the blood rushed up from his neck. Leaning on her elbows her small breasts appeared more ample across his eye-line.

"Really?" he said sipping the cool liquid from the tumbler as his hands shook ever so slightly. Without moving her head those huge eyes flashed up at him.

"It's about the final show. All that remains is the Market Square performance. This is different and I am worried for him."

"Worried?"

"You must have heard the rumours? About the announcement?"

There was an uncomfortable silence before she took a sip and continued. Dabbing liquid from her deep red lips with the back of a finger she coughed nervously. "Nova trusts you, having worked together a long time."

"Yes, likewise yourself," he said feeling the heat and unbuttoning his jacket.

"Our relationship is virtual of course. You know that?" What was she suggesting, that he was accusing her of being physical or simply confirming it wasn't?

"Of course," he acknowledged indicating some surprise she might even need to say it.

"I have to discuss something with you, it concerns Nova. It concerns us both and I need to know I can," she cocked her head and flashed an embarrassed smile. "Rely on you?"

Speaking the last statement in a question she was unusually vulnerable and evasive. He wanted to take the stress of this from her. If he was being manipulated by a well-choreographed performance of impishness it was surely working.

Then just as the Professor had predicted she would, Bluu went on to explain about the Migration Project. How it was about to be launched, how it was such a wonderful opportunity for everyone in Heathen. The Doctor did his best to be surprised and excited at the prospect as he would if it was the first he had heard of it.

She continued with how it had transpired that it would be launched on the last night of the tour the night of the live performance in the Market Square; Bluu and Nova having the opportunity to be the very first to Migrate and in effect be together forever in V-world to be together and set an example to everyone.

"I think it's a wonderful opportunity for us both don't you agree?" clearly a probing question.

"It sounds very interesting." Remembering this was allegedly the first detail he had heard of the project.

"Nova and I, we have a very strong relationship in V-world you know."

This wasn't a question, this was a statement.

"I have told Nova about this opportunity and he naturally has a lot to think about. We have to remember he is from a very different world to ours. It would be natural for him to have concerns and he will probably.." She nodded at him involuntarily as she sipped from her glass, shaking slightly as she did so. Once more the Doc was impressed, nerves from a drone.

"You think he may come to me? Is that it?" How perceptive I am, he thought even though the Professor had already made it clear this conversation would happen.

"What would your opinion be of such an act?" She looked concerned now. Would he disapprove, accuse them of being physical. He had no idea whether Bluu was even aware she was a drone that is if she was? It was a ludicrous notion but it appeared her feelings for Nova were genuine.

"In what way?"

"Would you support such an action?"

"I don't know much about the Migration Project," he lied. "It sounds amazing and as for the two of you, yes I would certainly agree it would be a great idea to take it up, it will be a historic occasion."

She slowly looked up as the smile radiated across her face and her eyes lit up in relief. She almost leapt across the bar to hug him. She grabbed him around the shoulders and his face pushed into her neck. He could smell her hair and feel the warmth of her flesh. He thought he felt the pulse of a heart beat as he was pulled against her. He was starting to doubt what the Professor had told him. This was really just too much, he shuddered at the physical contact and yet it gave him pleasure at the same time.

He pulled away and she still held him across his shoulders. "I should go now. I think it's a wonderful idea and I can't wait to hear more about Migration."

Bluu watched him leave, hands clasped in front of her face glowing like a bride on her wedding day.

Sitting in the Magpod on the way home he got to thinking. Let's say that Bluu wasn't a drone, that she was actually organic. It would serve the Professor and the scum if they could convince him she wasn't; being much more likely to help shut Mother down if they could get him as paranoid as them. Bluu might be organic, if so then she and Nova could go into V-world. But Feng was right, it's over anyway. Like plunging a knife into a sleeping baby they would drop the virus into the cloud whilst Mother was defenseless.

The show in the square was going to be the biggest real world event in memory. If it wasn't for that then there would be no reason for Mother to open up across all sectors. The show would have to be cancelled before Mother could defend herself and there was little chance of that.

Moments later as he walked towards his block an idea started to form in his mind. Something the Professor had said when they first met. The more he worked it out the faster he walked, loosening his tie his pace quickened in line with his thoughts. His excitement grew until he broke into a run, his overcoat waving in his wake like a cloak.

First he needed to get home and then he needed to find Nova. He had one last thought for Bluu. Seeing in his mind's eye how happy he'd left her. The realisation he would never see her again filled him with a deep sense of regret.

TWENTY TWO

Vic stared out of the transporter as he'd done so many times before whilst it crawled along the outer limits of the city. The final show of the tour was only two days away. After that and ironically not for the first time he'd die and be reborn. He considered the words of Paul, the man who'd been the first to go inside, something like "it was seamless," but couldn't shake the feeling there was unfinished business here. The incidents weren't helping either, coming at different levels at different times. What was so frustrating was that in those moments he knew the answers. After an incident it was like he forgot, he simply couldn't hold the information. Like being given the winning lottery numbers only to find the memory had faded away later.

Since the note there'd been no contact from the rebels. Vic wished there had been something, he wanted to judge for himself, see them eye to eye. Security had been tighter since the V-world shows but if there was a message he didn't get it.

The virtual warm up shows had been an incredible experience and in two days' time it would be the real thing. Amazing to think that it will feel exactly the same except it won't be the same. The 'futures' are more aware of that then he is. "Nothing is real" had been the mantra and yet in two days' time everything would be real. To the futures, being in reality by default entailed some form of risk. Whatever happened in V-world, crashing a car for example would never hurt you but in reality it was a different matter. He let out a little giggle at the memory of Bluu's little joke that first time in V-world.

It had become habit after the shows to log into his private sim to relax. The reality show had closed in fast and he wanted the time alone, time to think.

Earlier in the week there had been a proposal from Bluu. It made him realise how lonely he was, how different to everyone else here. There was a huge decision to be made without anyone 'normal' he could talk to. What Bluu had said sounded like a fantastic idea.

As his experience of V-world had grown Vic had understood something. It wasn't just the reality of V-world that made it so amazing, there was something else. Bluu had said how pain is limited and other emotions could be accelerated. Maybe it was that or maybe it was just that feeling you get when everything goes your way which it always would if you wanted it too. It was as if emotions were deeper and more powerful. He knew this was a quirk of the system but it could be quite subtle. That was one of its addictive properties. It was ironic to live in a world where the possibilities were endless only to find it was the simple things that gave him the most pleasure. In V-world emotions were in technicolor and Bluu had chosen just the right moment to open up about the Migration Project.

The two of them had gone inside to another sim after the show. Cruising across miles of dusty desert roads in an open topped Cadillac, music blaring and not a soul for miles. The horizon rippled in the heat of the Sun as it belted down on them both. They'd pulled off the road and arrived in what looked like a dusty Australian town.

They were in a public travel sim, designed for adventure and exploration. The Cadillac slid to a stop in a pool of dust outside what looked like the only bar around. A road-train cattle truck passed covering them and the car in a layer of dust. Hopping over the doors and passing a lone tethered horse the pair made their way inside. There were around twenty or so people chatting along the bar but in a town like this it could have been the entire population. A few locals eyed them from bar stools and Vic had ordered at the bar whilst Bluu checked out the jukebox. Being an open sim these were live residents and not automated bots, it was clear that they'd recognised him. Being polite enough to keep that to whispering amongst themselves the pair were left to their own devices. Vic thanked the lady and carried the drinks to a table nearby. As he did so a record clunked into place and the music broke the silence of the place, covering the gossip between a couple of older looking gents on stools at the end.

"Let's dance," she whispered taking each hand and pulling him towards a space on the floor.

They were already hot and baked from the desert sun and Vic's bronzed face glistened with sweat. Bluu looked cool and relaxed despite the heat as her light dress dipped and span in time to the music. Dancing for a while they'd provided a source of entertainment for the locals; one or two occasionally mimicking them at the far end of the bar to the amusement of the others. At last they collapsed onto chairs around one of the old wooden tables. Vic was hot and the air felt stuffy, the ice crystals clawed against his throat as he drank. He'd never felt better in all the time he had been here, he laughed to himself for thinking of this being somewhere else. He was staring through the door at the haze rising up from the dusty road whilst some mischievous local kids eyed his car. Knowing how he was always completely safe in V-world made him feel an internal warmth.

Bluu leaned across him, looking up into his eyes as if to answer his thoughts.

"What if you could?"

"Could what?" he said surprised pulling his head back to look down at her.

"Love me, for a thousand years?"

"I meant it," he whispered, kissing the side of her nose. Remembering for a moment her complete lack of sexuality in the real world and how strange and natural it was that in here he absolutely loved her. She was a complete and beautiful woman in every way.

"I mean it too. But I am not talking about just in the sim."

"I am not sure what you mean?" he said melting into those huge eyes of hers.

"Do you mean reality, physical?" Vic said excitedly. Was it possible that she had been suggesting a relationship in the real world, a physical relationship? It turned out that what she was suggesting was the exact opposite.

"When we are back in reality then our love ends," she explained. "We go back to reality." She looked down, as his smile and excitement ebbed.

"But this is good isn't it?" he said, "being here right now, the two of us?"

"It's the most wonderful thing."

There was a long pause as they both stared through the doorway at the kids fooling around his car, taking turns in the driving seat.

"The Salvation Project, when the time comes would you?" whispered Bluu.

He thinks, looks at her. The audience at the bar were losing interest now and returning to their conversations.

"Would I choose this over reality? Is that what you're asking? Or this over death?"

"Yes," she said deliberately.

"Right here now, being together? With you I would choose this forever." When he said that he meant it so sincerely, but like a hasty drunken promise he was having doubts now. He wasn't drunk when he said it but he was drunk on the emotion of that moment.

"Then what if we could do it now?" said Bluu sitting upright.

"Euthanise? Now?" Vic was puzzled. He guessed they were a similar age. Vic had planned on enjoying his extended life here in the future. Believing the need to top himself was some way off.

"I mean the Migration Project, the project that is being launched at the reality show in the Market Square." Then he realised. His live show was going to be the launch of the new project, the next stage from Salvation. It will allow anyone to go into V-world at any age at any time.

"You're not thinking? We could actually do it right now?"

"We could and what's better is that we can be the first, if we want to." Nervously she waited.

He thought, eyeing the line of characters at the bar who like them could log out in an instant.

"So we go and live forever in this ga.." He stopped himself from saying the word game.

"In V-world."

"You said our love was lost when we are back in reality, but it never would if we were to stay." She smiled at him.

"A thousand years?" he said almost to himself.

"Maybe more."

He had thought about it before saying yes but not for long. Did any of it matter anymore, really? His shows were a success and he was a superstar in both worlds and that meant something here. His final show was days away and would play in front of thousands of real live organic humans and then what? He was becoming one of them anyway he even dressed like one after Pierrot had brought in his goon squad to help him with his fashion sense. In V-world he was still very much a twentieth century boy. Out there in reality he dressed in future clothing, a full range of what would have seemed futuristic? Now with thanks to Pierrot he had a show that would be the icing on his musical cake. With Pierrot's choice of costume for him and the Spiders it looked like nothing he had ever seen in his own time.

Pierrot may have fallen in the personality barrel as a baby but that's why he was Heathen's biggest presenter. His loud voice and louder personality had enabled him to be at the top for decades. Right now Nova and the Spiders were the biggest act the planet had seen in living memory. Pierrot was not threatened by Vic and he had told him so.

"Nova my good fellow, music has a short lifespan. You're my favourite flash in the pan but I have been around for forty years and will be around for another forty," he had confidently boomed.

Vic took that as a compliment, not least because he said it with a tiny hint of concern.

So in V-world with Bluu, looking into those eyes of course he had said yes, absolutely, but now he wasn't so sure.

What was out there in the mist? Is there a question unanswered, an itch he needed to scratch before he did this. Vic was running out of time. He was going to live in virtual reality forever and this was a big decision. He had said yes but really had better speak to someone. Since that day in V-world his brain felt rammed, like a warehouse with no room to spare.

He stared out once more in vain, nothing.

"Home," he whispered and the pod pulled away.

## TWENTY THREE

Twenty minutes later Vic's magpod was pulling up outside his accommodation. It'd been another long day and he was mentally shattered. He slumped out of the transport and sauntered towards the block entrance. As he walked along the short public area between the towering buildings he became aware of a presence behind him. It could just have been a waste drone but something made him feel uneasy. Vic didn't look back but suddenly the world closed in and darkened, he felt very alone.

These people had seemed non-violent to him but he couldn't be sure. Every race has crazies his fame might be too much for them to cope with. On top of that there were these humanists, maybe they'd found him after all, perhaps they were dangerous? He felt, rather than saw the figure that dropped out of the shadows and was walking directly behind him. His heart was pounding, recalling images of those before him, left for dead for no reason other than fame. It takes just one lone head-case. Lennon, Kennedy and Reagan could tell you that.

There was no reason to target any particular area because this was no affluent part of the city. Heathen just didn't work like that there was no real segregation because any affluence that existed took place within the homes rather than the outside. Relatively speaking it was possible to live next door to a high spec accommodation or average without knowing. The main front facade of any apartment was academic, there was no way of knowing what lay behind it. He'd certainly heard rumours that one or two people suspected he lived here but they would never expect to find him in the street, alone. Suddenly he felt stupid for leaving himself so exposed. He heard the footsteps behind him break into a trot as he lunged towards the DNA scanner. His only chance was to get behind the security of the block and ask questions later. He reached out placing his flat palm against a plate on the door which simultaneously read his DNA and unlocked. The door gave instantly and Vic stepped across the threshold as the figure bore down on him. Knowing that no unauthorised person could follow him across the doorway boundary he stepped inside. The scanner would have detected any unauthorised organic bodies and set off the security. The hairs on his neck seemed to bristle as he crossed to the safety of the interior.

"Nova!" a familiar voice shouted.

He made sure he was across the door line before spinning round to see the Doctor standing in the centre of the path illuminated in the yellow light. He held out a palm to stop the door closing but stayed inside.

"Fuck man. You scared the shit out of me!" he screamed in annoyance. The Doctor looked breathless and sinister in the darkness. "Apologies, I had no intention," he stuttered. He had stopped a few yards back from the doorway as if not wanting to come closer.

"What the hell are you doing here? How come you didn't broadcast or something?"

"Old school you call it?" said the Doctor nervously grinning. "Just stopped by to see if you were interested in some real world travel?"

Vic laughed. It was probably one of the reasons he liked Dr. Touchreik so much. He would really tune into stuff. Having spoken a lot about how things used to be with Vic telling how people would physically interact, call round to the house and hang out. He'd explained that's how they did things 'old school'. It was typical that the Doctor would try and please him in that way. Vic had been off grid for a long time and Bluu would want to be able to detect him soon.

"It's kinda late now, the shows and everything?" he said slapping his forehead.

"The thing is," said the Doctor taking a step closer.

Vic waited, looking up the stairs knowing that Bluu might be concerned about him.

"I hope, you don't mind, I just wanted to talk?"

Wow this was kind of unusual, not just for the Doctor but for any of the futures. In fact it was outright odd that any of them would use that language at all. Nova took a single step outside, letting the door close behind him with another whispered whoosh. Late as it was, maybe the Doctor could help him out a little too? Why not?

Pausing he glanced upwards and stepped forward. "Ok, let's hit the road," he said stepping outside as the door closed behind him.

They grabbed a pod and headed out towards the edge of the Natural History Park. Modern transport was not allowed inside and so, as they often did they began walking amongst the dark wooded area. It was illuminated by false moonlight and would be almost completely devoid of organic life on the fringes. This area seldom drew crowds in the daytime and so now it would be mostly deserted unless they travelled a lot deeper.

"So, The Migration Project you say?" They strolled along the wooded path amongst the trees some areas almost pitch black whilst beams of bright silver light broke through others.

"Bluu told me about the Migration Project, how you were planning to go inside early," he said nervously.

"You know about that then? I wanted to talk to you about that."

"Oh."

"Yeah, Bluu thinks it's a great idea, I was interested to know your thoughts?"

If Bluu is a drone then it certainly would be a good idea for her. Perhaps she is, but even if he told Nova he'd never believe him, no one would. He'd studied her intently and found nothing that would give her away. Whichever way things went in the coming few days whether 'Bluu Gene' as they'd called her was actually non organic or not was going to make little difference. The Doctor felt a deep affinity with this primitive man in the time they'd worked together. Some of the Doctor's views drifted towards Moonage and that's natural in light of the work he did. He could not publicly condone the principles of physical relationships but he understood them. Given how things must have been in those days what option had humans but to behave as animals did.

"I think I'll miss you?" said Nova.

"We can continue our work in V-world can't we?"

The Doctor looked away, grateful for the dim light anxious not to show the tear that was pooling in the corner of his eye.

"Well that's what I wanted to talk about."

The Doctor didn't respond, he heard the tone of apprehension in his voice but couldn't make out his features.

"I'm going into an enclosed sim, myself and Bluu. To live and grow old, perhaps even die there it's how things are meant to be."

"and Bluu?"

"We've discussed it."

"You understand an enclosed sim would be impregnable, no communication with reality unless you chose to open the firewall?"

"I know all that. You of all people must understand how I don't belong here?"

"I do, it's merely selfish reasons," the Doctor whispered. "I think it's a good thing, if you have the opportunity to Migrate then you should." He realised that with these words he had reached a tipping point, his decision had been made. He was going against his older self and the humanists. He was deciding to follow his own agenda. The Doctor really cared for Nova but as so often is the case, the discovery of a rare species will often result in its destruction.

"I've been thinking, once you're inside, it's going to be like you're euthanised and there's still a lot for me to learn," said the Doctor as his fingers clasped tighter at the device in his pocket, feeling the cold metal in his palm. He rubbed his fingers across its form, feeling its power run into him.

"I've thought about that," smiled Nova.

"You know what this project means to me?" Becoming conscious he took both hands out of his pockets and clasped them in front of him.

"I've thought about that too," he said, "I believe there's a way you could continue to work after I go into V-world without ever needing me."

"Really?"

"Yes."

The Doctor was consciously trying to keep calm, could he be suggesting what he thought he was suggesting?

Nova continued, "A complete trace of my brain has been taken. They had to do that so that I can still be the same person in V-world. So I can take every experience and memory with me." Nova laughed nervously. "That's one of the things that scares me, that my personality exists on a hard drive somewhere," he said waving upwards as they reached a fork in the path, taking them in a circular route back.

The Doctor laughed. "Oh don't worry it's not activated until you go inside, all very straightforward."

"I believe so, I wasn't too sure about the technical aspects but my thought was," he rubbed the back of his neck as he walked. "With my permission you could access a copy of that trace, you could continue to work on your memories and all the other information that's in there."

Vic stopped walking and looked at the Doctor. The night had darkened under the trees and he struggled to see him, they were two silhouettes deep in discussion.

"So you would kind of have a copy of my personality, would that help?"

The Doctor once more took a long breath. "It would just be data, not a personality but wow, a lifetime's work for me to interpret, but it would mean I can continue to help the people of Heathen rebuild their history, those that care that is." The Doctor set off walking and Nova followed. Vic thought for a moment and then realised how ridiculous his initial objections had been. Here he was planning to spend the rest of his known life in a giant Xbox and this idea had bothered him? It hadn't take long to see this wasn't a much bigger step. After all there had been a lot of nutcase things go on since he thawed out.

"No comebacks, no secrets revealed or anything like that?" he enquired.

The Doctor smiled. "Every single secret revealed I'm afraid but only to me and no comebacks, I promise that would never happen and I would never share it."

"Well if it's as cool as you are saying, let me talk to Bluu."

"You're going to do it then, Migrate?"

"Why not? I'm happy there and it's as close to home as I want it to be."

"Home," smiled the Doctor, realising the irony of that word.

"I'm an earthling just like you, but I feel like an alien."

"I understand."

"Ok well," he sighed. "I never thought I'd say this but if you want a copy of my brain then God help you." They both laughed once more and shook on it.

"You seem to miss your time and yet from what you have told me it seemed a difficult life, why do you want it back?"

"It's what I know."

"Can I ask you something?" said the Doctor stopping once more and plunging both hands into his overcoat pockets.

"Sure."

"What if we had a choice, right now, if we could go back to how things were in your time if we could switch everything off."

"What like get rid of Mother, no Cloud? Are you crazy?" Nova laughed. "I miss the world I knew, personally the answer is yes. But you guys wouldn't stand a chance. No offence but you're all just too soft, even softer than the first time it happened." The Doctor knew the answer to that before he even asked it but still. Here it was coming from an ancient being that had experienced both worlds.

Vic continued. "It's funny but it's not like I'm dying in a couple of days, it's like I'm being born."

"You're both very lucky."

"Soon you'll know everything about me."

"Well it's not that straightforward really, remember you told me about written books all stored in rooms like paper servers before digital?"

"Libraries," Nova corrected.

"That's right, well it's a little bit like ripping all the pages out and throwing them out of a window. In a storm," he added. "I'll have to build the data into something. It will be a lifetime's work."

"Sounds pretty awful."

"It's what I do it's very exciting to me."

Vic was unsure about asking what he wanted to know again but it seemed like a good time, maybe now.

"Ok but if you're having all my secrets, I want to ask you something I have asked before. Could I ask you a second time about the humanists?" he said inquisitively.

The Doctor felt himself redden in the cheeks, glad of the cold draft in the air. This had caught him out and he took a moment to steady his nerve. He needed to be calm, act natural.

"Sick people. Everything bad you ever heard about them is true."

"Have you ever met one of them, spoke to them?"

The Doctor stuttered a little, did he know? Is this why he was probing because he knew about the plan? Suddenly he felt unnerved. He had to keep his trust, get his hands on that memory trace.

"It's hard to say, you can't always tell. They range from hardcore lunatics to general sympathisers. Their venomous messages, sly symbolic references are around but, spoken to one of them? I don't think I could bring myself to knowingly do so."

He said that with complete honesty, the Doc's feelings for them remained unchanged regardless of the position he found himself in.

"Are you worried about the cloud! Once you're inside?"

"No, I'm just curious."

"Forget them Nova. They can't harm you. In a couple of days you're going to have the greatest night of your life. You and Bluu are going to be very happy."

Doctor Touchreik understood even more what a terrible dilemma he was in, he had decide who he would betray. He held the world in his hands like it was something he could buy and sell. He was glad he'd spoken to Nova he knew now what was right.

"Thanks Doc."

"My pleasure and thank you. I am very excited about our project and can't wait to get home and start working on the data. You should get a permission request later."

Vic smiled. "Dr Touchreik requires permission to access your brain," he said in a comical voice.

The Doctor took a long hard look at the caveman. Unconsciously he was fingering the device in his pocket once more. He was genuinely going to miss him.

"Come on," said the Doctor. "Let's get back."

"I ordered a Magpod to head home directly, I'll walk to it from here," said the Doctor. "By the way," he said as if a passing casual thought. "Black-Star."

"Sorry?" said Nova.

"Have you heard of a thing called the Black-Star?"

Nova shook his head in the darkness, clearly puzzled. The Doctor was satisfied he'd never heard that phrase before. He hadn't heard of it before until that moment but he felt a wash of what could only be described as anxiety. He was about to ask about it but the Doctor spoke again. "Never mind," he said and began walking off.

Nova shouted after him. "Will you be there? At the reality show?"

"I sure will," he heard him reply but he was gone now, leaving Nova squinting into the darkness.

The Doctor waved over his shoulder to Nova for the last time. Their chat had confirmed everything he suspected. His decision was made, he wouldn't be at the live show, that's a certainty and neither would Nova, it was for the best.

TWENTY FOUR

A physical show brought its own unique challenges, more so than any physical activity. Nova and the band would have to physically get to the stadium to perform for a start. As it was going to be the busiest place on the planet they had arrived very early in the day. Arriving around midday Nova was initially concerned, there wasn't a single sign of any crew or equipment. By 4.30pm he knew he needn't have worried. This crew were all drones, hyper efficient and fast too. No hangovers or Polish whores to worry about with this lot. After the sound checks it was all about waiting. The rumours were already rife about tonight's announcement even though they were completely without foundation or fact, as it happened most guesses as to its nature were uncannily close to the truth. Live tickets could have allocated many times over and the Market Square outside the stadium itself would act as an overflow, this too would be filled to capacity. The performance would be shown on huge 2D screens outside and there were virtual 4d facilities available elsewhere. The 4D feed would go live into V-World simulations across the City, enabling thousands the same front row seat without leaving their armchairs. There would be over a hundred thousand real physical people crammed inside later and similar numbers outside. It's estimated that 95 percent of the population would experience the show live in some way. It was going to be beamed into every sector of Heathen utterly live.

The dressing rooms were more like a Hyde Park apartment than anything Nova had experienced. Usually smelling of smoke and beer next to the toilets, sometimes the dressing room was the toilets. Huge white leather settees, allowing for perhaps 20 guests, there were state of the art entertainment systems and even soundproof bedrooms. The whole place was tastefully decorated and Nova's suite housed a sauna and jacuzzi, games and a fully stocked kitchen with waiting staff. Three of the walls in the main lounge were glass offering a choice of views, one across the City another over the Market Square and a third which was high on stage left. The tinted glass would hide anyone from those who cared to look up from the excited throng below. There was no sign of Pierrot but he wasn't particularly expected as they'd made no plans to meet before the show, they'd surely all get together afterwards instead. Pierrot had similar facilities of his own, if they were allocated by ego then God only knows what his would be like by comparison. There were a lot more humanoid drones around mainly these were security and waiting on. Bluu was incredibly excitable all day whilst Nova had been surprisingly relaxed. They'd spent the final hours chatting about future plans after the show, after the announcement. Nova had a feeling of inevitability and no real concept of what he was going to do tonight, he pushed that thought away. Instead he wallowed in the beaming happiness that burst from Bluu all day.

Beard, Gilly and the rest of the band were in the adjoining suite enjoying their own time before the performance. He still hadn't told them his plans to migrate and only now considered whether he should but quickly decided against it.

Nova hadn't expected the Doctor to arrive as early as them but he still hadn't arrived and it was getting late. He still hadn't arrived by the time the doors to the stadium were open to the public, already the streets looked busier than Nova had ever seen them. Nova stood in front of the tinted wall of glass and surveyed the square below. In the centre was a huge hexagonal tower which looked like a huge goblet. The top was made up of 2D screens on every side so the crowd could view from any vantage point. They blinked and went through tests then flipped back to generic support performances and chat. He could see but not hear an interview on the screen and recognised one or two of the team who had regenerated his new body. Although it was a permanent fixture in Heathen the tower had never been used for its intended purpose. Small groups of people were standing and chatting below, most looked like vendors of various kinds. There were flags and banners as well as high tech memorabilia such as Nova-world sim access and virtual avatar codes which would enable users to imitate the Nova style. The Nova style was accepted as the dress he'd become known for, a bizarre mix of style from across the centuries. In truth most of the credit for it belonged to Pierrot and his goon squad. There were still teams of engineers confidently making final checks on screens which would occasionally light up with enormous audible and visual countdowns. Groups of revellers would join in, count along and sigh in frustration when it abruptly ended at three or two. Sudden and deafening sounds would occasionally crash out of the sound system causing people to jump in fear. Nova felt no apprehension about tonight, it was natural to him and he wasn't concerned. Not being nervous can be a bad thing in his experience and many performers agreed.

"Is the Doctor here?" he said without looking round at Bluu who was relaxing on one of the bed-like sofas. "He's not on grid, hasn't been since this morning."

Nova scanned the milling bodies below as if he might spot the Doctor down there somewhere, which would be all but impossible but he tried anyway. Unseen and behind them was the main stadium and stage area. At last the sound of rock and roll filtered up from the distance and it never failed to get his heart racing. The distant thud of drums and the echo of guitars during sound checks one, two.. two.. two. The dressing room apartments were amazing but he knew that once he was outside he'd smell it too. Rock gigs had a particular smell and sound that even five hundred years would never change.

☐

Jak Samian had distributed members of the group around the Square in readiness for tonight's event. Only those dedicated to the cause at the higher levels had been briefed. All the others would appear out of the woodwork and fall into line after tonight's success. Like soldiers behind enemy lines they hid their rebel symbols beneath civilian clothing. Lightning symbols and red attire buried under hooded tops and shirts until they could reveal themselves. Jak for one was both excited and apprehensive at the possibility of finally being able to reset the clock, at being on the brink of freeing humanity from manipulation by technology. The reality of how difficult this was going to be had already hit him. There was going to be a great deal of responsibility upon the humanists to complete this bloodless revolution. To bring everyone along and ensure they were weaned off their reliance on technology. This was the end game and he knew that now was the time to be on guard. This was not a time for being stupid or impulsive. Jak was exposing some of his most dedicated people here in the square. With his entire hierarchy within a hundred yards of this spot he felt very exposed. Still he was proud to be at the head of this battle, being seen leading the group come success or failure. Sitting here waiting for the time to move, his mind drifted. Of course he'd considered whether this whole thing may have been a trap and so had some of the others. But the prize on offer was too big to turn down. He'd been cautious in his dealings with the Professor ever since he arrived in the Chase and very willing to listen to his story of time travel and the horrific news from the future. After meeting the Doctor it was clear that they were one and the same. The Professor's predictions had to be proof he really had come from the future, unbelievable as that might be. Trust him? He certainly didn't, however he trusted him a lot more than he trusted the Doctor. They were two sides to the same coin but without a doubt the Doctor was the most dangerous. Jak still had concerns about Feng too. It was the Professor who'd suggested he seek him out, telling him how in his future they would become close friends. Jak preferred to choose his own friends but having done so he had given Feng who was almost a stranger a short cut to the heart of his organisation. If it wasn't for the fact that Feng was so unstable and undoubtedly dedicated to humanism then that too could have aroused his suspicion. On the positive side he'd been offered a silver bullet that could shut down Mother for good. Hearing that the humanists were right all along may have diminished his normal sense of caution. The rebels had no idea how or why the reliance on technology would be so harmful in the long-run. It was more a sensitivity, an awareness of what might be coming. In all their assumptions they never predicted that it would be her love that was humanities downfall, a machine that might one day smother her own children with love. This opportunity was too good to miss, too tempting. Regardless of tonight's outcome he was right here in the thick of it. He stared up at the high tinted windows of the stadium and across to one of the huge screens on the tower. It had just finished another mock countdown to the cheers of the crowd before returning to a huge digital display.

To performance,
4 HOURS 32 MINUTES 45 SECONDS 44, 43, 42..

TWENTY FIVE

It was going to be a long night. The Professor had multiple channels of media coverage on in the life area. Tonight was the only news in the world right now and no media channel dared talk about anything else. The whole city is almost on shutdown in preparation for the biggest single live event in history. Here he was again decades later experiencing the same event from a totally different perspective. In his first experience he was already at the stadium with Nova and the rest of them just as the Doctor would be now. The memory of that night still caused the hairs on his neck to rise and yet it was sullied by what he now knew about the future. Yes the show would be amazing but he smiled to himself, remembering the excitement at having secured the memory trace from Nova's upload. He smiled at the enthusiasm of those days, feeling like pushing Nova out the door so he could get started. Desperate to get to work deciphering the memory trace and the treasure trove of history it contained. Completely unaware of what he would discover in the decades to come. So much has happened since then, decades of work, there was the Ramona incident and all his other achievements. Ramona entered his thoughts once more, like she was calling him one last time before she was finally gone. Ramona would be another one of the thousands of victims from tonight's actions. Strange that all the times he remembered sharing with her from this day on, she would never experience. As a precaution he had asked Duke to hibernate and it felt quite lonely here just waiting for news. It would be four hours until the event actually started and even longer until the power failure. After that it would be a short time before they'd know if they'd been successful. From then on a new challenge for mankind would begin and he wondered for a single moment, did they have the right to make that choice for them? Were they really in a position to decide what form humanity would or should take for its future.

Too late for that now.

His younger self would not return until way after the performance tonight. It would be a new world in which humanity would survive as it had done in the past. That's when the seed of a thought struck him he

165

started to think that maybe he could reinstate Ramona just for what little time remains. He knew the codes and she was right down the hallway. Just a few hours with her would be amazing, to be able to explain what he was doing. They could chat and pass the time, it was so tense and quiet here, as if he could sense the emptiness of the whole block. Surely this would be better than letting her shut down whilst she's in hibernate mode. It was like putting a cushion over the face of a lover while she sleeps. What harm could it do to laugh with her once more? She'd understand, of course she would, he desperately wanted to feel her against him one last time. Ramona was his, wasn't she? He and the Doctor were one and the same.

The Professor stepped cautiously into the corridor, still unsure where he was going as if his body was on autopilot. Behind him the sound of Pierrot's voice dimmed and echoed across the media in the life room.

Stopping for a moment he stared down the hall before continuing on to the Doctor's quarters. At the moment he pushed the door panel there was a huge roar from the crowd behind him, as if in response. The door instantaneously detected his DNA imprint and allowed him access. His excitement gathered pace at the prospect of seeing her open those beautiful deep eyes and smile at him one last time. He opened the wardrobe door and slid back the clothes hanging there. Punching in the code a broad welcoming smile spread across his face as he stepped back and the buff stainless steel panel slipped open.

The smile turned to horror and the Professor almost screamed out at what he saw covering his mouth he began shaking like a child. His eyes widened as tears poured down the back of his hands. His Ramona, his beautiful Ramona was..

He reached out to touch her cold dead cheek with his shaking fingers. He stroked her long flowing hair and located a small panel under her right ear. It was flipped open and the tiny drive inside had been removed and lay on the floor in front of him clearly crushed by the heel of a boot.

Why?

He dropped to his knees holding his head and sobbed. "Not again, please not again," he whimpered to himself, shaking his head. He thought he might be physically sick but resisted the urge. After a few moments he shakily got to his feet and dropped backwards into a sitting position on the bed. He stole himself to look up at her cold dead form.

Wiping the tears from his eyes he looked around the Doctor's room and for the first time noticed something at the end of the bed. A pile of clothes sat on the floor as if someone had stepped out of them. He felt dizzy and took a moment to question what he was seeing but he already knew.

That was when it hit him like a lightning bolt.

The urgency of what was happening brought him back to life. He jumped up and running into his own room ripped open the wardrobe. Pulling out a holdall he threw it on the bed and tipped its contents out.

"Shit, shit shit!" he said in frustration.

It was gone, it was definitely gone.

He ran into the life area where the media channels seemed to have gathered in volume and excitement. The biggest show in living memory was about to begin and Pierrot was already on screen.

"Duke activate please," he said.

"Good evening sir, how very exciting it is don't you think?" Duke, as always reactivated as if he'd never been away. As if unaware he'd ever been placed in shutdown mode.

"Duke can you show me some holographic security media from earlier please," said the Professor trying to remain calm. He was sweating now and his breathing increased. He knew what he was about to see and wanted to be wrong.

"Sure, where and when would you like to review?"

"The last couple of days at triple speed."

"Of course."

The Professor ran into his room and sat on the bed. There were holographic images of himself as expected. After a few moments a holographic blurry image entered and began whizzing around the room.

"Rewind five minutes and then normal speed," said the Professor.

A hologram of the Doctor entered and began searching the various storage areas. He followed him around the room until finally pulling the bag from the bottom of the wardrobe. Peering over his shoulder he could see the Doctor had found what he was looking for, the back-up time travel device which he quickly thrust deep into his pocket. He rummaged around some more before returning the bag to its rightful place. Presumably he was trying to find the other device, the one that the Professor had with him.

He left the room and the Professor followed him into his own room as he left the building with the device in his pocket.

"Stop please," he said and went back into the Doc's room and sat on the bed opposite Ramona. "Today Duke, quad speed." He knew what was coming and could hardly bring himself to watch. It wasn't long before a high speed hologram of the Doctor appeared in the room and approached the wardrobe.

"Single speed."

The Professor watched in horror as the Doctor opened up the door behind the wardrobe. He winced and turned away as the Doctor opened up the sync card space in Ramona's head, kissed her and then crushed it beneath his boot.

He then went over to his desk and started to examine some data on his screen. It was clearly the memory stream from Nova. Looking over his shoulder the Professor could see he was focusing on a tiny area of memory. He would not be able to interpret the data fully but he didn't need to. Having found what he wanted he took out the time travel device and input a destination date. It was clear he didn't know exactly how to use it but being as it was effectively a prototype it was simple enough. The Doc's hologram then stood over the pile of clothes and he pressed launch. He disappeared and the non-organic portion of his clothes remained in place for a second before falling to the ground. The hologram and the real clothes piled on the floor becoming one.

"Stop. Thank you Duke."

The Professor stood staring at the place where the hologram had stood seconds ago.

"Is there anything else?" said Duke calmly.

"No," he said in a daze.

The Professor went back into the main area and even though he wasn't taking in any media he felt its tone was building. The stadium was filling and the Market Square was busy too. The mere sight of so many people physically in one place was mind blowing. He tried to calm himself, he had to think clearly. He knew the plan was in motion but what could he do? Communication was risky but he had to warn Jak. He tapped his AR communicator but there was no signal. Of course they were off gird, why wouldn't they be? Firstly to protect against Mother but he imagined it would be a safeguard against a double cross.

He paced around, trying to think.

There was nothing else for it he'd have to get over there. He ran around the house throwing items into his bag and started towards the door. As he was about to leave he stopped and turned around.

"Duke."

"Yes sir."

"Close down and hard delete please," he said.

There was a long pause. "Could you confirm that your instruction is for a hard delete?" He questioned with some concern in his voice.

"That's correct."

"Are you aware a hard delete is unrecoverable?"

"Yes I am aware, carry out the instruction," he said frustrated.

"Certainly sir," said Duke calmly. "If you would be kind enough to DNA scan I can do that for you right away. I'm obliged to inform you that the company cannot be held responsible for any loss of data or services associated with a hard delete. Shall I proceed?"

The Professor opened the panel near the front door and placed his hand on it. "Proceed."

"Thank you," said Duke cheerfully. "It's been a pleasure serving you."

The Professor picked up his bag and left through the open door. It remained open and he was way down the corridor before the lights went out and apartments systems started to shut down.

Out in the street it was clear that things were already very different in Heathen. The transport system was in no way capable of coping with so many people actually being on the streets. It had ground to a halt and there was no alternative but to walk. He needed to find a way of getting to the busiest location in Heathen and warning Nova and the others. His only consolation being it wasn't more than a few miles and if he hurried he could still make it in time.

TWENTY SIX

Jak felt exposed arriving so early but they'd soon been absorbed into the growing crowds. Becoming more and more anonymous amongst the masses as the time grew nearer. As a precaution they stayed in visual contact so there was no need to be on grid or have communicators on. The Square had filled up quickly as people streamed in from the surrounding alleyways and streets. In no time at all this enormous space started feeling compact and claustrophobic. As the excitement grew so did Feng's tension, his eyes darting around rapidly. After hours of waiting the unmistakable figure of Pierrot had appeared on all five of the screens enabling them to relax as all eyes switched to tonight's host. The footage had begun with 2D cameras shadowing his movements backstage. There was no sound just the over the shoulder shots, smiles and backslapping as the crowd shared the back stage preparations. The loudest cheer had come when Pierrot had knocked on a dressing room door which was answered by a smiling band member. Gilly had waved to the camera before ushering Pierrot inside leaving the camera and 200,000 audience members outside waving back. After a few moments Pierrot had theatrically opened the door, waved to an unseen figure inside and continued his backstage tour. After numerous similar scenes he'd given the final thumbs up into the camera and was clearly heading for the stage. The sound was switched to the stage as the larger than life figure of Pierrot took to the stage to the rapturous approval of the crowd. Heathen had never seen anything like this, for organic humans to physically gather together was both incredible and nerve wracking. Jak was warmed by the idea of people physically being in each other's presence once again. Pierrot's voice echoed from every corner of the square.

"Good evening people of Heathen, where have you all been?" he said followed by his trademark booming laugh. The crowd roared in approval. This whole thing was just as exciting for Pierrot. He was without doubt the biggest entertainment host in Heathen and yet people had seldom seen him in the flesh. Most often he would have been on screen or holographic form.

"Where did all these people come from?" He put his hand across his eyebrows as if looking into the distance. "I thought there were only ten people living in this beautiful city?" he exclaimed and once more they screamed.

It was time.

Pierrot continued to warm the crowd, teasing and cajoling them ready for the big event.

Jak gave a subtle nod to Feng and the pair started to push their way towards the centre of the square. The tower that held the screens was so big that it was impossible to see any of the screens close up and so as they got nearer to its base the crowd thinned out. There were random groups of people underneath getting some temporary relief from the people around them or meeting others. The two humanists were well rehearsed in guerrilla action and didn't hesitate. They marched confidently across the 100 yards or so towards the maintenance access gate. Both wore just the trouser portion of grey boiler suits with the empty arm sections hanging limply by their sides. On top their open neck black shirts were open to the chest. There was nothing official about their dress but it was as nondescript as they could muster. As they approached, Feng pulled out a laser slicer and cut through the lock in an instant movement. Even if anyone had been looking directly at them they might barely have noticed what he'd just done. Jak pushed the gate open with his backside and rolled inside followed by Feng who slammed the gate behind them.

Up above the echoing voice of Pierrot continued toying with the crowd below and they were responding with vigour. The tower was a little like a lighthouse structure except it widened at the top to accommodate the screens and looked more like a gigantic chalice shape from a distance. One more locked door at the base and they were inside the inner core. Dim lights illuminated the dusty air and highlighted a spiral stairway that disappeared into the darkness above. Their boots echoed on the steel steps of the hollow tubular structure as they ran endlessly upwards. The roar of the crowd outside was muffled but still it shook the structure under their feet. Finally they reached their goal and pushed the door open into the unmanned control centre at the top. They were now below the screens and were able to see the real scale of the crowd spread out below. Tens of thousands of eyes on the outside all seemed to be staring up at them when in reality their gaze was fixed 20 metres higher. Every last one mesmerised by the face of the greatest entertainer in living memory, Pierrot.

Jak surveyed the crowd below with no fear he would be spotted in the darkened room. Feng went to work pulling panels out from under the

control desk. He produced an old palm sized physical interaction computer from his bag and opened it up.

Jak smiled. "Wow, where'd you get that?" he said laughing.

Feng narrowed his eyebrows insulted. "Code man, that's how it used to be done, real code."

He put a small torch between his teeth and started to carefully examine various wires before unplugging one and attaching a lead from his own machine. He stared tapping away at the keys and two of the desktop screens came to life. They showed the images of Pierrot on the screen then a green screen of digits. Finally they settled back to the original images. The screens inside were now showing what everyone else on Heathen was seeing.

"Is this it, are we on?"

Feng was too busy to answer, entering code, looking up and back again.

"Oh what kind of magic spell to use?" he said to himself before gracefully tapping one last key and then standing up to bow like a ballerina.

"Slime and snails or puppy dogs' tails. Phase one complete comrade," he said with a sigh of relief.

"Is that it?" said Jak surprised at the speed.

"That's it," said Feng standing upright and joining Jak as he surveyed the crowd.

"Are we in?"

"I think so."

Jak sighed and shook his head, thinning his lips. "What now?"

"This sector is locked into the broadcast in every sector. It's going out to all sectors and they can't switch us out of the grid."

"So now what?"

"Now we wait," said Feng with a proud smile admiring the view. He grabbed Jak around the shoulders with one arm and squeezed. "Once the power fails we can start administering the virus. They cannot turn us off locally. That will need a command from Mother on Mars and she is 14 light minutes away." He pulled Jak close and kissed the top of his head.

☐

The Professor was still some way off and the crowd was getting tighter around him. With so many people on the streets the transport system was incapable of moving at even a walking pace. The closer he got to the stadium the bigger the flow of people, like a mountain river it gathered pace. In some places there were physical parties where the group spilling onto the road intended to stay put. They were watching on media screens locally and so only served to cause log jams on the pavements. Even those who found automated transport were giving up, because it was programmed to allow pedestrians right of way. The smart option was to get out and walk. The Professor did his best to move slightly quicker than the flow of the crowd but it was difficult. As he approached the stadium from the East side most people who intended to enter had done so, which meant the crowds thinned out somewhat. By the time he arrived at his destination the outside was almost deserted except for small groups of stragglers. He stood and looked up in awe at the towering grey walls of the stadium before him anyone intending to be in the Market Square for the performance was on the opposite side of the stadium by now. He could hear the roar echo from inside as he skirted around in search of the stage door.

He ran around the outer edges of the structure trying doors until finally he found what he was looking for. He approached the security console where a young man was watching the events on his own 2d screen he looked up irritated as the Professor approached.

"My name is Doctor Algeria Touchreik," he lied as calmly as he could.

The man hardly looked up at him. "You listed?" he said.

"Yes," said the Professor. The man simply nodded towards the door, knowing the DNA scanner would soon pick him up if he wasn't. Of course it was the Doctor's DNA scan on the guest list so he wasn't lying. The Professor placed his palm on the unit and the door buzzed open. "Straight up the stairs," the man said as an afterthought before returning to his screen.

There was another distant cheer from the enthusiastic crowds. This time it shook the building as he heard not so much the words but the tone of Pierrot's final announcement introducing Nova and his band. The Professor leapt up the stairs two at a time, following the signs and partially his memory to the main dressing room. Finally at the dressing room door he composed himself and calmly placed his palm on the panel as it hissed open.

He stepped through into the plush hallway and walked forward into the lounge area. Now he felt like he really was travelling back in time. He hadn't seen Bluu for over 40 years and there she was. She was so engrossed in the spectacle she was witnessing below she hadn't heard him come in. She had her elbows on her knees and was leant forward as if watching a movie. The seams of her dark flowered dress tightened across her shoulders. Through the glass in front of her a hundred thousand humans were crammed into a single space. The Professor purposefully coughed to gain her attention above the euphoria she was witnessing. At that moment Nova had taken to the stage for the first part of his performance. Bluu spun round, startled and almost jumped to a standing position her back to the window behind her.

"Oh my, who are you? How did you get in here!" She made a dive across the settee and lurched towards the room controller to press the button for security.

"Wait!" called a familiar voice. "Just wait. It's me."

Bluu had her finger on the button as she slowly climbed upright from the couch to look at the figure in front of her. Studying his features intently the realisation spread across her face as she calmed, throwing her hand up to her chin in shock.

"Holy mother. Doctor, what happened to you?" Recognising the face of someone she knew well but who seemed to have aged maybe 30 or 40 years in a matter of days. This was the Doctor, there was no doubt of that, even the voice.

"Doc, is that really you?" slipping her hand from her open jaw and craning her slender neck forward as if the few inches might give her a better view.

"Sort of," he whispered still panting heavily from the rush up the stairs. The distance he'd covered on foot had been impressive for a man of his age and had left his clothes feeling sweaty and damp. He was still trying to contain his breathing and reduce his heart rate so as not to appear over anxious.

Bluu looked confused her pretty face wrinkled her attention torn between the spectacle behind her and the sight in front of her. Doctor Algeria Touchreik had aged almost overnight by decades; she had seen him only two days ago. Not just his features but the posture, the skin and eyes were greyer. His crisp long hair now dangled lifelessly over his face.

"What happened to you? Nova was wondering why you weren't here," she managed to say.

"What do you mean?" he said as she followed his gaze over her shoulder.

"You look," she paused. "Older."

"How old are you, Bluu?" he whispered stressing the word 'you' as he regained his breath. She shrugged her shoulders and gave out a quick breath, almost an involuntary snigger. The Professor detected a slight look of concern on her face again she glanced over her right shoulder as if looking for support from the people outside, maybe from Nova himself?

"I asked you a question," she responded with a matron like tone, cocking her head slightly. The Professor approached her speaking gently once more.

"I want you to tell me your age," he said firmly.

"I think you should leave." Holding up the controller with her finger poised over the security button once more.

This threat unnerved the Professor, if she pressed that button he'd be thrown out without any chance of explanation. He knew he had to persist if he was to gain access. Letting her see the doubts, letting himself see the doubts if there were any. Casually walking around the room, deliberately putting more distance between them. "When Nova came out of quarantine you were the only one who was allowed physical contact with him for some time." Her eyes were darting around nervously. "Why do you think that was?" He continued.

"That was my task for Heathen why would that not be the case?" a slight throaty quake in her voice.

"Have you never wondered why it was you?" he paused, "in light of the possible germs, microbes you might have been exposed to?"

"I'm best qualified to look after him," she said confidently.

"What were those qualifications?" he walked around with his hands clasped behind his back under his overcoat like a giant bird. He even faced away from her so he could keep her talking without making her feel threatened in any physical way.

She spoke out deliberately loud giving an air of false confidence. "I think you might leave Doctor, I think you are unwell, maybe the citizens?" She did have doubts, he could see it, he had to try.

He interrupted her. "I want you to repeat something for me." Pools of tears welled up in her eyes. She slowly shook her head and mouthed the word 'no' but there wasn't any sound came out, she looked into his eyes pleadingly raising both hands to her mouth in horror.

"I don't want to," she whimpered through them like a child at bedtime. The tears formed enough to run down her cheeks and she rubbed them away with the back of her hand. "Don't make me."

The Prof stopped and spoke directly to her. "They are just words."

"We discussed this only last night, you know how I have true emotion." Yes they had discussed it, he remembered that conversation and to him it was decades ago.

"You don't know do you Bluu?" slowly shaking his head.

"Know what?" Bluu wished she didn't know what he was talking about but maybe she did? But even so, would it really matter in a couple of hours? Soon it would be over and Bluu would never need to know because she would be with Nova in V-world able to be free and together forever just like they had planned.

Him as a boy and she as a girl they had talked about it so much, he would be king and she would be his queen.

Bluu spoke calmly and slowly as if addressing her executioner. "Doctor, don't do this, please," she pleaded. "It doesn't matter now does it? You'll have what you want. Nova is going to give you his memory trace."

The Professor steadied himself, he was hurting too. He liked Bluu very much and had always found her pleasant and if he chose to admit it very attractive. He gathered his thoughts, of course she was attractive to him, that's how she was programmed to be.

He turned and shouted at her. "Repeat access code initiation." Stopping abruptly her eyes glazed over. "I love Nova, I have real emotion for him." she said. "Wait before you do this." Her palms held out in defence. "I will do anything, absolutely anything. Think of Nova, you're friends and whatever you're thinking I want you to stop. Just please give me a chance to explain."

The Professor began, his bottom lip quivering.

"Victor, SF 8287," the Professor said loud and clear.

"Victor, SF 8287," she repeated her hands still out pleadingly, shaking all over.

"Mercury, Gemma, 6052, 011," he said.

"Mercury, Gemma, 6052, 011." Her body stiffened for a second and her eyes blinked rapidly and then she switched back to normal as if nothing had happened.

"8446, 94483, 3853" She said nothing.

"How old are you?" said the Professor.

The pain and fear he saw in her only seconds ago was gone. "I am 2 periods and 7 months old beginning operations in TVC13." Smiling she looking down as if caught out in a white lie.

"You understand you are a drone?" he said.

"Of course I do, thank you," said Bluu in a matter of fact way as if not a care in the world, she grabbed an electronic Vmag from the table and slumped down on the chair.

"We don't have much time. There's something you need to know about me."

Bluu looked like a spoilt child turning pages rapidly as if looking for something. Trying to make it quite clear she didn't want to listen. He began to speak but everything went black and they were plunged into darkness, he paused. The lights flickered as the power was restored and the emergency system took over seamlessly.

TWENTY SEVEN

The vile speech made earlier by Pierrot only served to enforce the feelings Jak had about how far humanity had fallen. Even if everything failed tonight this was surely the end of the human race. Whether the Professor was right or not didn't matter anymore because out there were hundreds of thousands of people celebrating their own demise. Jak was too young to remember how men had become slaves to machines and to hear Pierrot, it was machines that were worshipped. How had we allowed a human invention to govern our lives? To Jak Samian it looked like a hundred thousand condemned men celebrating their execution. Feng had been so engrossed in the spectacle below he hadn't noticed his stare. He'd proven to be a valuable if not volatile ally in the battle for humanity. The Professor had arrived from the future claiming that they'd eventually be future leaders and friends. No doubt their paths would have crossed at some point even without his introduction. Those people out there were not the only ones whose destiny was being changed tonight, his was too. If the old man was telling the truth he'd met them both in TVC26, 11 years from now. By then, he and Feng would be leaders of what was left of the humanists. Meanwhile right under their noses the entire organic human race was being coerced into living a virtual existence inside a machine. What might have happened to them next gave him goosebumps. If as the Professor described, Mother stopped reproducing organic life then they could eventually have been the last. All this had proven that they had been right and had to succeed tonight. Jak Samian may be young but he wasn't stupid, he knew this could be a double cross to root them out, but that was a risk he would have to take. Jak had become lost in thought, having watched the fat clown whip them all into a frenzy. Explaining how tonight was special and tonight's announcement would take us to the next level. The great Nova was here physically, and the crowd felt it as if in the presence of an ancient religion god.

At last the moment all of Heathen had waited for had arrived. Pierrot finally left the stage and the lights dimmed. Pierrot's voice echoed across the cavernous space only just heard above the screams.

"Ladies and gentlemen," drawing out his words. "Please." Another pause. "Welcome." Longer this time. "Nova and the spiderrrrrrrrsss!" he screamed with the crowd. In the darkness on stage there was movement, figures.

Suddenly, in an explosion of colour and sound the caveman appeared on the stage. A hundred thousand souls jumping in unison to worship at the church of a man. His aura and charisma were contagious and almost physical both inside and outside the stadium. The opening music and song were electrifying and Jak felt the hairs bristle on his arms. The pair were not immune, and from their own vantage point were mesmerised by the performance they were witnessing. The event had relieved some of the tension and shortened the wait. Jak even had time to daydream about the future whilst under the caveman's spell. If all went well he'd soon meet him, they would be kindred souls for sure. It wasn't lost on him that the pair had some affinity with the distant past. If the caveman joined them and became part of what they were trying to achieve then they might all replace the Major. It was they who could be heroes. They would be able to destroy the Major's myth and replace it with the men who really saved the world. After an incredible performance lasting maybe forty minutes Nova announced they would be taking a break after the next song. They had only played a few chords when it happened.

The pair were slapped from their individual trance as the power failed and everything went dark, seconds later the emergency backup kicked in.

"Was that it?" shouted Jak.

Jak leapt off the desk excitedly as Feng got to work.

"Me thinks so." His fingers stabbed at the old interface he held in his palm. Numbers and letters of code overlaid the screens inside the tower with show proceedings outside providing a background. None of this was visible on the outside main screens, at least they hoped so.

On the monitors the caveman had begun singing an acoustic tune whether as part of the program or not who knows but the people were enthralled and mostly unaware of the brief power failure.

Meanwhile Feng went back to work. From inside his jacket he produced a tiny fingernail sized memcard and inserted it into his device.

He pressed a few keys then frowned, looking up concerned. After shaking the device he went through the whole process once more. He took the card out and for a third time he did the same things in succession.

"Fuck!" he slapped the small handheld device. Jak didn't need telling, he could see the overlay on the monitors around the control room.

FIREWALL: SUSPECT FIGMENT DENIED

"What?" screamed Jak knowingly.

"It's fire-walled!" the reality of the situation hitting him like a slap in the face.

"How the hell, you said you could do this?" Jak screamed angrily slapping his forehead with the heel of his hand.

Feng's eyes seemed to spin in their sockets and he exploded with rage. Jumping up he had Jak pinned against the wall by his throat in an instant.

"You said the system would be open," he growled through gritted teeth.

Jak put both palms up in submission, spit dribbling from the corners of his mouth. "Calm down ok, let's try again," he croaked, struggling for breath.

"I know what I'm doing, the firewall is up. We've been crossed," he spat the words in his face. He opened his fists and released Jak who slid down the wall allowing the full weight back on to his buckling legs.

"No, it can't be a cross." Jak straightened his shirt and began rushing around the windows trying to see outside. He didn't know what he was looking for, perhaps the citizens' arrest of his comrades? This was a pointless exercise he'd no chance of making anything like that out from up here.

"We wouldn't have got into the signal, would we?"

"Of course you fool, that's local. We need to get into the cloud fella." He was right, they had got into the feed and hopefully had frozen it so it would continue to broadcast but with a firewall up there could be no virus upload.

"The citizens could come for us, sat up here like rats with the rest of our people out in the square. I should gut you and that Professor."

Feng lurched forward again with incredible speed but Jak was ready for him this time using the split seconds advantage to fend him off with an instinctive hard punch to the midriff. He stumbled to the floor coughing and gagging for breath, shocked that his violence had been countered with such a calculated move. He reached inside his suit and pulled out his ray gun as if expecting another attack.

"I am on your side, remember?" said Jak tapping the side of his temple. "Let's just think for a moment." Opening his arms he slapped his upper thigh and turned his back on Feng as he observed the crowds below. The hairs on the back of his neck bristled as he waited for the shot.

None came.

Feng lay on his elbow clasping his lower body and spitting onto the dusty steel floor.

Jak thought for a moment. Turning his back on him had worked to diffuse the situation for now. "It's over, grab the device and let's get out of here, we need to get everyone back up to the Chase." Jak was already out the door and heading for the stairwell.

Feng slid the weapon back inside his clothing and rolled onto all fours still panting.

◻

The roar of the crowd rose and died in unison with the opening and closing of the door as Nova burst through. He was mid-sentence before he noticed the Professor standing over his lover.

"Holy.. Holy did you see..?" looking up his voice trailed off as he froze in his tracks, looking the Professor up and down intently. Nova recognised him immediately but it was as if he'd aged considerably in the last 48 hours. The premature wrinkles were intensified by the distressed look on his face. The opposite was true for his lover who sat below him in the chair a wide eyed childish grin on her face like a 12 year old on barbs. Sweat was still pouring down Nova's exposed pounding chest, the adrenalin rush fading fast, realising something wasn't quite right. He'd expected to see her jumping up and down with pride after what she'd just witnessed. The situation was incongruous and the atmosphere in the room heavy, like he had disturbed something private between two people. It clearly was the Doctor, but the way he looked was weird. Sitting on the chair still staring straight ahead, Bluu hadn't even acknowledged him.

"Are you alright?" She clearly wasn't. The Professor looked down at her. "I'm sorry," was all he could think of to say.

"Doc is that you?" Squinting as he strode forwards to be sure of what he was seeing. It really was the Doctor but something was amiss. His long overcoat hung across his slumped shoulders and his posture was less imposing. He wore a scruffy unkempt beard below his red tired eyes. The exposed skin below his white shirt was greyer as were his wrinkled hands.

"Yes," he said watching Bluu intently. "I'm Doctor Algeria Touchreik but perhaps not as you remember me," finally turning to face Nova.

"You can say that again, what the hell happened?"

The Professor looked him up and down, thinning his lips as if in pain. "We don't have much time. There's a lot to explain and almost no time to do it."

Nova ignored him, pushing past he crouched down beside Bluu, shaking her by the shoulders. Aware of the odd role reversal, a flash of memory from when he was first thawed out and she had cared for him.

"Bluu speak to me." She looked at him but there was no expression she simply stared.

"What the hell is going on here? What's wrong with her and what happened to you?" he said anxiously.

After what Nova had experienced in recent months, the odd culture, the experience of V-world, situations like this were especially unnerving. Along with the 'incidents' there was an odd palpable atmosphere now, of blurred reality as if the different worlds overlapped.

The Professor looked deep into the eyes of his subject from all those years ago an interesting subject in the beginning but as time passed Nova had become human and later even a friend to the young Doctor. The years he'd spent sifting through the memory trace had increased his respect for Nova. In time understanding he was a real person just like everyone else.

"Do you remember a conversation we had recently? We spoke about the Migration Project?"

"Of course I remember," said Nova keeping one hand on her shoulder in concern as he stood.

The Professor braced himself. "To you that was days ago, to me it has been over 40 years." Nova looked confused and kept glancing down at Bluu and back at the Professor.

"He came back in time," she blurted and began laughing hysterically then gripping her sides rolling sideways on the chair.

"Look at me," shouted the Professor urgently trying to snatch his attention. Nova's head shot round and their eyes locked Bluu slowly regained a little more composure, reduced to random giggles squirting uncontrollably through her nose as if drunk.

The Professor continued slowly and purposefully. "What I am about to say to you will.." The level understatement was mind boggling but he had to try. "It will sound crazy but please believe me. There will be time for explanations later. The person you had that talk with days ago was a younger version of me." The Professor swallowed and considered the ridiculousness of what he was about to say. "That was the person who belongs in TVC15." He paused but there was nothing in Nova's face he could read. "I don't belong in TVC15. I have travelled back in time. I belong in the year TVC57."

There was a long silence Nova looked closer at his old friend then back at Bluu. She smiled vacantly up at him. "If that's true then where's the Doctor?"

"He's gone, he stole the other device and went back the same way I got here," replied the Professor.

"So you're saying there were two of you?" He was interrupted by another childish snorted laugh from Bluu. "Where's he gone?" Correcting himself. "When has he gone to?"

"That's why I am here tonight and not him because he went back." The Professor ran his fingers through his tired greying hair. "To your time, the same way I travelled back from my future."

"You are the Doctor but." Nova trailed off then took a moment to realise he laughed at the idea. "Ha, you travelled back in time to see him and he has now done the same?" Nova shook his head. His real concern was for Bluu. "So there are two of you an older and younger version?" Nova wondered about the citizens, perhaps Bluu was on some kind of drugs.

The Professor sighed. "There was, the Doctor you knew has gone back to the year 1967."

"Is he ok?"

The Professor appreciated the concern for the Doctor because by default it was concern for him but now was not the time. Nova stole another quick glance at Bluu. "That's before my time?" Looking outside and then to the door as if he might walk through at any moment. "Why would he do that, he liked it that much?" Nova knew it was his experiences here that allowed him to even ask such a bizarre question.

"I expect he's gone." The Professor paused swallowing hard. "To kill you."

Those words hung in the silent air and they felt the stadium vibrate under their feet.

"Kill me? He's no reason to kill me?" he said.

"He wants to stop you doing what you might do tonight." Nova looked around in surprise, opening his arms. "It's just a show man, he was excited about the show we all were."

"It's not just a show anymore." Nova followed his eyes as they both contemplated the waiting masses outside. "I came back in time because of what I saw in the future. The reason he probably went back was to prevent you doing what we need you to do."

"You're not making any sense?"

"I don't know how much time we have, or what the consequences are. He has gone back to your early life, presumably to kill you before you could come here. That's why he accessed you brain trace so that he will be able to intercept you easily at the other end."

"He used my memory to find a way of killing me? But you said." The Professor interrupted him.

"It's the most likely explanation. In June 1967 you released your first and only music album as you call it, he'll find you easier during your brief flirtation with fame," he paused. "Vic!"

Nova's blood froze at the use of that name. How utterly stupid had he been? Of course his memories were bound to reveal everything about him and he'd never stopped to think for one moment. He'd been faking it for so long and in light of his success maybe he lost track of its importance to the futures. The fact he was Victor Robert Jones and not Nova had become meaningless.

"You know then?"

The Professor shrugged his shoulders. "I know lots of things I spent years on your memory trace. There's other things I can't explain but none of that's important right now."

"So what happens if he kills me? Do I just disappear?"

"I am fairly sure that won't happen, there's something my younger self was either unaware of or ignored." The Professor felt a twinge of guilt for even involving the Doctor now. "All my experiments seemed to show that it isn't possible to travel outside one's own lifetime."

Nova spun. "So you don't know for sure?" he said. "I might just drop dead or disappear?" He was becoming more excepting now. Perhaps he was genuine he certainly looked to be willing to accept what was happening.

"There's no exact science here, no certainty. Myself and the Doctor are the same person remember, ok we are made of different stuff, different molecules but who knows. My early experiments with the device seemed to indicate that some very basic laws of physics come into play when using it. Matter can be neither created nor destroyed only transformed. There's a finite amount of matter in the universe and we are all made of some of it." The Professor tried to dumb down the science as best he could. "It's possible to steal a few billion, billion atoms from another time without too much disruption. Go too far or outside of your own lifetime and it quickly falls apart as if the bits are not there waiting for you at the other end." There was another stupendous roar from the crowd outside and it sounded like Pierrot was leading some kind of chant or sing-a-long.

By now Nova was considering these consequences, amazing himself at how easily he was excepting this story. He was overcome by a deep feeling of destiny, like being in a film that he'd seen a thousand times before. The fellow standing in front of him was claiming to be an older version of his friend the Doc and ridiculous as it was, he knew it to be true.

Nova was starting to feel like an actor running through his lines in a play. "What is it I might do that would make you want to kill me?"

"It's not me it's the Doctor," he stressed. "You have to remember we are different people."

Nova looked confused, he walked over to the window rubbing the back of his neck and stared down at the crowds below. The Professor's words echoing and overlapping in his head.

"In the future I experienced, you went into that machine with Bluu. However in time more and more organic humans followed you until there are very few left. After around five years Mother slowed production of organic life. The Migration Project was the beginning of the end. I was witnessing the elimination of humanity through natural wastage. Homo Sapiens were obsolete."

"Isn't this Machine of yours supposed to be reliable, to love humanity?"

"If anything the Saviour Machine is too good. It thinks it's what we've always wanted. It's a primitive desire that has existed in humans since they could think."

"What is?"

"To live forever, eternal life, immortality call it what you want. Mother believes that inside V-world the Migration Project will provide that for us."

Nova flicked his hair and dragged down the zipper on his red and green body suit to cool himself.

"What's this got to do with me?" he said turning with his hands on his hips. He knew the answer to that question before he asked it but could never express it. He needed to hear it said, had to wait for his next line.

"I don't know for sure but it's possible that your brain trace was confirmation of that desire. You are more primitive than us." The urgency of the situation didn't allow the luxury of subtlety. "In around ten minutes time you're going out there to launch that project and effectively set in motion the destruction of humanity. We cannot allow you to do that."

"We?"

"The humanists."

Realisation spread across Nova's face, he nodded.

The Prof continued. "Right now as we speak a virus is being uploaded to her servers on Mars. The red planet is 14 light minutes away and every sector is open for tonight's show, we can ensure it stays open. Mother is closing down and if you go inside then so are you."

"Holy shit, so that's it?"

"Nothing can stop it. You're one of us, an organic human being. We need you to go out there and deliver a different message."

"Which is?"

"To explain that everything is going to be ok, that Mother is being shut down and we can," he paused. "We will survive this." How sure he was of that he didn't know. "We've got five years, that's all we've got. After that the decline of humanity begins."

"So what's left for us?" said Nova stabbing his chest and pointing at Bluu becoming angry as he realised the implications. "You crazy bastards are destroying everything. We were going to be the first, tonight. This fucking nightmare was over for me. We were going to live in my time in V-world and now you're just going to turn the lights off?" he said raising his voice and glancing at the door.

"The virus is already on its way." The Professor stared down at Bluu and Nova followed his eyes. "Whether you decide to go or not there's something you need to know." He swallowed hard. "Something you need to know about Bluu."

The Professor's mind flashing back to the cold empty features of Ramona he'd witnessed earlier. He knew in detail the pain felt in losing a physical partner.

"There's no easy way to explain this," he paused and pulled the hair over his head. "Bluu is not organic, she is a drone."

"That's ridiculous," Nova said pleadingly. "That's not true I would have known." Even as Nova said those words he had doubts. It was true they'd shared their lives but how much had been in reality? The memories from their time together in V-world felt real but they weren't. Bluu's lack of any discernible sexuality her lack of physical interaction with him were both completely normal for TVC15. Despite all that he'd grown to love her right here in the organic world too. Bluu had always been open about how she was androgynous and Nova had always placed her in his consciousness as a girl. Was it because he felt foolish that he protested against what he knew to be true?

"We are in love, we love each other," he said looking down at her, his eyes moistening.

"I'm sorry, so sorry but," he nodded over his shoulder towards her. "That's what she was programmed to be, to be the person you'd fall in love with."

## TWENTY EIGHT

Nova surged forward and grabbed the Professor by the lapels and threw him onto the settee. The frail older man fell backwards, looking pathetically up at him, elbows up to defend himself. He wanted to hit out but what was the point, who else was there to blame but himself?

Nova walked over to Bluu and grabbed her shoulders, looking into her eyes but what he saw frightened him, as if she could see right through him. He shook her lightly as if she might snap out of it but she was gone. The Bluu he fell in love with wasn't there anymore.

"What have you done to her?"

"I accessed her intel, she's functioning in a safe mode."

"That's nonsense, have you drugged her or something?" He walks over and is towering over the Prof's face now and that's when he sees. Unblinking the Professor looks back at his old friend and recognised the realisation in his eyes.

Nova unclenched his fists and walked back to her.

"Bluu," he whispered quietly into her ear. She looked up at him sharply as if he'd screamed, looking like a frightened child her eyes stripped of any of her personality. The Professor pulled himself upright and touched Nova's shoulder. Time was running out and he could already hear the distant roars as Pierrot wound up the crowd for part two of the show and the special announcement.

"Do something, help her. I won't do this without her."

"Nova see sense, she's just a drone and that's it. You can't love her and she certainly can't love you." He didn't truly believe that, remembering a time he almost confided in Nova about Ramona all those years ago.

"So now what?"

"The virus is on its way to Mars. In minutes her automated systems will shut down. The people of Heathen trust you. They need your reassurance."

Nova squeezed his temples with thumb and forefinger as he considered his options. The Professor opens his mouth to speak but is interrupted by Bluu. "Firewall activated, virus blocked!"

"What did she say?"

The Professor approached her. "Bluu what did you say, what's happening?"

She giggled a little. "Mother has blocked the upload."

"Oh no," whispered the Professor as he collapsed into the chair that Bluu had been sitting in, putting his head in his hands, shaking his head slowly.

"What does it mean?" asked Nova.

The Professor ran his fingers through his straggled tired locks. "It's over. The humanists are right. Even if we were to try and warn people they would either not hear it or not believe it."

The situation started to fast forward for Nova and he felt a kind of synergy with what was happening. The Professor jumped to his feet pacing up and down pushing his hair up across his forehead and standing between them both.

"How?" he was asking himself but Bluu answered him all the same.

"Doctor Touchreik had sent a communication to a drone called Ramona A Stone, its trending."

"Of course, I never thought," he said. "The Doctor, the younger.." he paused so he could make himself clear. "The younger me, the one you saw recently has sent a message. He knew it would never arrive but it would eventually share and trend before warning the citizens and Mother." Hand on one hip, biting his thumb he continued to pace, trying to work out what the implications were. How much danger were Jak and his comrades in, how much danger was he in for that matter.

Bluu burst into hysterical laughter. "It's failed," she screamed out to the sky.

"How does she know?" Nova asked.

"I'm plugged into Mother's grid aren't I?" That familiar matron tone again. "The fix is on its way and the entry point has been detected."

"Holy Mother!" said the Professor into his hands. It sounded like the humanists had been found, it wouldn't be long before the citizens were able to pick them up. If only he could have warned them but he was probably already too late.

"What does it mean for us? If Bluu and I go inside then your friends will always be on the outside trying to switch Mother off?"

"How can we know? It's possible that the world will revert to a version of the future I knew. It can't be exactly the same now, but close." The Professor needed time to think but there was none.

"I need her back, can you get her back? We had plans we were going to share a life in a twenty first century sim, but now?"

The Professor tapped his communicator, still nothing. Pacing again he continued rubbing his chin frantically.

Nova was still confused. "She is gone isn't she?" he said looking at her vacant expression.

The Professor still ignored him he had a lot to work out now. He had never considered what would happen if this plan failed. He needed to get out and warn the others.

"Yes you'd be safe," he replied. "In fact with the likelihood of the rebels succeeding in another attack being zero who knows how long you could both live in V-world. Maybe Mother is right after all? Humanity may well migrate into V-world and exist for as long as the servers are functioning on Mars." For a moment the Professor even allowed himself to imagine a time, thousands of years from now when the residents forgot they were not real organic beings 70 million humans living on Mars and not a single soul to be seen. Then he dared to ask himself the question, would it really matter. Perhaps the existence of organic life wasn't as important as he imagined.

Nova made a decision. "I am going to finish the show. Carry on." Nova turned to leave. "I am taking Bluu with me tonight and we're going to migrate."

The Prof grabbed his arm. "I don't think that's wise," he said. "We need to go, to find a way out of here."

"But why?"

"The Doctor's message. Who knows how much he has implicated us. We should find that out before the citizens catch up with us."

"If what you say is right, the Doctor is toast way back in 1967," said Nova unblinking he stared into the Professor's tired red eyes. "I only wish he'd taken me with him," he paused. "I suggest you leave." He turned for the door.

Then suddenly it hit the Professor, something that had bothered him for decades.

"My Heathen that's it," said the Professor his eyes widened and he was grinning like a madman.

"The Doc in 1967 is toast. But you wouldn't be."

"What do you mean?" said Nova turning at the door.

"You're right, he could have taken you with him. It's starting to make sense now. The problems I had with your memory trace."

"I have to go."

"Wait."

The immense difficulty he had in pulling Nova's brain trace into any kind of order. Falsities, gaps and pure fantasy had made the job incredibly difficult. He'd even been forced to put false placeholders into the gaps in his life and in many instances there were multiple, duplicated memories. In short his deep memory had been a mess.

"Of course now, it makes sense," he said at last.

The crowd in the stadium roared once more as the building vibrated. "What does?" The amber light flashed in the dressing suite to indicate two minutes to stage time.

"In your trace there are memories that didn't belong there. Deep and hidden but I had put them down as just fantasy. What if they weren't?"

"What kind of memories?"

"Memories of you, Nova performing," he paused still trying to make sense of his theory. "Performing in your own time," he finished.

"That's not possible?" Quieter he added, "I'm not Nova, I am Victor Robert Jones?" looking down at the stage and seeing the figure of Pierrot waving and agitating the crowd. It would not be long now.

"Block theory!" he yelled clicking his fingers in the air.

"What the hell is block theory?"

"It's an ancient idea, completely unable to prove. But if it's true then it explains everything." His mind was in overdrive now as he pulled everything together. The more he explained the more it made sense. "We naturally think that time runs concurrently. The day starts in the morning and ends at night, days years and months pass us by. But block theory says that it's just an illusion."

Nova turned and furrowed his eyebrows as he continued. "In actual fact the future is as fixed as the past. Everything that has ever happened and ever will happen exists in a single block of space time. There is no future or past. We can only experience the moment and so we believe we are moving through time."

"That's clearly not true, I have a choice?" said Nova, "I could choose to go on stage or not too," he said pointing to the door.

"You don't have a choice, you had a choice," he said pushing the tips of his thumb and fingers together in front of Nova's face. "You already made it at the birth of the universe, the future already happened, we are just experiencing a tiny slice of it right now. Then tomorrow another slice and another until?"

"What's this theory got to do with my memories?" said Nova frustrated and looking up at the flashing amber light.

"What if those memories in your trace are real? What if you're going back to your own time. Taking your new body, your new music and.."

The Professor went almost white, his heart pounding. "Maybe even our influence?"

"You're not making sense."

"Don't you see? Look around you at our clothes, our style, our culture then look at yourself. Those things are all influences from the past." He could hardly breathe he was so excited.

"Nova!" the Professor had an insane look in his eyes putting his face close up to his. "What if it was you who was that influence upon us? What if I was to send you back to your time, say 1968 and you lived your life in a different way. Wore the clothes, played the music?"

"That's nuts, I'd remember." Nova could hear himself saying the words. But he had remembered hadn't he? He was remembering now. What if the 'incidents' were snippets of those memories? He hadn't told anyone about those but he knew there was something.

"Wouldn't I have to go back in time for that to happen?" He laughed. "So you're saying I take influences back in time and then those influences are still around 500 years later, then I arrive and take them back again?"

"Exactly that."

"This could go on forever, I could be followed by others."

"That's almost impossible," said Touchreik.

"But?"

Touchreik put his face up close to Nova. "The Black-Star is unique, there's only one left and it's in this belt. Believe me you have done this infinite times before," he snapped.

"There's no beginning and no end?" he said puzzled.

"Take this and put it on," said the Professor excitedly.

"What is it?"

"My time belt." Unbuckling it he swung it around Nova's waist. He fiddled with what looked like a combination lock on the oversized buckle. "It's all set and will take you back. Don't you see? Only you can go back five hundred years and still be within your own lifetime, you'll be completely safe. Back before any of this ever happens, your 22 year old body can do it all again. You have the cure you came for and can relive your life."

"But what about?" Nova was playing the scenario through in his head. "What about Vic?"

"There's a fold in time for you. Vic and Nova are one and the same existing in identical but different dimensions. When you go back there is no Vic, just like there is no Nova for him in his life."

"If what you're saying is true, the block thing, then I would come back here and do all this again?"

"It's already done you could have lived this life a thousand times before for all we know."

"So whilst most people live in a single slice then mine will repeat itself forever with no beginning and."

The Professor interrupted excitedly. "It's as if your slice of space time is creased or folded."

Nova paused and stared upwards. "That means no end, no death?"

"It's never over for you Nova. You'll sacrifice your death to save humanity every time. You'll be back I'm convinced of that and everything will happen in the same way. You'll meet Bluu and fall in love again and again. Both of us have travelled in time therefore we have experienced the slices in the wrong order."

Nova knew it was true he had lived this life so many times before and would do again. He was Nova after all he was the musician from the 21st Century that they intended to thaw.

He was unsure whether it was the emotion he felt that had pushed him over the edge but the 'incident' he was having now was powerful everything was harmonising in a single moment. He could make sense of everything as he always did, this time he was desperate to keep that knowledge. The 'incidents' were giving Nova his memories back in full but only for short periods. He saw his lives, every one of them. He was going back to when he was twenty two just like he'd done a thousand times before. He also knew that this 'incident' was going to end soon and when it did this knowledge would be gone. Drifting frustratingly away like cigarette smoke in the wind leaving him with the feeling he'd known something important. Like an incredible idea conceived in a dream that was gone in the morning. Whilst this knowledge was here he knew what he had to do next. Nova rubbed his eyes hard with the back of his hands and saw the symbol of the lightning stripe, deep flashes of red.

"You have to go Nova, go now before it's too late." The Prof reached over to press the button on the belt.

"Use me," whispered Bluu to herself. "You could use me."

The Professor looks up now, frozen with his finger hovering on the button slowly the colour returning to his cheeks. "What?"

Bluu spoke out again. "I'm connected to the grid, you can use me to upload the virus."

Nova was still in shock. "What do you mean?"

The Professor became even more animated, perhaps there was a chance. "Holy Mother she's right, she is connected to the cloud. She would have to.."

Bluu answered his question. "I would have to switch to manual and drop my firewall," she said in a matter of fact tone.

The Professor laughed and grabbed Nova almost jumping for joy. "She can do it as long as it's voluntary, Mother would always assume her data is clean because of her local firewalls."

"What about Bluu, it'll kill her. We can't do that."

"Understand, Bluu is just a non-organic machine, we are talking about the human race here," he said angrily.

"I love her."

"She can't love, don't you see she's just a drone?" Clenching his fists in a prayer motion as if to hammer home the sense of what he was saying.

"Then why am I breaking my protocols, why am I willing to self-sacrifice? Offering my life for his? Isn't it because I feel 'emotion' for him?" Bluu smiled mischievously revealing a tiny peek of the personality that lay within. The Professor was dumbstruck, she was right. He had no answer, Bluu was effectively offering herself to save them all. He looked at Nova and then at the floor. Some error in programming perhaps, too much love not enough logic but who cares now. It was their only chance.

It couldn't be done here that's for sure. It would be too easy to trace the upload. Perhaps under the circumstances the opposite was true? Maybe if they had too many signals it might shield them long enough. He would need to contact the humanists in the tower if they weren't in the hands of citizens by now.

Nova turns to Bluu and grasps her around the shoulders for support as his legs buckle.

"So it's true," he cries into her ear.

"Yes," she whispered.

"I know what I have to do now but trust me, we'll be together again," he sobbed.

"My emotion is true," she whispered as if begging him to believe her. The Professor turned away as she physically kissed Nova.

"I know," Nova smiled, pulling away and rubbing her cheek with the back of his hand. "It always is."

The Professor was forced to interrupt the pair. "If we're going to do this we have to move fast," he said stepping in between them." He touched the belt. "When the time comes just press, it's all set. We have to get Bluu into the crowd so we can upload without detection."

The buzzer sounded for stage time and Nova made his way towards the dressing room.

"Give me five minutes, there's something I have to do." He disappeared inside.

The Professor turned to Bluu. "Do you have access to the public areas in the Market square?"

"Yes."

"Go there and wait, I will send you a loce to meet my friends."

She made her way towards the door without a word before the Professor shouted her. "Bluu!" She stopped and twisted her waist to look over her shoulder.

"Thank you," he said in a whisper.

Bluu paused for a second and without any acknowledgement she turned and was gone.

The Professor tapped the side of his head and finally Jak answered. "Thank Heathen."

"You better," said Jak pushing his way through the crowds with Feng close behind. "Keep your mouth shut and stop squawking, I'm coming for you."

"We had a problem with the Doctor I haven't got time to explain."

"You said.."

The Professor cut him short. "I know what I said."

Feng is raging and has hold of Jak's shoulder indicating he wants to communicate but Jak waves him away.

"You need to get out of there as quickly as you can, I don't have time to explain just do what I say."

"Oh really?" Jak replied ironically. "Could that be because it's fire-walled? Don't worry we did, and it looks like mama's coming for you too."

"I know she is. But I have another access point, straight in. Get down to the market square and into the busiest part of the audience. I am sending you a location for a drone, she will have yours."

"No way man. No way are you giving my loce to a drone are you nuts?" screamed Jak, attracting attention he lowered his voice. Feng was shaking his head furiously on hearing this. "It's a fix up, there ain't no drone gonna drop its firewall, it doesn't happen," said Jak rolling his eyes at Feng. "Believe me we've tried."

"We don't have time for discussion. This ain't 'no drone'," he said mockingly. "It's Bluu." Jak's silence was enough to know he understood. "Now get out of there and into the crowd, find her. She will allow you to upload through her port. Mars already knows we have locked all the sectors in. The fix and instructions are on their way back and you are being picked up locally. I need you in a crowd understand? That's all we got, take it or leave it. Yes or no?"

There was a long pause and the Professor was catching his breath, resisting the urge to say anything further he waited.

Jak stared at Feng knowing the seriousness of this decision. It was all or nothing, high risk and high reward. This was leadership.

"Yes," came the reply.

The Professor hung up his communication and forwarded Bluu's loce. There was a whoosh from the door as Nova appears from the dressing room behind him. The Professor turns to speak but is immediately silenced. His jaw drops in shock at the sight before him.

"Nova!" he says "Oh by holy Heathen!. What have you done?"

TWENTY NINE


A hundred thousand human beings were physically in the stadium with a similar number outside in the Market Square. The millions who weren't physically at the show were watching in 3 and 4d simulators and virtual representations. There were physical gatherings taking place across Heathen using old style 2D silver screens. There was barely an organic human on the planet who wouldn't experience tonight's show in some way. The bringing together of so many people was not without its problems, resulting in a small number of casualties. Mainly through those who had partaken in behaviour which might ordinarily have been safe enough in V-world. In the physical world however, falls, bumps and in one case attempted flight had real consequences. In light of tonight's announcement it was ironic how humanity was revelling in the experience and novelty of physically being together. The word was that Mother was opening up the Salvation Project to everyone and that Nova along with his V partner were to be the first. Behind the scenes the heart of Heathen continued to beat as the robotic infrastructure continued its work. Wherever humans gathered tonight the atmosphere was electric and the hysteria created by the first part of the show still hadn't died down. Nova's music had blown their minds in its complexity. It was in awe that they heard songs written by a human who was over 500 years old and yet his music was about them. Having been here for such an incredibly short time he'd gained an incredible perspective on their lives within his lyrics. Nova's music and songs reflecting his experiences in their time since he was thawed. A buzz was going around the crowd as they realised Nova was late returning. Obviously a ploy, some said to help build the tension before the finale.

At last on the huge 2D screens there was some movement and a roar went up before it was quickly drowned in the groan of disappointment as Pierrot walked on to the stage.

"Ladies, gentlemen and drones," he screamed and the crowd laughed along with him, waving and screaming excitedly. He took a deep breath and spoke slowly and with purpose. "Are you ready for the final part of tonight's performance?"

From the noise they made it was clear they definitely were. "Please be patient, I am told that Mr Nova will be with us very soon." The announcement was followed by further groans and sections beginning the slow hand clap. Pierrot carried on with his improvised entertainment in an attempt to fill the unscheduled void.

"I can't believe Nova is late either," he said with arms spread in genuine concern. "They told me he was 'Early Man'." Even the slow hand clappers laughed as they continued to protest, at this Pierrot's laughter almost fed back the sound equipment it was so raucous. Sections of the audience beginning to re-engage with him whilst others continued their own conversations which manifested as a low hum of words and conversation.

Feng had stopped in the crowd until Jak gave him a sharp dig in the back. They cautiously moved deeper towards the executive area where special guests could enjoy the clearest view of the stage. According to the loce she was close and would be just on the other side of the invisible barrier in front of them. At last they spotted her but Jak grabbed his shoulder and pulled him back.

"He was right, she don't look like any drone," he whispered in his ear.

"Let's find out," said Feng shrugging him off and approaching her from behind. Bluu didn't look round as the pair positioned themselves behind her. "Hello Bluu, nice to meet you," he whispered into her ear. She didn't respond and just stood staring up, sniggering at Pierrot's jokes. Feng looked over at Jak and reached inside his pocket pulling out a small knife. Jak moved closer so as to block the view of anyone stood around them and opened the blade. Quickly looking around Feng put the tip under her right shoulder and pushed it into the material. Sharply shoving the blade upwards he tore a hole in her dress big enough to slip a fist into. Bluu didn't react as he put his hand inside and began fumbling around inside her clothing, feeling the curve of her breast until he found what he was looking for. He took a wire from his small handheld device and pulled the end inside. Pinching a piece of skin under her right breast he popped out a receptacle and plugged in. He tapped a few keys on his device and nodded to Jak. He dropped the device into an inside pocket and reaching round he grabbed her hips backwards into him.

He tapped his head to check the time. Mother knew the sector was locked in and if that was the case they would be working on a fix to break free. If that happened then they were screwed and their virus would remain local. Calculating the light time to Mars there's a chance that the fix is already heading back and could hit Earth at any moment.

That was when people started to look around suspiciously at each other and were becoming more agitated. Feng and Jak comically mimicked this behaviour in the hope of buying a few minutes. One or two citizens were grabbing at each other and they would soon zero in on them. Locally there was a fix on the signal but with so many people compacted into a tight space they could not pinpoint where it was coming from, for now. Jak silently applauded the stroke of genius from the Professor in sending them here but it might not be enough.

Feng stood behind Bluu and gripped her tightly round the waist. If the citizens zero'd in on them he wasn't letting go. The few seconds it might take to separate them might be enough to finish the job. His eyes met Jak's and he nodded in acknowledgement, that moment was a mental contract between them, neither were going anywhere till this was done. Jak sensed the agitation around him but tried to appear enthralled by Pierrot and his humour. He spoke to Feng through gritted teeth.

"How long?"

He laughed loudly at another of Pierrot's poor jokes and said,"Nearly there."

Feng looked at the device in his pocket as two or three citizens on Bluu's side of the barrier began moving in their direction.

"Come on," whispered Jak to himself. One of the men pointed at Bluu and they began pushing through urgently towards her. She continued to look up at Pierrot laughing at his poor humour. The men were only yards away now and beckoning to people around her, pointing but to no avail. One man was shouting something but it was drowned out by the cheers of the crowd. At last Feng pulled the wire from inside her torn dress and kissed her on the cheek. That definitely did get a reaction as he pushed backwards and disappeared into the crowds followed by Jak. One or two had seen the physical kiss and grabbed at him as he pulled away.

Pierrot continued improvising. "Mrs. Pierrot wanted me to be more caveman in the bedroom, wait till she sees the pictures I painted on the.." He didn't finish his punchline and he didn't laugh, he fell silent as he stared stage left. His eyes wide and his jaw gaping, for once in his life Pierrot was genuinely speechless. At that moment, along with everyone else Jak and Feng stopped dead and could only stare in wonder at what they saw on the stage. As the crowd followed his gaze a wave of silence filled the stadium and no doubt filled Heathen. The whole City and by default almost every human being stared in utter disbelief. There were pockets of nervous laughter but only from the few who hadn't picked up the message trend the Doctor had sent to

Ramona. The Doctor's lost message had done its job in providing warning of what was to come should he fail in his attempt to kill Nova.

At first there was disbelief that the figure who nervously walks onto the stage was actually him, surely not their Nova. If only it was a joke or parody or perhaps an imposter.

The screams and cheers quickly turned to shock and tears as the man they have worshipped steps towards the microphone for part two of the show. He stood before them as a living breathing insult to every decent human being on the planet. Slowly they realise it actually is Nova under the bright red spiked wig. Painted across his face is the red lightning stripe that symbolises the humanist movement. It couldn't be clearer where his allegiance lay, even if in jest it was in very poor taste.

As if broken from a spell the media and news networks burst into life. Broadcasting pointless news flashes to the mere handful of residents who were not witnessing this event live. The media too are starting to trend the message from the Doctor. One of the news guys actually wept as he told how the Earth was really dying as mentioned in the Doc's message. By now almost everyone knew that this was part of the evil, plotted by the rebels. Random screams, tears and shouts of anger spread across the crowd both inside and out.

Nova slowly raised a hand and a wave of silence swept across the crowds except for occasional outbursts from individuals. Their feeling of betrayal insurmountable.

The confusion was as strong as the shock. Why is this happening? Why has Mother not shut this down?

Feng stopped to admire the view first looking up at the screens and then around at the faces. He wanted to jump for joy and scream out. The smile on his face said it all, it was the most beautiful thing he'd ever seen.

Nova paused at the microphone and if it were possible for an entire planet to hold its breath, then it was now.

Finally he spoke. The world listened.

"Everybody.." he said nervously. "This has been one of the greatest tours of our lives. I would like to thank the band.. I would like to thank our crew. I would like to thank our lighting people."

They waited, he waited.

"Of all the shows on this tour, this particular show will remain with us the longest."

Silence.

"Because not only is it the last show of the tour, but it's the last show that we'll ever do. Thank you."

Someone in the crowd screamed out, "No!"

Nova looked tiny and isolated as he began strumming his acoustic guitar, playing his final song to tears in the crowd and all over the City. A song he had written to celebrate the new life that he would have been starting with Bluu. A song that had a completely new meaning now.

☐

Nova had taken little time to explain to the hundreds of thousands of silent ghostly faces staring up at him where their future lay. Having no way of knowing how they'd feel when they learned the background to his motivational speech. Never believing he'd find himself offering a rallying call to humanity yet here he was. These people were in need of some tough love but if they did nothing then human organic life was doomed to extinction.

It was for Nova to offer the reassurance, to try and explain that in his time humanity had thrived in the physical world and had spread across the planet. His words may have fallen on many deaf ears for now but he hoped that they would offer comfort in the tough times that lay ahead. He was sorry he'd never had a chance to meet the people who'd made this happen but he praised the humanists too.

It was probably at the very moment he finished speaking and looked around he realised the hypocrisy of his own words. Cynically assuring them everything was going to be fine before he left them to fend for themselves. Meanwhile he'd head back to his own time and take his new body, his songs and everything they'd given him. By now Bluu would be gone too and his mind was in no man's land. He turned and walked from the stage in eerie silence save the occasional cough echoing off the walls. In his memory he'd hear his own footsteps clopping across the floor as he left. All the pieces were now in play, the virus was hurtling towards Mars at light speed as Mother's digital brain frantically searched for an antidote to the firewall.

He didn't make eye contact with the small group by the side of the stage as they parted to let him through. Climbing the stairs he soon found his way back to the luxurious dressing room area as the door slid open in front of him.

As he did so the very last person he expected to see was standing right there in front of him.

"Bluu!"

"It's done," she said. "I wanted to say goodbye."

She had always appeared more masculine in reality but now she looked more beautiful than she ever had. Her dress torn down one side exposing her pink flesh did nothing to diminish how she looked. Nova knew it wouldn't be long until his 'incident' faded completely and robbed him of the understanding he now had. The way he felt, he wanted it to go right now. He wanted his ignorance back so he wouldn't know any of this. He was meant to go home and when he did he would lose the knowledge just like he did every time. The future he'd experienced was about to be shut down but he knew one thing for sure. He always went back to another slice of time as the Professor called it. Back over 500 years to live the life of Nova, he and Vic different people living different lives yet the fold in time made them the same. If time and space really were like a loaf of bread where we experience a slice at a time then he was trapped. The travel through time meaning he lived in a tiny imperfection in its crust that folded back on itself. Whilst history was being created he would travel back and live the life he dreamed of, as a true rock star. Not one who plagiarised the hits of the past but those of the future. His knowledge was fading again, he was clawing at it as it drifted. He'd live and grow old he knew that, but the day will come when he had to face death once more. At that stage he'd want no gravestone and no epitaph, secretly whisked away into Cryogenic suspension. Loyal friends able to hide the pod and its identity by changing the name on the outside and so the circle was complete.

Nova's knowledge was fading fast but he was certain of one thing, this time he'll express his freewill, he'd prove them wrong. He wasn't going back in time, he wanted it to end here naturally, the way it should be.

Unlike all the times before where it would end with him being right here, with the knowledge that block theory was not a theory, it was real.

When he got back to 1968 he'd have no idea that in the future humanity would build a machine that loved. That machine would build Bluu and a single human would travel forward in time to love her. She would give her life for him and humanity, whilst ironically he must give his death.

"Thank you," he whispered and they kissed physically and despite everything they had shared as lovers, it was the first time physically.

"See you in a thousand years," she said, her lips touching his ears as she spoke.

"I'm so thankful," he said hoping she'd understand. "We'll be strangers when we meet." There were tears in his eyes as he held her against him.

"Because we can do it all again, like we always do," she said with a hint of that impish grin and the personality beneath.

"Not this time," said Nova.

"What do you mean?" she said looking up into his eyes.

"I'm not going back. I have freewill and I'm staying here."

Touchreik was on the other side of the room attempting to be discreet as he stared down at the emptying stadium below. Watching for any signs that they had been successful, a power outage was most likely or drone shutdowns but there was nothing. He span and raced across the room towards the pair.

"What did you say?" he shrieked, throwing a glance towards the door as if it may come crashing down at any moment. Nova kept his arms around Bluu protectively as if she were a porcelain doll that might shatter at any moment.

"You said we all made our decisions at the birth of the universe, that we expressed our freewill then?"

"Yes, yes I did," he said slowly.

"You're wrong, I'm making some different decisions this time," he said.

"I don't think you can, I honestly don't think you can."

He let go of Bluu and walked over to the window and pointed down at the thinning crowds in the square. "I've just been out there to tell those people it's all going to be fine, that I survived and they can survive without Mother. I told them they could live and thrive across the planet in their billions. So now you expect me to just leave them."

The Professor pulled at his beard and turned away before walking over to the window to look down. He turned to look in Nova's eyes.

"I think you always do, that can't change no matter what you think."

"It's changing this time Professor, it's changing this time." He held out his arms to Bluu and she ran over to him throwing both her arms around his waist and locking them tightly around him till he almost stumbled backwards.

Bluu felt a shudder as the virus ravaged her circuits. "It's worked," she said as she looked up at him. "I'm shutting down."

Nova wanted more time to explain, to tell her how he felt but time was the one thing that they didn't have.

Nova sobbed. "I'm going to miss you. I never felt for anyone in any time like I feel for you."

"Do you believe my emotion is true?" she said.

He stared deep into her eyes. "Yes I do."

Nova thought he saw the impossible, as if her eyes were filling up with tears. The Professor ran over to the door and hit the lock switch before turning to face them both.

"Nova, there's no future here, please understand that you can't change your mind. When you come back it will be the first time again, the first time for Bluu. You will both experience the same love once more. If you stay then.."

He broke off as the door camera showed a small group had gathered outside the door. The device was locked from the inside and they were banging hard, rushing from side to side and shouting up at the camera.

"It's over," said the Professor and walking over to the armchair he fell backwards into it with his head in his hands.

Nova looked down at Bluu. "Does it hurt?" he said

"No, not in my physical feelings, it hurts my mind. It all hurts my emotion and I don't know what to do."

"You don't have to do anything honey, it'll be over soon. I'm staying right here."

She pulled slightly away from him and looked across at the Professor, then the door and back at him.

"I'll be gone soon, a shame I only knew you once. My emotion hurts so bad."

In what he realised was their first physical embrace he felt her slender fingers slip inside the front of his belt.

"I love you," she whispered.

"I love you too," he said

"I'm sorry," she said and as the final parts of the virus ravaged her electronic circuits she pressed the buckle with her thumb. Nova had time to realise what she'd done but he froze for a second and it was too late. He saw the world in rewind as if everything was being played at high speed in reverse. Finally everything became a coloured blur, the stadium disappeared and he felt himself being bumped around in the environment, falling to Earth. The sky was visible and the Sun whizzed across the sky faster and faster until day and night became one single purple haze.

The Professor looked up in time to see the non-organic parts of Nova's outfit fall to the ground in a heap and he was gone. Bluu was now alone yet lifeless, staring blankly into space. A second later her legs folded and she collapsed in the same spot on top of the remains of Nova's clothes.

She was gone too.

The Professor stood up in time to see the door open and several citizens burst through and stop inside the opening. The leader of the group stood panting as he eyed the Professor and the crumpled heap on the floor. The lights seemed to double their brightness for a second before everything went black.

EPILOGUE

There wasn't another vehicle in sight when Nathan Adler swung his Jaguar into the labs empty car park. The admin block was situated in a large four story Victorian building upon a small hill. The smell of pines along the landscaped path was always incredibly up-lifting. There had been numerous additional buildings added in the seventies. For some reason these were semi buried beneath large grass slopes and at ground level the windows made them look like giant staring eyes.

Although the remembrance service was some weeks ago he'd known there could be no real closure for him until today. Once he completed this final act then perhaps his sleep would settle down again. Nathan was unsure whether it was illegal or whether any law even covered it. Even if it was a crime then anyone who might be a victim would be long dead before or if it was ever discovered.

He unlocked the front door and involuntarily checked down the corridor towards the library where some weeks earlier he'd arrived to find his dearest friend slumped in a chair. Almost as if his dear friend might walk out of that room and bid him good morning. He supposed metaphorically speaking he had intended to do that one day, although that would likely be beyond Nathan's lifetime. He started up the wide oak stairway to his right and thought back to the words he'd offered in Vic's his memory.

"There are some human beings for whom their ullage writes itself," it was with those words that Nathan had proudly opened.

"Victor Robert Jones will be remembered as a great man in both life and death," he said projecting his voice towards the packed congregation. "A man who took control of his death in the manner he controlled his life, with absolute certainty and commitment. He chose to leave us because the time was right for him and it was no selfish act on his part." Nathan's voice breaking up as it echoed through the church's towering space. "In his early life he'd shown great talent as a musician, something he was very humble about." There had been good natured sniggers from one or two who remembered the song that has brought Vic what might be more notoriety than fame. "This in itself had been a blessing and had allowed Vic to pursue his other passion, physics. Vic's success in business and technology made his company a household name but had never delivered the prize he sought above all else. I believe he hoped to find a way to see his dream a reality. He has provided his company with the remit and finances to pursue light processing technology. His wish to be held in Cryogenic suspension was certainly a measure of that belief and gave him the hope of one day being able to witness that success."

Comforting words to colleagues and relatives but he knew them to be true. Still he'd tortured himself that he'd provided the means for his dear friend to do what he did. Being a director of a cryogenics laboratory Nathan had been enthusiastic about its potential. After it had all happened he'd never showed anyone the letter but had carried out all his friend's instructions precisely, except this final one.

Nathan's computer fired up and illuminated the dim wood chip walls. As is his habit he went next door and put the kettle on whilst it slowly booted into life. Returning with a steaming mug of tea he felt the chill of the room. Running a hand across the bulky Victorian radiator he felt a hint of warmth, it was early but the place would heat up soon. He tried sipping his tea but it burnt his lips and he dropped it down on the desk. Nathan pulled a well creased piece of paper from deep in his wallet and opened it up on the desk. On it was a single word:

'Nova '.

Within a few dozen mouse clicks he had opened up the cryogenic pod I.D. of his good friend Victor Robert Jones. Then he opened up a file he'd downloaded and the detailed profile of his friend before proceeding to swap one for the other. A moment's pause before he closed the windows and a small box popped up.

'Save changes? - Yes/no/cancel' it said.

Nathan paused before hitting 'yes' and the windows closed.

He snatched the scrap of paper from the table and crushed it in one hand. Standing he pushed the chair with the back of his knees and walked over to the window. He peered through the steam rising from his cup out towards the main gate. The morning mist was clearing and the sun was struggling through the grey cloud. He could almost make out the lake from here.

'It might well brighten up later,' he thought as he raised the steaming mug to his lips and dropped the crumpled paper in the basket.

## ABOUT THE AUTHOR

Michael Mendoza is the name given to an award-winning author for film, stage and page. Revelling in his reputation for unique concepts, tireless research and fact based writing. Behind Michael Mendoza there's a vegetarian athlete and geek from Cheshire in the UK. Shortlisted in two National Channel Four writing competitions as well as a number of regional accolades.

www.michaelmendozabooks.com

www.blackstar-redplanet.com

35505799R00127

Printed in Poland
by Amazon Fulfillment
Poland Sp. z o.o., Wrocław